Ken Decato

Copyright © 2009 Ken Decato
All rights reserved.

ISBN: 1-4392-4992-X
ISBN-13: 9781439249925
Library of Congress Control Number: 2009932654

Visit www.booksurge.com to order additional copies.

DEDICATION

I wish to dedicate this book to my family, those who supported me in my endeavor from the start. To you I say thank you. Especially Bobbie and Sarah who read and offered constructive criticism as well as making their own contributions to the spell and grammar check on my computer.

Special thanks to Stephen Hawking. While I never contacted him, I read his book, "A Brief History of Time" and was duly inspired. Please know that any errors in the subject matter regarding time travel, paradox and quantum mechanics are mine, this is fiction afterall!

PROLOGUE

The Yankee soldier sat leaning with his back against a great chestnut tree. The sun shone on his face as he remembered how if felt to be up there, looking down on the beautiful blue and white planet. He wondered how he had come to be here; and if he would live to see it again.

A Johnnie Reb hurdled the stone wall near where the Yankee had taken cover. Upon seeing each other they both felt immediate regret. Neither of them expected to find the enemy where they were, only someplace to rest before returning to fight. The war had been waging on so long and they were both tired, so very tired.

But this was after all, war.

The Yankee lunged at the man in gray with all he had left in him. He had long since run out of powder so with his bayonet from his muzzle loader in his left hand he reached at the rebel's coat with his right. The rebel had an attack of his own in mind and charged as well. The two men flailed at each other with fists and bayonets. When the fighting finished the rebel soldier lay in a pool of his own blood on the ground, twitching in his death throes. The Yankee lay across the stone wall with a gaping hole where his left eye used to be, and a rebel bayonet buried deep in the muscle tissue of his left leg. He was unable to walk, and he was bleeding heavily from his leg and his head. He felt his face and realized that his eye had been gouged out. He knew that once gone an organ could not be repaired or replaced. He tore a piece of cloth from his fallen foe's shirt and wrapped it about his head, covering the empty orbit. Then with the last bit of strength he possessed he gripped the bayonet with both hands and pulled it free. The pain was white hot and exquisite. The trees and sky began to spin. He passed out.

The sun had settled low over the western horizon when the Yankee soldier came back around. He sat up and looked around him to determine if he were still alone. When he felt sure that he and his dead enemy were alone he sat and relaxed. He took a piece of hard tack from his mess kit and unscrewed the cover to his canteen. The repast, while brief, proved adequate to give him the energy and strength to move. Before getting up to go he checked his leg. The wound had closed and only a faint scar remained visible where the bayonet had done its work. However as he flexed his leg he realized that he must have lost some muscle tissue in the fight because he didn't have full mobility. He used some of the water to wash his eye socket. The lid was fully closed and he felt no pain from the injury. This would be the way he would live out his days. He stripped the rebel of anything useful; powder and balls, the water from his canteen, hard tack. The dead man's shoes were in much better condition than his own but they were a full size or more too small. He loaded his own weapon and sheathed his bayonet. He also took the scabbard and bayonet from the rebel and hung it on his side with his own. This would do.

As the Yankee began limping toward the last known whereabouts of his battalion he looked upward again, and remembered.

CHAPTER ONE

Cy stood with his back to the kitchen sink; the window behind him open. It had been a long day at work and he felt ready to call it a night. Morgan sat beside him with his head against Cy's thigh letting his ears get rubbed. His tail in perpetual motion as it thumped against the cabinets in easy rhythm. The cool night air rolled across Cy's shoulders making him feel that something lived in the ether that caused the hair on the nape of his neck to stand up on end. Morgan felt Cy's uneasiness and his head lifted a little higher. The thump-thump of his tail stopped, adding to the night's stillness. Cy wasn't prone to believing in spooks in the night or alien invasions; those things were for horror movies and sci-fi nuts. He had too much practicality for that. Yet he knew instinctively that something more than a breeze moved on the air tonight. Cyrus Theodule Hill often wondered how his parents could have been so cruel at his birth. Honestly, 'Cyrus?' Who names a kid Cyrus? Nashville's Johnny Cash had his 'Boy named Sue' and Sheldon's Owen and Eve Hill had their boy named Cy. At least his kid sister Sarah had a normal name. When he was younger he always found himself the smallest guy in the crowd. Adulthood brought an extra few inches in height and a broadened chest and shoulders. These days, Cy looked the bruiser at about 225 pounds, a shaved head and face. His inner self was nothing like the image he projected. He wanted the same things most guys wanted; hearth and home, the love of a good woman, the perquisite 2.5 children running around in the backyard chasing the family dog, and so on and so on. Maybe someday, but for today, there was only Morgan. Dave's dog Morgan.

Morgan is a seven-year old Golden Retriever that Cy adopted two years earlier after his friend Dave Boudreau had disappeared. If anything in life had Cy befuddled it was how anyone as young and full of life with everything going for him could just vanish. Because Dave's body had ever been found, Cy felt convinced that he would one day see his friend again. It wasn't easy to put it out of his mind, not with an eighty-five pound reminder trotting around constantly wanting to play. It didn't take long, about three months for Morgan to settle in with Cy. It helped that Cy had known Morgan since he was a puppy. Now they were a team, and instead of reminding him of Dave's absence, Cy decided to just let himself remember Dave's life and friendship. But nothing could take the sting out of seeing Annie, Dave's wife. The sight of her proved that heart break is a physical event and not just a cliché term. For her, Dave's disappearance meant that he was dead, and that shook her more than anyone else. Even Dave's parents were certain he would show up one day, like nothing had happened, whether it was denial or a sixth sense, they felt their son was alive.

Annie could not sense Dave's presence in this world in her heart. For her that meant he was dead.

The faint breeze brought Cy back to the moment, the air felt balmy and warm but it sent a chill up his spine. He stepped out onto the back deck turning to face the air current, breathing it in and daring the boogieman to come out of hiding. Nothing, just the sound of Crickets, a nearby tree frog, freight trains in the old Depot Square changing tracks and a few late night trucks rolling down route 2 in the distance. Morgan took the opportunity to go for a trot around the yard. He bounded down the steps and ran to his favorite spot out in the back corner to do what dogs do. It's curious how the night can play games with your head. If there were anything in the breeze surely Morgan would have sensed it. Then again, Cy couldn't be sure if the dog would feel what he did. Soft rain began to fall adding to the nocturnal symphony. Perhaps it was just a breeze after all. Cy decided to move back inside, his pillow is calling and he felt ready to answer it. A quick short whistle and Morgan came faithfully up the steps and followed Cy into the house for the night.

Cy felt quite tired, and wanted very much to just close his eyes and sleep. He found himself laying on his side in bed just staring out the window listening to the rainfall and all of the other night sounds as his mind drifted back and he remembered how this whole business started.

CHAPTER TWO

Many years earlier, on a similar balmy summer night a very much younger Cy had been awakened in the middle of the night by a breeze that brought the same sense of foreboding. He was fourteen years old then and sleeping out under the stars with an old canvas tarpaulin as his only shelter. That night had been spent out in the woods near where he grew up. Cy had suppressed the memory of that night. His mind worked to forget, but his body still remembered. All people have an innate somatic memory that is beyond the cognitive: things that we do or experience without thinking about them or attempt through a conscious effort. This is the basis of martial arts training, to teach the body to act, without thinking, to defend itself. Everyone at one time or another has said, 'it's like riding a bike', the body remembers even if the mind forgets. So when that night something passed by young Cy, it was his mind that wanted to forget, yet his body would always remember.

It started out as a typical Friday night in late August. One last camp out excursion before school started up again. It had been dry all month, so even with the high humidity and the night's damp air, they had no fire in the pine grove that night. Cy and two of his friends, Dave Boudreau and Brian Wright were nestled in for the night. They had laid a large tarp out, placed their sleeping bags with the open ends toward the edge and folded the tarp at their feet over the top of themselves. This provided a quick and easy shelter in case it rained, and made for easy carrying in and out of the woods.

At around two in the morning the still night air stirred. The tops of the pine trees were the first to report it. The whispering in the pines is what woke Cy. Not voices, just whispers. There seemed to be words articulated in that whispering, just on the edge of his hearing. Cy looked at his friends. Dave quietly snoozed, just a faint rumble of a snore, oblivious to what Cy heard. Brian lay turned on his side facing away from Cy, so he couldn't tell if he was awake or asleep. Cy guessed asleep, anyway he wasn't about to wake either of them and risk being branded a sissy. There would be no reassurance from them, at least not if Cy had anything to say in the matter. The sound of the whispering grew even though the wind didn't pick up. That seemed odd, even without wind, the tops of the pine trees rustled on their own. Even though there were no twigs snapping or crunching of the forest floor under foot or hoof, Cy felt someone or something approaching. His eyes strained at the darkness in the trees, the only light from the stars in the hazy moonless sky. Cy tried not to move. He thought, maybe it's true that what you can't see won't hurt you. Right now Cy didn't want to see, but he couldn't close his eyes. He didn't want to hear but his ears involuntarily tried to glean understanding from the unintelligible whisperings in the treetops. And what the hell or who the hell is that right outside the tarp? Slowly he rolled over in his sleeping bag, being very sure not to make a sound. That's when the inexplicable happened. With his eyes pealed and his ears on high alert, something touched his cheek. It felt like fingers, but colder to the touch and even rough. When his eyes and ears told him no one was there, somehow there was, unseen, with only the whispers high above as evidence of the presence. He froze. What's on my cheek, he asked himself silently. He couldn't move, fear gripped him and had him paralyzed. The fingers or whatever they were coursed along his cheek slowly then simply slipped from his face. In the same way this apparition came, it went. Silently it moved off, away from the pine grove. The whispering grew fainter and the breeze subsided. The night settled into its stillness again and the three boys were alone as before. Only Cy had been aware that there were more than the three of them in the pines. Feeling emboldened, he pulled himself up and out of his sleeping bag and got to his feet.

Perhaps because of his movement, Brian stirred and asked, "What's up?"

Cy said, "Nothing, I just gotta take a leak."

Brian said, "Yeah, me too." He climbed out of his bag and padded barefoot across the pine needle carpet to his previously chosen and designated tree and started to water it.

Both boys entered into the almost ritualistic past-time and were now aiming high and pushing to make a higher arc than the other. There's something about being a teenager out with your friends that almost demands that you take any opportunity to have a pissing contest. They each claimed victory and returned to the warmth of their sleeping bags.

Cy decided he could take the risk and asked, "Brian, did you hear anything earlier?"

Brian yawned and said, "Nope, just when you climbed out of your bag. Why, did a bunny wabbit hop by an' spook ya?"

Brian's sense of humor could be as irritating as it was humorous. Cy enjoyed it when Brian would get on a roll joking around. Whenever it turned into a berry busting session, Brian was hands down the quickest wit in the land. "Yeah, that's the ticket, he left you some Trix for a midnight snack after you finished playing with your twig and berries."

"No little girl, you've got the twig and berries, I've got the branch and apples." Brian quipped.

Cy knew this could go on all night. He just decided to throw a shot that might be viewed as concession and get to sleep. "I never knew a girl to have a twig and berries, but then there's no accounting for the girls you date."

Settling in, the boys went back to sleep. When dawn came with dew on the ground and grumbling stomachs, Cy had chalked up the events of the night before as just a bad dream and didn't give it any further thought. He just chose to forget. But you can't really fully forget. Memories don't work that way. And sooner or later something usually comes along to stir them up and back into the forefront of your mind.

Cy was sixteen and a half when he next felt the breeze. He had just gotten his license to drive and the keys to his Dad's old Dodge on a warm early May evening. The snows had lasted into mid April, there were still patches of it about in the more heavily shaded and wooded areas. This night though, it was warm, hastening the melting and scenting the night with a clean spring smell that they keep trying to put into fabric softeners and soaps. The spring peepers were singing their chorale in the swamps. All of the birds were in their hiding places in the bushes resting from their long migratory flights back from winter nests in the south, and preparing to build their summer nests in the north. The leaves on the trees still only a little bigger than the buds they had just popped out of. Of course a night like this wouldn't be complete without the company of little black flies that swarm around you and try en masse to lift you and carry you away for dinner.

In the early evening he went driving with the purpose of doing a few drive by waves at his friends; an extension of the pissing contests. He was the first in his circle to get his license and he wanted to show off a bit. He had found Annie and Dave at Ray's Dairy Bar, the local DQ down on 2A. They had seen his Dad's car before, so that wasn't new, but Cy driving it alone made it new. Annie and Dave were steadies, which, as far as teenagers are concerned that meant they were next to married. They had been a couple since sophomore year and had an easy relationship, arguably better than many married couples. It was a comfort for some reason, for Cy to hang with them. He never felt like a third wheel, and to them, his presence never felt like an intrusion.

As he pulled into the parking lot they saw him and waved triumphantly to him seeing that he was evidently successful in getting his license. Cy, playing it cool and just jerked his head upward and called casually out the window, "Hey!"

"Dude, this is so intense, you've got wheels!" Dave said, as Cy got out of the car and strolled casually toward the table.

Cy remained determined to not let his own excitement show. "Hey guys, what's new?"

Annie saw through Cy's façade, but she didn't let on, instead she just fanned the flames, "Not much here, how about you?"

"Oh, you know…same old"

Dave sat there just shaking his head and wondering if it could all get much deeper. Of the three he showed the most exuberance and had had enough of the charade. "Okay, enough already, what's it like driving solo man?"

Cy finally let loose, content that he hadn't been the first to blow cover, "HO, man, it's really great!" Cy took a deep breath and added, "It's a bit scary too, having the responsibility with no one there to bail you out, like having the security blanket taken away."

Dave said, "Hey, ice cream is on me tonight!"

Ray's Dairy Bar had the tallest soft serve cones around. Cy got a large chocolate vanilla swirl cone and spent the next ten minutes furiously dispatching it to keep ahead of the melting. That was half of the fun with soft serve. Annie and Dave accepted a ride to Annie's home about a mile and a half away. He dropped them both off and found himself alone again. This didn't bother Cy much, given to solitude he could often be found off on his own even when at a party or dance. He decided to go to his spot.

He drove to a flood control reservoir near his home where he liked to go for quiet and solitude. The land on which the reservoir had been built, once had been part of a large estate that had been in Brian's family for generations. The State took four hundred-fifty acres some ninety years ago and built a dam to flood it. Brian's family had been compensated for the land, but there's really no consolation for taking away something so vast from a family.

Parking on the side of the road he walked in by a gravelly path to the edge of the woods. The sun had gone down some time ago but Cy didn't need much light to see… this path he knew well enough to walk blindfolded. Through a small field and over the dike he arrived at the water's edge and made his way to his favorite sitting rock. The black flies were swarming but they were still neophytes so they weren't biting yet. There's always at least a gentle wind near water making waves on the surface. This night seemed especially calm with only two or three inch waves lapping at the rocks on the shore. He could make out the voices of a couple guys fishing across the inlet about two hundred yards away. There was a small Coleman lantern lit and turned down low where they sat. The light was just high enough to see what they were doing while baiting a hook or removing a horned pout from their line to put on the catch line. Pout were about all that you could catch worth eating in this old pond. Every so often someone would brag about catching a big bass or you would hear about a pickerel or two, but mostly just pout.

While Cy was lost in thought about going pouting, the trees stirred. He felt the air move around him pushing his hair into his eyes. What really made him take notice is that the water's surface didn't change. Usually a breeze made a pattern across the surface of water disrupting the wave tops as it pushes past. The light from the fishing hole across the way glittered on the waves and didn't show any change.

He looked around behind him and up into the trees and could see the tops swaying with the breeze, whispering to him. Then he remembered… that sleep out a couple years ago when something in the breeze had touched him. Yes, something had touched him, he had remembered it as a dream, but tonight he felt otherwise.

Now again, something touched his arm.

Suddenly his body sprung up and he found his feet running full tilt boogie through the woods. He came out of the trees and into the small field and only slowed when he saw the car. Not sure what he should do, he climbed in and sat there trying to put together what had just happened and why he got so freaked. Out loud he talked to himself, 'What was that?' 'There was nothing there!' 'So nothing touched my arm?' 'Something touched my arm.' 'And those trees, they were whispering, just like before.' 'But there was nothing there!' Cy's mind raced with his heart but to no finish line, not in this race, and the racer didn't seem to be coming to any conclusion as to what he had just seen, or not seen… felt, or not felt. He decided he would just go home and come back in the daylight. Tomorrow is another day.

CHAPTER THREE

Tomorrow took two and a half years to arrive. Sometimes life is funny that way. You make a choice and then you find one reason or another to disregard following up on it. Call it avoidance, procrastination or whatever psychobabble term you prefer. If you really don't want to do something you can usually find a way out. Cy didn't have to rationalize to anyone about it anyway since nobody knew of the events of that night but him. As far as he was concerned there was something weird down there in the woods by the pond, something that he didn't like and he felt the feeling was mutual. It's easy enough to stay away. Now that he could drive the next step would be to get a job. Then there are girls. So when two and a half years passed, and he found himself home from college strolling through his old haunts with old friends he also found himself thinking how foolish his fears were. Or at least that's what he tried to tell himself.

The Christmas semester break had arrived, there's nothing like being home from school with family and friends after that first four months away from home. All the nostalgia pulls at the heart-strings. It seems that all of the things that he wanted so much to get away from when he left for school were the same things that he wanted to immerse himself in.

Thanksgiving really gets the emotions primed. The stores are all decked out with Christmas decorations, the city streetlights are covered in tinsel and wreaths, Santa Clauses on the corners ringing their bells for the Salvation Army. All of the private homes were engaged in the ritual silent competition to see whose house could draw the most attention. Then there's television. Cy remembered catching Rudolf the Red-nosed Reindeer and could barely hold back the tears when the Burl Ives snowman started singing "You know Dasher and Dancer and Prancer and Vixen…" Homesickness was hitting hard and by the time finals were over Cy felt ready to head home. Packing for home was no chore, throw some clothes, dirty or clean, into a big green trash bag and catch the train out. After all, Mom had been waiting all semester just to do the laundry. Home cooked meals waited and clean sheets were on the bed with that 'summer fresh smell.' Clean sheets! Won't that be nice?

When Cy got home and settled in, it seemed almost as though he had never left. Strangely this disturbed him. He thought that there should have been at least a modicum of a feeling that he was now an adult, but letting his Mom do for him and knowing that his Dad was there to cover his expenses just added to the feeling of being a dependant child, no matter that he had been away. It lifted the veil off of the pretence of independence that he had been living under. The nostalgia that drew him so powerfully home now worked as a repellant, making him want to get out. And this, only the first semester break with nearly four years to go before he actually went out on his own. He had some serious humble pie to eat.

His Dad had spent some time getting the snowmobiles running during the last few weeks and had already gone out for some night rides. Trekking through the woods at night on a snowmobile, it just didn't get any better than that. They went out to the fields that were about eight miles through the forest from home. The air felt crisp and cold, the night faintly illuminated by the light of the moon in its first quarter. When the sleds were shut off, the quiet of the night could almost be felt. This had become something of a ritual of theirs. Even though the machines ran perfectly all the way from home they would stop, shut down and open the hoods to check out the engine compartment and be sure all was well. Owen Hill worked as a machinist and had become something of a fanatic when it came to small engines. After the engine check, they sat on their seats in the silence for a few minutes.

Owen asked, "Well Cy, how do you like being out on your own?"

Cy wasn't sure how to answer this especially since returning home and facing that he was anything but out on his own. He also didn't want to seem ungrateful to his father. He said, "Come on Dad, you know as well as I do that I'm not really 'on my own.'"

Owen wore a subdued smile, he felt somewhat bemused by his son showing this maturity, "You know, there are a lot of levels of independence. Don't be in too much of a hurry to do it all by your onesies! For the time being just let it be what it is."

"Dad, I just don't want to be a burden to you and Mom." Cy said.

"Don't worry about being a burden. You're working part time at school for pocket money. We're okay here. Just concentrate on getting your education for now. That's your job. Got it?"

Cy said, "Yeah Dad, I got it."

It was two nights later when Cy got together with the whole gang. Annie and Dave were there, still together, no real surprise to anyone. The only real question was why they weren't planning their wedding. For the most part nobody speculated about whether or not they would marry, but when. They all gathered at Brian's rented cottage in the neighborhood, a small place near the pond, a five-room ranch with 1 ½ baths, and a fireplace in the living room. There were logs already burning in the fireplace when the gang started arriving. Brian introduced his new girlfriend from work; Charlie (short for Charlene) Baker. She, like Brian, went to work after high school instead of continuing on to college. They worked at the new high tech company, Forum Data Inc. that had recently opened up in an old factory building downtown that used to house a chair company. Chairs were the bread and butter product for Sheldon back in the 1800's. Different times for Sheldon, which don't bode well for the making of chairs. The overhead had simply gotten too high for the local wood shops to turn a profit. This left a gaping hole in the local economy. Unfortunately the younger people went to where the jobs were. The City elders were trying to lure in small businesses, like high tech specialty shops and situate them in the old existing factory buildings. Typically the buildings had adequate power and high ceilings, which allowed data cables to be easily routed as needed.

Sheldon landlords had an abundance of space to let, so rent was cheap and with tax incentives to the prospective companies the job market actually seemed to be showing promise.

Brian and Charlie met at Forum Data, and sparks flew. They were already talking about the future, including marriage and kids. This mystified Cy. He couldn't imagine getting married at this age and here they were talking about kids!

Annie brought a friend with her to meet Cy. She had made it her personal mission to be on the look out for an ideal match for Cy. There seemed to be a need on her part to see to it that he would not spend the rest of his life foundering alone. As to Cy, his biggest worry seemed to be that she would actually be successful one of these times. Annie's latest attempt may prove to be her triumph. Lexi was a classmate from Annie's accounting class. She made Cy think of that old song, 'five foot two, eyes of blue.' Her hair was long and wavy, jet black, it really set her eyes off. Cy was an instant admirer. He realized straight off that if a woman made you think of a song, it could only mean trouble. It would take some doing if he were to keep his heart in check.

Annie knew that she had done good, evidenced by her smug little grin when she introduced them. "Lexi, this is my wayward pal Cy, Cy, meet Lexi, and try live up to my build-up"

Cy blushed. Chatting up a girl didn't come easy to him. Annie tried to assure him that most girls actually found that endearing. Maybe so, but mostly an endearing quality in friends of their boyfriends! "Hi Lexi, it's nice to meet you." He managed to say with effort. Lexi had Cy feeling dumbstruck, but he determined not to embarrass himself. Heck, what did he have to lose?

During the course of the evening Dave suggested a walk in the woods. This being the middle of winter, a great deal of debate ensued about the wisdom of walking out in the cold of night. Lexi seemed intrigued by the idea so Cy was tossing his vote in favor of a walk in spite of the cold; who knows, maybe he would be called upon to help keep her warm. Brian and Charlie liked the warmth of the fireplace and were squarely of the opinion that such an excursion was contrary to the laws of nature. So the four of them, Annie and Dave, Lexi and Cy, went out all bundled up for a walk in the woods down by the pond.

To say that Cy felt apprehensive about going back would be a great understatement. He decided, however, that he was not going to let it show. He felt more afraid of showing himself in a cowardly light to Lexi than of any old memories of breezes in the woods.

The night air felt cool and a little humid. A hint of snow rode the air. Cy thought that would be a nice touch. A little light snow could be romantic. So long as it didn't turn into a blizzard, the evening looked quite promising. Their feet crunched through the hard packed snow as the troupe made their way along the snowmobile tracks. One danger with a light snowfall was that the new snow would cover icy spots, making them invisible and even more slippery. As the streetlights faded that became redundant. Darkness quickly engulfed them as they made their way into the woods. Lexi and Cy were in front under Annie's watchful eye. Dave held back, embarrassment for Cy because of Annie's romantic notions. But he knew when to go along. Annie patiently and deliberately slowed their pace, letting the new pair move ahead. She was coy in the way she kept her voice up as she bantered with Dave, but he knew what she was up to.

Cy struggled to come up with something to say or to ask so he wouldn't seem like a complete loser to this beauty by his side. "Where are you from Lexi?" He hoped to get her talking so he wouldn't goof up.

"South Bay, Michigan." Lexi answered, "I have an aunt that lives in Boston, that's where I'm staying while I go to school."

Cy asked, "What are you majoring in at school?"

"Business."

"How do you like it so far?"

"Well, the jury is still out on that."

Cy actually found that the conversation flowed easier than he had expected. "Do you have a lot of snow in South Bay?"

"Not much different than here." Lexi said. With that she turned and gave Cy a little smile that even in the dark he couldn't miss. Just to encourage him a bit. Annie had told her that he was shy. She liked that, thought it was cute. And, she decided, she liked Cy.

The crunching of boots on the snow grew louder as the light snow accumulated. For Cy, the sounds were not enough to drown out the beating of his heart. He had to get control of himself, he knew, he was prone to falling too hard, too fast. This girl seemed special and that made it even more difficult not to fall. That's when he noticed that the snow had stopped flurrying around them. The air had taken on that familiar stillness that Cy recognized and had grown to anticipate. The pine tree tops were sighing in the calm, Cy felt sure he would be overcome with panic and felt every nerve ending in his body electrify as his senses heightened.

From behind him he heard the sound of terror as Dave yelled out; a throaty scream, not very loud, but then snow cover has a way of muffling sound. Cy and Lexi turned around and were surprised to see that they were alone on the trail. The others had fallen behind so far that they were out of sight around a bend through the pine grove. Cy took Lexi's hand to lead her and they trotted back the way they had come in search of Annie and Dave. When they came upon the scene they found Annie trying to calm Dave and get him to be still. Dave was crab-walking backward on his hands and feet trying to get away from something unseen. His mind had clearly left him, he was in a fugue state, it seemed almost as if Annie wasn't even in the same world as he. Cy knew Dave had been touched, but he had kept silent for so many years about the breeze in the woods. He feared if it got out what he had seen and felt people would think him nuts. Here now, Dave's mind had taken leave of his senses before his eyes.

"It touched me! Damn, what the hell was that?!" Dave ranted.

"Calm down Babe! It's alright!" Annie tried her best to calm Dave but obviously she didn't know what had happened or what bothered him.

Cy grasped Dave's head and got down next to him and looked straight into his eyes, "It's okay Dave, it's gone, you'll be fine. Come on let's get up and get back to Bri's"

Dave finally showed recognition, he got up, and with Cy's assistance they made for Brian's place.

It wasn't until they were out of the woods and back on the street when Dave looked at Cy and asked him, "Do you know what that was?"

"No" Cy looked at him meaningfully, "I only know what you know."

Nothing more was said and the rest of the way back to Brian's was trod in silence.

CHAPTER FOUR

Cy was completely mystified about what he had just seen. He had to think about how to proceed. He knew now that it was more than just he himself who could have been touched by the phenomenon in the breeze. He felt uncertain as to how to proceed. Dave had come back to his senses and seemed to be doing much as Cy would expect… downplaying the whole matter, trying to minimize what to everyone else must surely look like mental illness. Cy knew he would have to wait and get him alone, away from the rest of the crowd to talk.

There had been a noticeable change in Lexi as well. She seemed to still like Cy, but she seemed just a bit uncomfortable with the night's events. No one would blame her for that. Cy decided to consider his priorities and placed talking to Dave at the top of his list for tomorrow. For now, Lexi would get his attention. He asked, "Lexi, do you want me to take you home?"

She said, "Home, or to Annie's parent's house?"

"Where ever you would like."

"Okay" she said with a slight smile on her face.

They got their coats and started making the rounds. Annie was miffed, she had wanted to watch the pair all night, but Dave settled her and reminded her that Lexi would be at her parent's when she got home that night. That calmed her down but she maintained her disappointment.

Cy took Lexi out to his Dad's car. The old Dodge had been replaced with a three-year old Chrysler 300. It was still Dad's car, just a much nicer one.

When they were all buckled in Cy asked, "Would you like to go get an ice cream or something to eat at Friendlee's?"

Lexi smiled and asked, "Ice cream?"

"The most essential of all of the food groups!"

"But it's the middle of winter!"

"Soooo, it will just take longer to eat."

"Hmm," Lexi grinned, "that would be nice."

Cy felt elated, it was now a date. But tomorrow, he had to talk with Dave. No excuses.

9:00 A.M. the next morning the phone rang at the Hill's home. Annie felt almost desperate to talk to Cy. Eve answered the phone, "Hello?"

"Good morning Mrs. Hill, this is Annie, How are you this morning?"

"I'm well Annie, and you?"

"I'm doing fine thanks. Is Cy up yet?"

"Yes he is, let me get him." she called up the stairs, "Cy?" But he didn't answer. She put the receiver down and climbed the stairs to the top. When she arrived at Cy's bedroom door she knocked and again said, "Cy?" Again there was no answer, so she opened the door and looked in. Cy's room sat empty. She checked the bathroom; he wasn't there either.

Returning to the phone she picked it up and spoke to Annie, "Annie, he must have stepped out, but he didn't say anything to me about leaving."

"Oh, well that's okay Mrs. Hill, I'll get a hold of him somewhere along the line. Thanks anyway." Annie said.

"Good bye dear." Eve said.

"Buh bye." Annie said and they both hung up.

Now there were two very curious females in Cy's life that he would eventually have to answer to. And of course he had no idea. Cy had been home moments before Annie called, but had left on foot to get to Dave's house a quarter of a mile away.

Cy found Dave in good spirits and in total denial about the night before. "Dave, tell me, no, let me tell you for cryin' out loud what happened!"

Dave began to listen.

"You heard a rustling almost like a whisper in the treetops didn't you, like someone talking but not quite there, right? Then you could feel a presence, but like the whispers, there was no one there whispering." Cy implored.

Dave looked at him incredulously and couldn't quite tell what to think of his friend. Had he become clairvoyant or did he speak from a shared experience?

"Dave listen, the next thing you felt was something touching you, like a finger dragging across your skin, right?"

Dave's eyes were widening and it became clear to Cy that he touched a nerve. He said, "Whoa, wait a minute Cy, what are you saying, how could you know to describe that?"

"First, tell me, has it ever happened to you before last night, ever?"

"No, Cy, what's going on?"

Cy breathed a deep sigh, a sigh of relief or concern he wasn't sure, "Dude the same thing has happened to me, twice, out in the woods. The first time it happened we were camping out about five years ago. The second time came almost three years ago when I first got my license and went out there just to sit and contemplate my navel."

Dave asked, "What do you think of it, whadaya think it is?"

"I've got no idea. I'm just glad that I'm not alone anymore."

"What do you think we should do?"

Cy didn't answer right away. "Same answer, I haven't got a clue, nothing right now. We have no idea what it is, and it's not like we can call Ghostbusters!" They sat in silence for a few minutes. Cy asked, "Did you tell Annie?"

Dave gave him a stupid look, "No, man, what would I tell her? You know how this sounds or else you would have told us by now. Have you told anyone about this in the last five years?"

"No. It's just been me, myself and I talking to each other trying to stay sane. Last night brought the first time I actually had hope that I wasn't hallucinating. And on the subject of seeing visions, where did Annie find Lexi, is she for real or did I dream that?"

Dave grinned for the first time since the night before. "You weren't dreaming man, Annie's been chafing at the bit for weeks waiting to get you two together. Did she call you this morning?"

"Not unless it she called after I left to come here."

"What did you guys do after you left Brian's?"

Cy grinned, "We went for ice cream at Friendlee's, then just drove around for an hour or so talking."

"Are you going to see her again?"

"Come on man, do I have 'Stupid' tattooed on my forehead?"

"When?"

"Tonight. What are you and Annie doing?"

"Nothing that I know of, but if Annie gets her way, we'll probably be shadowing you guys. So you tell me, where are we going?"

"Pizza and a movie is all I can do on my budget, and that's stretching it. Maybe my Dad will kick in for me. I just don't want to have to ask her to go Dutch.

"I got four passes to the Cineplex in my stocking from 'Santy Claus.' If we end up doubling, the flicks are on me. Like I said, knowing Annie, we're not leaving you guys alone. She's wanted to see you with someone for years now and she isn't likely to miss any of the proceedings!"

Cy grinned and said, "That's comforting. Its good to know someone's looking out for me. Now if she could just stop what's out in the woods from getting under my skin." The mood went back to serious. Cy recounted in more detail the events of the sleep out and of the night he got his license. When he had finished Dave felt more inclined to talk about what he had experienced.

"We were just following along. You know, Annie wanted to watch you guys but give you some space too. So we were dropping back a bit. The snow was falling and it was dark and we were just enjoying the whole thing. Then the snow just stopped. The air got still at first then I noticed like you said that the treetops were almost sighing, they were moving but there seemed to be no wind. I swear it seemed like something being said but just on the edge of my hearing. Annie didn't seem to notice anything so I started thinking it was in my head. Now I'm more convinced that it was, 'in' my head. Cy, I could feel someone or something right there, in front of or around me, but I couldn't see anyone. The air got crisp and still. That's when I felt something like a finger poking at me, right on my shoulder, no, that's wrong, more inside than out. I couldn't think of anything but that movie, Alien, it was like that, some thing inside of me trying to poke it's way out! Annie got all confused. She had no idea, she only had eyes for you guys and I don't think she noticed all the other things going on. Evidently she didn't get touched."

Cy said, "I just wonder what the whispering is all about. It also seems to only happen out in the woods." The manner in which Dave had been touched differed from Cy's experience. That fact wasn't lost on Cy as he tried to reason his way through all that had happened.

"Do you think the woods have ghosts?" Dave was half joking and half serious.

"No, man I don't believe in ghosts, you know that."

"Yeah well right about now I don't know what to believe."

That evening after showering shaving and spending an inordinate amount of time in front of the mirror, Cy decided he couldn't improve any more and to head over to Annie's to see what the plans were. Eve Hill would have no part of it until she had an explanation that would satisfy her. As Cy came trotting down the stairs, his sister Sarah raised the alarm for Mom. Sarah could always be counted on for that, Cy thought, the little turncoat! They gave each other the sibling look of consternation as Eve called out to Cy to come into the kitchen. When he came to her she knew by his appearance that there was more afoot than just hanging with his friends. She gave her son the motherly eyeball from top to bottom. This is a gift reserved for mothers and has the same bemusing effect on sons and daughters of all ages the world over. Soldiers in boot-camp typically have an easier time with a full barracks inspection and an angry Drill Sergeant than they do with their mother eyeballing them with scrutiny.

"What did you want Mom?" Cy said in as casual a voice as he could.

"Cyrus Theodule, where are you going this evening?"

"Out with Annie and Dave. Why?"

"And?"

"And?"

"Yes, and?"

Cy sighed, "a friend of Annie's."

"I knew there was a reason Annie called you this morning." Eve was enjoying having the upper hand with her son, even if her tone hinted at playfulness. She respected her son's privacy and knew that as a young adult his answers were voluntary. She also knew that he would give her full disclosure if she pushed for it. "Who is this girl?"

Cy grinned, "Her name is Lexi, she's a friend of Annie's from school. I met her last night."

"What's she like, this Lexi?"

"Well, she's very pretty, but what she is like is something that I am going to be too late to find out if I spend too much time here."

Eve acquiesced, "Alright, alright, but I want a full report in the morning. You only have a few more days before you go back to school and I think I'm entitled to know a little about the girl that takes you out of my company for any of those evenings."

Cy stood erect at attention and snapped a salute to his mother. "Ma'am, yes Ma'am."

"Give your mother a kiss and get out of here! That's an order." Cy relaxed and gave his mom a kiss. As he was going down the hall toward the back door, he saw his eavesdropping little sister at the bottom of the stairs. Quickly and playfully he put her in a head lock and gave her a noogie. Then he released her and went out the door.

Owen was in the garage tinkering on one of the snowmobiles. Cy always found himself fascinated by the way his father could always find something to be working on. That is just his nature, he found it to be very difficult to sit still. As Cy was passing though he smiled at his father and said, "G'night Pop!"

Owen asked, "Gotta date?"

Cy smiled sheepishly and said, "Sure do, an' I'm late."

"Hey Cy, do you need some cash?"

Cy felt ambiguous here. He didn't want to abuse his dad's generosity but on the other hand, he's going out with Lexi, and didn't want to get caught short. "Well, yeah, but I didn't want to keep hitting you up."

"How about I give you $20.00 and if you use it, fine, if not you give it back tomorrow?"

"I can live with that." Cy liked the agreement, hoping he wouldn't need the $20.00. He took the bill and tucked it into his pocket, "Thanks Dad, don't wait up!" And with that he headed out.

She was intoxicating. With each passing moment Cy felt himself losing more and more control of his heart. Lexi had him completely charmed. The evening started out with just the two of them. They dined at a small local restaurant. One of those little candles burned on the table, red glass with the white mesh surrounding it. The lights were subdued so that the flickering of the flame danced on Lexi's face and played on her skin. She had worn her hair up, tied loosely with little ringlets hanging down carelessly in all the right places. Cy knew, if she were to shake her hair loose and let it fall about her shoulders it would devastate him. He was in trouble, deep. They both ordered the fish. Because they were still underage for alcohol they had cola with lemon. Cy was very conscious of keeping his breath as neutral to hers as possible, tonight he wanted a goodnight kiss. They kept the conversation light: more of the night before when they had gone for ice cream. Then they discussed where they were from, what high school had been like, parents, brothers and sisters. Tonight they went a little more in depth. More vital stat's like middle names, Alexis Ekatarina Iachovelli. Mom is Ukrainian and Dad is Italian. She grew up Byzantine Catholic, a strict orthodox branch with a lot of chanting and incense. Cy soaked it all in and allowed himself to be immersed in her world. His greatest fear in life had been to fall in love before he was ready, now he found himself living out that fear and doing so with enthusiasm.

The fish dinners arrived with little flair and the conversation lulled a bit as neither of them wanted to be impolite and talk with their mouths full. Coffee followed and the time neared when they were supposed to go and meet the others.

The waiter placed a small tray on the table. In the middle of the tray sat a small portfolio folder with the bill inside. "Will there be anything else?" He asked as he put the tray on the table.

Cy thought the question out of place. Why did they ask that after the bill had been rung up and they were handing it to you? He thought to himself, 'here's your hat, what's your hurry?' and grinned as the waiter left them to contemplate his tip.

"What's going through your head Cy?" Lexi asked as she noticed his grin.

"Nothing, they must need the table. It always seems that the check is ready before they ask you if you want anything more. Maybe next time we should wait until after the check is rung up before ordering!"

"Next time?" Lexi rebutted coyly. "So, you've decided there's going to be a next time?"

Unbelievable, Cy thought, as he felt a blush come up from his toes. "Well, I've decided for myself anyway."

"I'd like that too." She didn't leave him twisting in the wind. "But with school it's going to be difficult keeping in touch. I'm worried about starting a relationship now."

There it was, stated simply. "I know, I feel the same way, but..." He trailed off, not wanting to finish. "Look, lets not worry about tomorrow right now, let's just enjoy the evening."

"Deal." She said, and smiled that smile.

Already Cy could feel the fish unsettled in his stomach.

They finished their coffee and left the down town hovel in search of the crew. Cy took Lexi's hand as they left the restaurant. It was a much colder night than the night before and the wind gusting only made it seem cooler. Ears, noses and cheeks got bright red on nights like this, but Cy was generating so much heat he hardly noticed the chill air. Breath streams poured out of the mouths and noses of passersby as they walked the street to the car. The snow crunched under foot and under the tires of cars driving past in the night. The moon glowed dimly overhead as it coursed toward morning. It wasn't late, only 9:00, but Cy was painfully aware of how short the time had grown that he had to spend with Lexi. They were going to meet the others at Brian's, a farewell party for the returning students, just the six of them. One thing for certain, nobody would suggest going into the woods for a walk.

CHAPTER FIVE

Annie gave Dave a kiss and told him that she didn't want to leave for school the next day. They were trying to be mature about their future and realized that continuing their education now would be much easier than cutting it short and trying to finish it later. That meant time away from one another, and being apart for months at a time was quite difficult for them both.

That afternoon she had arrived at Dave's parents to find Dave in a sullen mood. Cy had just left and she could tell that whatever they had discussed had disturbed Dave. They were in the game room down in the basement. Dave's father had finished the cellar years ago and put a pool table down there. He set the room up with a dart board and a vintage pinball machine, a 'Charlie's Angels' game that he had found at a flea market in southern New Hampshire. Of course it was only appropriate that there would be a vintage Farrah Fawcett poster hanging on the wall along the side of the pinball machine. They were sitting on an old sofa along the wall by the pool table. The sofa had seen better days, the fabric on the cushions had become worn and frayed at the edges. The middle section sagged more than the two outer sections and so most people tried to avoid it, but not Annie and Dave. That section had become their pocket; worn by their cuddling it had conformed to their bottoms over the years. Annie wanted to pry the lid off of Dave but met with resistance. "Don't you want to talk about it?" she asked.

"Talk about what babe?" doing his best to avoid her interrogation.

"You know what I'm talking about, last night. I was pretty shook up by what was happening to you and could see that you were too, so I didn't want to push last night, but come on Dave, talk to me."

Dave looked at her for a moment, admiring her pretty face and short blonde hair. She had the look of a living kewpie doll, all of five feet even and usually about ninety-five pounds. When she smiled the corners of her mouth just kind of curled up and her cheeks swelled revealing a pair of dimples that could melt his heart. She wasn't smiling now, and Dave wasn't ready. "Annie, I just don't want to go into it right now, okay?"

He wouldn't open up, he told her there wasn't anything to say but she knew better. All she wanted to do was help. She resigned herself to this not being the time. Somehow Cyrus knew more about last night than Dave seemed to and definitely more than she did. So Dave must have opened up to him even though he wouldn't share with her. Guys don't get it, she thought, its one thing to confide in your buds, but this time it hurt her and angered her, and she would not simply lie down and let it go on. She would crack this nut wide open and that would be that. Tonight at the party, after all, it's just going to be friends.

The events of the night before were frustrating because now instead of focusing on enjoying one another the whole group was distracted and trying not to talk about what had happened in the woods. She and Dave had picked a spot on the floor near Brian's fireplace and were cuddling together. It should have been a perfect atmosphere but this thing hung in the air thick and relentless. Cy and Lexi had just arrived and were showing signs of affection toward one another. Annie could tell they were falling for one another. She shoots, she scores! Unfortunately she didn't feel like celebrating. There would be time for gathering details from Lexi later when they were back at school, for now there were bigger fish to fry. When there was a lull in the conversation, Annie said, "Alright boys, it's time to spill it!" While this got everyone's attention, there were no volunteers to start talking. She decided to focus on Cy directly. He felt the burn of her stare even across the room. "What happened in the woods last night?"

Cy looked at her, then to Dave and back to Annie, He feigned ignorance as best he could and shrugged his shoulders and said, "Why are you looking at me Annie, I didn't do anything?"

Annie said, "I'm not buying it Cyrus T., you know more than you're letting on, and I want to know what's happening. And I didn't say that you did anything, I asked you what happened." Then she turned her attention to Dave, "And you're not coming clean either!"

Cy and Dave looked at each other and both of them knew that there would be no avoiding the subject. Dave drew in a deep breath and let it out slowly. He leaned back against the wall, straightened his legs and settled himself in.

Almost subconsciously he reached for the fire poker and started poking at the log in the fireplace, knocking some embers loose and sending sparks up the flue. Playing with fires had always been a part of Dave's persona. Whenever they had gone camping Dave could always be found poking at the camp-fire. While he gently prodded the log with the poker he started to retell the story of the night before; only this time with the benefit of having some time for the fear to wear off making the accounting a little more detailed. If it hadn't been for Cy telling him of his experience he probably wouldn't have had the courage to go into it.

While Dave talked Cy paid attention to Brian. He found it hard to believe that living this close to the woods, and having grown up out there like he and Dave had, that Brian would have escaped any contact with this mysterious touching breeze thing. All of that along with the fact that the land has been in his family for generations made Cy suspicious that Brian knew something that he wasn't sharing.

When Brian stood he was the tallest of the gang. Right now six foot three and he weighed about two hundred ten pounds. He hadn't had a haircut since before high school graduation and had started a braid down his back. He had a gentle demeanor, so even though he should have, he didn't look threatening. Maybe it was the blonde-ness of his hair with the blue-ness of his eyes that rendered in him the demeanor of a lover and not a fighter. No matter, for the most part nobody bothered picking fights with him, so he lived a freely peaceful lifestyle. It was easy to see what Charlie saw in Brian. They were sitting close together on his sofa, her arms wrapped up with his and holding hands. They made a good couple, Cy thought, they complimented each other. She was also tall, about five foot ten, 130 pounds with brown hair and hazel eyes. She didn't seem to get excited easily, very laid back, but quick-witted and intelligent.

Presently Brian looked pensive. Cy had difficulty reading what Brian may have been feeling. Then he noticed Brian's gaze fixed upon him. Not only Brian, but the whole room seemed to be intently staring at him. He had been lost in thought and could not recall the last few words that Dave had said.

Charlie broke the silence when she said, "I don't get it, what does that have to do with Cy?"

"Yes, tell us Cy, What do you have to do with this?" asked Annie, her voice terse.

Cy knew that the time had arrived to come clean, no matter how guarded he had been about it. Anyway, there was nothing to do now but tell his story. So he did. He related the events of the sleep out five years before and the evening that he got his license two and a half years ago. This brought the touchy feely breeze thing encounters to a total of three. It also changed the overall mood of the party. No one had come out expecting to hear ghost stories or be in the mood for Ouija board games or a séance. Cy in particular felt distraught over the change that his stories had affected. He really didn't want to spoil the chemistry between he and Lexi, but he was beginning to fear that the damage had been done. When they had arrived, the only seating available were two separate chairs. They were side by side but not in a real intimate proximity as he would have preferred. They were able to hold hands but it was over the armrests and it began to feel awkward, especially when the time to begin telling his tale had come.

When he finished he looked at Annie and asked, "Are you satisfied now? I told Dave about this earlier today but I really didn't want to go into it tonight."

Brian ignored Cy's irritation with Annie and said, "So lets get this straight, Cy, you were touched twice by this thing but you say it felt like it was on the outside, and Dave, you were touched once but you said it felt like something inside of you poking outward?"

Both Dave and Cy nodded in acknowledgement toward Brian.

"That's kind of weird, don't you think? I mean the whole business is weird but there's an obvious difference in the experiences."

"What's your point?" Cy asked, and as he did so Lexi let go his hand and rose, she crossed the room toward the bathroom quietly.

"Well, nothing more than to state the obvious, your sensations were external Cy, while Dave's were internal." Brian was stating this as a matter of fact, trying to lend an analytical tone to the conversation.

Cy asked, "Do you have a theory?"

"No, nothing at all. Do you?"

"Only that I think you had an experience that you aren't telling us about."

Brian looked back and forth from Dave and Cy, then around the room. There were four pairs of eyes looking very expectantly at him. He said, "Look guys, I don't know any other way to put it than as bluntly as possible, I've never had any kind of experience like you're describing."

At that moment Lexi came into the room and with an almost guilty voice said, "Cy, could you bring me home now please."

Cy was taken by surprise by the request and it's being made at this particular time. He didn't want to leave the conversation but he also felt disinclined to cause a rift between he and Lexi. He looked back toward Brian and said, "This isn't over!" Then to Lexi, "Sure, Lexi, if that's what you want."

They gathered their coats and bundled themselves up. The air outside was chill and felt humid. Breath hung in the air as they slowly made their way to the car avoiding the icy patches. Cy opened the door for Lexi and made sure she didn't slip on the ice getting in. When he had gotten in on his side and started the car he asked, "Lexi, are you alright? Are you not feeling well from supper?"

Lexi looked down toward her knees. She had a sad and perplexed look on her face. She said, "Cy, I don't think this is going to work out between us." She turned her face toward him. "I think that a clean break now would be easier than allowing things to grow and become painful down the road. I really like you, and I hope we can still be friends."

Cy hadn't expected this. "What made you change your mind? Earlier when we were talking you seemed to like the idea of us as a couple. I thought we were on the same page about taking it slow and all…"

Lexi reached her gloved hand over and took Cy's hand and said, "Cy, look, I don't know what's going on with you and your friends, but it's kind of weirding me out. I don't know if this is the typical thing when you all get together, to talk about paranormal phenomena or what, but I'm just not into it and don't really want to be."

What could Cy say? From his own lips she had heard him speak of his two encounters with something that could only at this time be called a ghost. Feeling dejected, he put the car in gear and drove her to Annie's parent's house where she was staying until the next day. They went the whole way in silence. It was only a mile and a half but it seemed like it took an hour and a half to drive. When they arrived, Cy put the car in park, he turned to her and said, "I wish there were some way I could change your mind."

She looked sadly at him and just reaffirmed what she had told him earlier, "I really think its better this way." She reached for the door handle. "I'll see myself in. Good bye Cy."

"Bye, Lexi."

And with those words she walked out of his life.

CHAPTER SIX

Cy sat up in bed. As near as he could tell he hadn't fallen asleep in the two hours since he had gone to bed, only laid there remembering. Morgan lifted his head and looked at him from his dog bed on the floor. A very slow, lazy thump of his tail was the only noise in the silence. The clouds outside had broken and the third quarter moon rose slowly from the horizon. A soft melancholy glow dimly illuminated the bedroom through the blinds as Luna began its course in the night sky. It was 1:00 A.M. It had been almost a year since the memories kept him up all night. He didn't need this. He had a busy day ahead. Of course he knew the nature of his demon. October 1st approached, that would mark the two year anniversary of Dave's passing. Maybe it would be good to call Annie and get together with her for coffee. Cy had a hard time knowing if seeing her would be good or not. On one hand she is an old friend and someone whose friendship he valued. Yet, on the other hand, her pain and his together in one place seemed more than he, or she, could bear for long. Then there's the other thing that hung in the air like a dark cloud, why did so many people think that now with Dave gone, Annie and Cy would get together as a couple? They had both been nudged toward that arrangement by folks that didn't know them very well. While Annie and Cy were great friends there was just no love connection that could be made there, any more than one could be made between he and his own sister. The same people overlooked that minor detail not taking it into consideration, Dave is listed as missing, not dead. Still, the time had come, a call was in order.

With that resolved he lay his head down to fight round two with his pillow. Perhaps sleep would find him, but his mind would dream consciously first, of her. Lexi's memory set an impossible standard for anyone who followed to live up to. Impossible at least where Cy was concerned. It had been eight years, still he was alone and spending too many nights with her occupying his dreams. He constantly reproached himself for a sap the way he still pined for her.

Cy gave up, rolled out of bed and made his way downstairs. He lay down on the sofa and reached for the remote, hoping to find distraction on the television. For all he knew she had married and had ten children by now. He hoped to himself that her husband was ugly. A Saturday Night Live rerun was on, a show from around the fifteenth year. Hans and Frans were pumping up the audience. Ten kids would really have taken their toll on her too. She must have let herself go. Arnold Schwarzeneggar was the guest host and had joined Hans and Frans as they made fun of girly men. Cy didn't believe it, not for an instant. He felt sure that she looked beautiful as ever.

So it went until finally around three-thirty, Cy eventually dozed off with the TV still on, his mind still thinking of all that had happened over the years.

After college Cy had taken a position in a local company. He had earned his degree in Manufacturing Engineering. He specialized in taking old blueprints and translating them into a computerized drawing editor and from there, generating programs for the CNC machinery that would manufacture the parts. This proved to be something of a niche position. It presented Cy with a challenge mentally and paid him pretty well.

Brian and Charlie were married by this time and had been for a year before Cy had graduated college. Another wedding loomed ahead of the old gang, this one for Annie and Dave. Cy and Brian were co-best men for Dave. Annie told Cy that the girl from South Bay would not be coming. He felt ambiguous about the news.

When the wedding day arrived, the weather made for postcard perfection in an early October New England countryside. The leaves were at their peak, the sun shone through oversized cotton ball clouds creating a textbook autumn day for the occasion. Annie and Dave exchanged vows at the little church they had both grown up in at 10:00 A.M. The reception followed at The Wright Family Farm, Brian's family farm that had been converted into an inn by his parents. There were mountain views, a lake with rolling nearby fields and a stream on the property. Cy found himself thinking that if the day were any more perfect for his friends it would probably seem too cliché.

There were no girls there that caught Cy's eye, not that he spent much time looking. He had long since decided that he wanted simply to be a bachelor. His mother would fight the notion at every turn. She had tried in vane to push her son toward this ones daughter or that ones niece. She wanted grandchildren and her son wasn't cooperating.

It was at the reception that the new manifestation occurred. There again came the eerie stillness in the air, especially noticeable during the outside reception. Dave sat at the head table, alone for at the moment, when from his plate a single pea arose. It seemed to levitate about three inches over the rest of his meal. This caught Dave's attention. After about fifteen seconds the pea began to spin. No warbling or sound coming from it. It just floated there spinning. Dave looked around quickly, and saw Cy at the end of the table. They made eye contact and Dave nodded toward his plate. Cy had noticed the atmosphere as well and had been wondering what if anything would come of it. He got up and made his way toward Annie's empty seat. He could see the spinning pea as he approached. He felt as though he were moving through molasses on a cold winter day. As he sat next to Dave they tried to act as though nothing were happening.

Cy smiled as a man smiled at his best friend's wedding, he clapped his hand on Dave's shoulder and said, "So what's happening here, man?"

Dave's face didn't match his voice, smiling back he said, "Oh, brutha, we don't need this now, not here, not at my wedding. Annie will freak!"

Cy said, "Let's just wait this thing out and see what happens, maybe this will be over without anyone noticing."

"I hope you're right, Cy"

They acted as though they were making idle chat, trying not to stare at the pea over the plate. Waiting; one, two, three minutes went by, as if the phenomenon were saying to them that it could continue as long as they could wait. As they waited through this microcosm of an eternity they were looking about them, trying to notice if the event in Dave's plate had been noticed by anyone else. That's when someone did that annoying thing that is so popular at New England weddings. Clink, clink, clink, the silverware tapped the glass cups and bottles all around the reception dining area. All eyes were searching out the bride and groom to witness a kiss.

Cy said, "Go find Annie."

Dave didn't need to be told twice. He rose to his feet and headed around the table, drawing all the attention away from the specter of the spinning pea. With everyone's attention following Dave cross the dance floor toward Annie, Cy decided to take an action and tossed Dave's linen napkin onto the plate to sink the pea… big mistake. The napkin caught hold of the pea and began to spin with it, waving around in rapid clock-wise revolutions, the edges flailing about, flapping and creating a small clamor at an altitude of three inches over the plate. Cy immediately reached for the napkin to put an end to the spectacle without considering what might happen. The instant he touched the napkin he felt that he too might be taken up and spun like a toy by the pea. But instead, he felt as though he were blacking out. Everything and everyone around him faded from his sight. All sound became muffled, although in a strange way he could still hear the sounds of the wedding. They sounded like a reel-to-reel being run at fast forward giving the reception guests an Alvin and the Chipmunks appeal. He could see his own self, and the napkin in his hand, and there were shadows moving about him very rapidly. The sounds accelerated and grew to a high pitched timbre. The napkin grew still and seemed to be rigid, suspended in the same flailing way that it had been when spinning above the plate. Cy let go of the napkin and it fell to the dewy grass in the otherwise empty yard. The dark starry sky had pink fringes on the horizon.

There wasn't another soul in sight. Cy was at a loss at first about what had just happened to him. He determined that he must have been taken into the source of energy that had caused the pea to spin. He knew that he had to come up with some kind of cover story for disappearing in the middle of the reception. Dave would understand and want to hear what had really happened to him. Cy knew however that Annie would be a little less enthusiastic about this phenomenon intruding her wedding.

He made his way around the farmhouse. That's when he noticed that the pink fringe on the horizon glowed in the east. It was the dawn, the sunrise, not the sunset after the reception. He had been spinning with that napkin from when... two o'clock in the afternoon, and here it was dawn, somewhere around 6:30 A.M. That's approximately sixteen to seventeen hours, in what seemed like no time at all. His mind was having a hard time wrapping around that concept. He made his way to the parking area and fished his keys from out of his pants pocket. When he came around the barn he realized that the keys would be more useful if only his car were there as well. He remembered driving it and parking it along the edge of the lake. Yet, now the entire parking area was empty. He thought perhaps it had been towed away, but why would the Wright's have his car towed?

A five-mile walk back to his apartment as it turned out would be just the thing he needed. Cy had to come up with a viable story for his disappearance. He realized that he also had to avoid being seen. It wasn't normal to be out and about strolling in a rented tux in the early morning hours. The police would ask him for some kind of explanation should he encounter them, and Cy felt at a loss for anything resembling a viable story.

He made his way down the dirt road to the main road below the farm. At the entrance he turned east and started the trek back to town and to his apartment. A story started to roll around in his head; 'he had met a girl at the reception, they left together and got a room. While nobody that knew him would be inclined to believe that he had had a one-night stand with a total stranger, and some would likely want a name, he determined that it would be a decidedly better alternative to having been hurled into the future on a napkin spinning around a pea on the Groom's plate! There were bound to be some men in white coats somewhere that would believe him. Besides, he was only concerned with satisfying the police if he was asked.

As he made his way into town he felt pleased that he wasn't encountering any traffic. He approached his apartment and was almost shocked to see his car parked right there in front of the building, just like he had always parked it. Someone must have moved his car, not towed it, but why?

Cy quietly climbed the stairs to the second floor. He didn't want to wake his landlord. Turning his key in the lock, he opened the door to his apartment and stepped inside.

Something was wrong. There was someone here. The hair on the nape of his neck prickled up, as did his ears, his eyes widened and every muscle tensed. Whoever had moved his car had also likely invaded his home and now he could hear the mystery guest in the bedroom moving around quietly, almost, Cy thought, too quietly. He stepped into the bedroom door and looked for the first time, eye to eye, at the perpetrator.

He looked at himself.

As the sun rose and shone into the window it mercilessly stabbed at Cy's eyes causing him to come full awake. He could hear his alarm clock upstairs in his bedroom. The morning news played on the TV. The time on the cable box read 6:36 A.M. Three hours sleep had to be better than none. The coffee brewer, set to an automatic timer, had already kicked on. The smell of coffee filled the house. Cy rose from the sofa with an appetite for a cup of coffee and a bowl of cereal.

CHAPTER SEVEN

As Cy drove to work he remembered talking to himself. He thought that perhaps he may be the only living human to have had that experience. The cost of therapy that he should have for all of this would be astronomical. But all things considered he felt he was holding it together quite well without a shrink.

At first they had just stood there looking at each other. Remarkably there was no panic on either of the two Cy's faces. Almost as though they both knew that the other was in fact himself, and that as long as they could remain calm, they could work this odd turn of events out. But neither of them knew where to begin.

Cy #1 who just walked in started, "I know one of us doesn't belong here, and I think it's me. Just tell me, what day is this?"

Impatiently Cy #2 said, "It's the ether isn't it?" Then without waiting for an answer, "It's Saturday morning."

The look on Cy #1's face was that of realization. He hadn't gone seventeen hours into the future as he had supposed, rather he went back in time about seven hours to when he was just getting out of bed that morning. His other self was just awakening as he had walked from the farm. He looked around the room and remembered everything that was presently taking place in front of him just as it had with him just a few hours ago; the bed still in disarray from a fitful night, the coffee brewing in the kitchen, the morning news on the television. He looked at his other self and smirked, "I'm going to need some of that coffee." Then he chuckled and added, "This is one morning that I'll need two cups!"

"Ayuh!" Cy #2 said. They went into the kitchen and awkwardly sat across the table from one another. "Would you mind explaining how you got here, how I got here, across the table… from myself?"

Cy #1 recounted to his earlier self the events of the day as it happened to him. The story of the pea and the napkin was the high point and he was careful not to leave any details out. When he had finished he said, "Isn't this what the scientific community would refer to as a paradox?"

Cy #2 said, "Wouldn't one of us have had to kill the other for that, or at the very least one of our grandfathers?"

Cy #1 thought for a moment and grinned, "Fortunately we don't believe in suicide."

Cy #2 turned serious. "Or patricide! So if I avoid the pea, wouldn't that just put things to rights?"

Cy #1 said, "I don't think so. If you avoid the pea, then I won't be here to tell you to do so. This whole scenario wouldn't take place and you wouldn't know to avoid the pea and napkin. We would get caught in a loop. You would do the same thing again and I would be here again. That's the conundrum, that's the paradox."

"Right, how about this then; we both go to the wedding reception, obviously you stay out of sight, until the pea pops up, then you go and repeat what you did while I take a powder. Perhaps we'll remerge into one being."

"Or we'll be having this conversation again only with a third self to make things more complicated. Who knows, maybe another one of us is about to walk in the door at any time." They both paused for a moment and looked at the door. "I don't know for sure what to do, but that's as good a plan as any."

Cy #2 decided to be the one to say it. "So this is a new thing with the damned breeze."

Cy #1 looking back said, "Yeah, I think so. It's like nothing from before though, I mean, we talk to ourself, as you know, but nothing like this."

"Any tips you can give me from the day that might help me along? Lottery numbers? Girls' phone numbers? Anything?"

Cy #1 laughed and shook his head, "You know that I don't pay attention to the lottery. And as far as girls go, she won't be there and neither will anyone else of interest."

Cy #2 nodded knowingly. "I think, just the same that I'll take notice of the Mega Millions numbers… just in case we do this again!"

They couldn't leave together so Cy #1 stayed behind to await an opportune time to make his way to the wedding reception. Cy#2 left and, aside from not looking forward to the entrée at the reception, enjoyed witnessing his friends' nuptials. When the meal began at the reception Cy #2 noticed from the corner of his eye that Annie had left her seat at the table to go to the ladies room. It must have been the ladies room, two of the bridesmaids went with her. He wondered to himself at the reason why women always go to the ladies room together. Then he noticed Dave looking at him. Dave's eyes looked as if gesturing toward the plate in front of him, just as his other self had told him. There he saw the pea, hovering in a spin about three inches over Dave's plate. Cy got up and made his way toward Annie's empty seat. He could see the spinning pea as he approached. He felt as though he were moving through molasses on a cold winter day. As he sat next to Dave they tried to act as though nothing was happening.

Smiling, Cy clapped his hand on Dave's shoulder and said, "So what's happening here, man?"

Dave's face didn't match his voice, smiling back he said, "Wow, Déjà vu. Oh, brutha, we don't need this now, not here, not at our wedding. Annie will freak!"

Cy said, "If only you knew. Let's just wait this thing out and see what happens, maybe this will be over without anyone noticing."

"I hope you're right, Cy"

They made some idle chat, trying not to stare at the pea over the plate. Waiting. One. Two. Three minutes went by, as if to say to them that it could continue as long as they could wait. As they waited they were looking about them, trying to notice if the phenomenon in Dave's plate was being noticed by anyone else. That's when someone did that annoying thing that is so popular at New England weddings; clink, clink, clink as the silverware tapped the glass cups and bottles all around the reception dining area. All eyes were searching out the bride and groom to witness a kiss.

Cy said, "Go find Annie."

Dave didn't need to be told twice. He rose to his feet and headed around the table, drawing all the attention away from the specter of the spinning pea.

Cy #2 looked around, wondering if his other self had been able to get there, and if so, get there without anyone noticing. Then he saw himself, behind a balloon bouquet. Cy #1 was waving him off. He got up and hastily crossed away from the head table to the bar hoping to blend. He would know soon if they were going to be successful or not.

Cy #1 made his way across the crowd, hoping the dual presence wouldn't be noticed. He rounded the table from the direction that his other self had gone to make it look like he was returning to eat. As he approached the Groom's dish he saw the pea still in a hover and spinning away as he remembered. He picked up the linen and tossed it as he had before onto the pea... as before it began to spin around, attempting to call attention to itself. With great trepidation he reached down and caught a corner of the napkin. At first he didn't notice anything happening. Then, curiously, he started to remember waking up that morning to find himself looking at himself. He remembered the whole conversation, all of the days events, from both perspectives. It seemed to him that the plan that he and himself had come up with had worked. As he pondered all that had happened, Annie and Dave returned to the table. Dave seemed nearly in a panic, Annie looked almost suspicious. That's when he realized he was standing at Dave's dining place with a napkin in his hand that partially draped over Dave's plate. Cy seemed to be scavenging Dave's plate. This may seem inappropriate behavior at a wedding.

Cy said, "Didn't like your dinner Dave?"

Dave followed Cy's lead, "Oh, yeah it was good, I just took off looking for Annie and I must have tossed my napkin on top of my plate."

Cy put the napkin down next to the plate and said, "Ah, okay." He smiled and looked at them both and said, "I'm really happy for you guys!"

Annie gave Cy a hug and Dave shook his hand at the same time. The two men knew they would have to talk after the honeymoon, but there would be no more discussion about the spinning pea today.

As Cy parked his truck in the parking lot he drew a deep breath and blew it out slowly. He had to go to work and decided he had to do his best not to think about it. But no matter how he tried, he couldn't help but think about the unknowns surrounding Dave. Was there a connection between Dave's disappearance and the ether? Was Dave actually dead? Or was it as Brian had once speculated, he had somehow been taken by the ether and moved through time? What is the nature of the ether, anyway? Could it be manipulated, mastered? At one time this phenomenon seemed to behave more like a ghost, trying to scare them, then it changed... why? The 'why' list kept on growing and growing. Cy felt surprised as he pondered this, at the automatic way in which he had started his truck back up and drove out of the parking lot. He would return home and call in sick.

CHAPTER EIGHT

Cy would have to call work from home. He could call Annie from his cell. He took it out of his pocket and flipped it open. Knowing that cell phones and driving weren't the best combinations, he pulled over and attached the hands free set. Annie was #9 on speed dial. He pulled back into traffic as he waited for her to answer.

"Hello?" Annie said, over the phone.

"Hey girl, it's Cy, How're ya doin'?"

"Cy, hi. I'm well, how are you?"

"I'm alright. Hey what are you up to, care to have coffee with an old pal?" Cy asked.

"Hmm, I think I could squeeze you into my tight schedule…old pal!" Annie retorted.

Cy felt gratified to hear what sounded like a normal tone of voice for Annie. He asked, "How about in an hour? Tee's?"

"Tee's it is then, in an hour."

"Great, see you then, Annie."

"Bye."

Annie was surprised to hear from Cy, although she felt she shouldn't be. She decided it would be nice to sit and talk with a friend. In the last few years, she had withdrawn. She found it easier to just cope on her own than to feel the uncomfortable tension that seemed to prevail with well meaning friends and family. It was the pity that bothered her the most. She didn't want it. She felt repelled by it. Cy was an exception to this because if anything he and Brian were every bit as devastated as she. Annie found that she pitied them as much as they pitied her. Perhaps with them, pity is the wrong word, commiseration seemed more appropriate. That shared loss made their similar sadness tolerable. But for them, they had lost a boyhood friend, for her; her soulmate, friend, husband, the man she had wanted to have children with and grow old along side of. Brian still had Charlie, and Cy, well, Cy still had Lexi in his head. If Annie had known how things would turn out between those two she never would have introduced them to each other. She often wondered if she ought to tell Cy that Lexi was still single, and of all things, living locally. They kept in touch by email, Christmas cards and such. Lexi hadn't been able to make it to the memorial Service but she had called and spent time on the phone with her a few times. She got the sense that she wanted to ask about Cy, but Lexi never did, so Annie just left it alone. Then there was Cy who was always on the edge of asking about Lexi, but he never did, so again Annie left it alone. She wasn't, after all, in high school anymore and neither were they. If they wanted to get together it was their business. Yet, while Annie felt responsible, she had her own troubles to work through.

It isn't easy trying to understand who she is when for most of her life she had been identified by others, and had even identified herself, as one half of a couple. She never expected to be trying to come to grips with these emotions at this young age. Nor had she ever thought of what she would do if she found herself suddenly alone. All of these feelings were real and in her face demanding her attention. It was nearly two years since Dave's disappearance. That was why Cy had called. Maybe he wanted to talk about Dave. Maybe he wanted to talk about that, damned breeze, or ether or whatever they had called it; the very thing that drove Lexi away. The very thing that nearly drove her away; that should have driven her away! In retrospect, it really wouldn't have mattered, the end result would have been the same, at least she had had some time with Dave.

It would be okay now. Annie felt ready to talk about it. A part of her didn't want to, but that was just the old jealousy rearing its ugly head. Even after they were married Dave, Cy and Brian would get together and go on about this thing like most groups of guys would go on about baseball or football or whatever. With them it was always the ether. A lot of talk about thin air! Alright, so she had seen what happened with Dave in the woods way back then, but could that have been reason enough to become obsessed? Needless to say it was a bone of contention between she and Dave during their marriage. That was then, this is now.

They arrived separately at Tee's Diner. Cy arrived first, and had ordered two coffees. He was acquainted with waitress, Sandy, from many breakfasts there. They were friendly but really didn't know each other. She was short with long blond hair that she usually wore braided while working. Cy thought she had a nice figure and at times even thought that she was flirting with him. He ultimately chalked that up to maneuvering for a good tip, which Cy was known to give. Sandy brought the coffee and asked, "Would you and your imaginary friend here like to order breakfast?"

Cy grinned and shot back, "We're just going to sip our coffee for now, but don't go to far, I might imagine a third friend soon and maybe then we'll order."

Sandy smirked and said, "Alrighty then, you just holler." She turned and strutted it back to the kitchen area and made herself busy.

Cy indulged himself and enjoyed the spectacle of her retreat. While he watched Sandy, he missed Annie coming in the door.

Annie of course could see what Cy was watching and she quietly approached the table and said, "Busted! Men are so transparent."

Cy laughed and stood up. He gave Annie a hug and helped her into her seat. Then he sat back down across from her. He said, "You're looking great Annie! How have you been?"

Annie just smiled and looked back at Cy. She tilted her head slightly to the right, which for Cy was trademark Annie, and said, "Oh, I'm doing as well as can be expected. How about you?"

Cy said, "Well I've slept better, but all things considered, pretty well."

Annie asked, "How is Morgan?"

Cy said, "I think he's adjusted. I bet he would shake his tail if he saw you though."

"Oh, you mean like that waitress was shaking hers for you?"

Cy laughed and said, "Man, you're quick to point out how transparent men are, but you women are catty!"

Annie just grinned and poured some half-and-half into her coffee.

Sandy came back to the table and looked at Cy and asked, "So do you two want to order this morning?"

Cy said, "I sure would like some breakfast." Looking at Annie he asked, "Are you hungry?"

Annie said, "Actually, I ate before you called, I'll make do with the coffee, thanks. But by all means, eat Cy."

Cy looked back at Sandy and said, "I'll have the Eggs Irish with wheat toast and a large orange juice, please."

Sandy snapped, "Oh watching your cholesterol?"

Cy said, "Yeah, watching it go straight up."

Sandy smiled and turned to go.

After Sandy had gone from earshot, Annie said, "Go ahead, enjoy the view, again!"

Cy looked at Annie and just chuckled, resisting the urge to watch Sandy walk away. He said to Annie, "You're taking all of the fun out of it. You're supposed to let me think I'm getting away with something!"

"Have you asked her out?"

Cy just looked down at the table and said, "No, I just enjoy the view."

Annie said, "Why not, she obviously likes you?"

"Nooo, I'm not into her."

Annie was contemplating mentioning Lexi, but it proved unnecessary, Cy seemed anxious to move on.

Cy said, "Listen, I wanted to talk with you. There are some things that you never knew about that I think Dave would want you to know now."

Annie had a look of consternation on her face. She said, "Are you saying that Dave kept secrets from me?"

Cy winced at that and said, "Maybe 'secrets' is a strong term, look you know that we were trying to figure out what was going on out in the woods, but I don't know that Dave had told you everything that had happened, and I thought that you would like to know more about what we had learned."

Annie looked down at the table top. She felt nausea creeping up on her. She thought that she was ready to talk about all of this, even now she wanted to hear what Cy had to say. But at the same time there was a gnawing in the pit of her stomach that threatened to burst a dammed up reservoir of tears. She struggled to keep her composure and looked up at Cy. He seemed to be reading her thoughts on her face as if they were written there in bold marker. He had gone silent. The tension at the table was thickening. Neither really knew what to say at that time.

Sandy arrived with Cy's breakfast. She placed the plates in front of him and turned to Annie and asked, "Are you sure I can't get you anything else?"

Annie looked up and forced a polite smile and said, "No, Thank you."

The mood at the table was evident to Sandy, but she pushed on anyway, "Can I top off your coffees?"

Cy said, "Sure."

Sandy said pleasantly, "I'll be right back." She turned and went to the counter where the coffee pots were. She picked up the first pot, it was less than half full and had a few grounds in the bottom of it. When she got back to Cy and Annie's table she poured coffee into Cy's cup first, then emptied the pot, grounds and all into Annie's cup.

It wasn't a blatantly obvious gesture, Cy missed it completely in fact, but Annie saw what Sandy had done and recognized the territorial overtones that came with it. Strangely, this seemed to bring Annie out of her funk. She giggled. A little at first, then it seemed to grow funnier and funnier.

Cy was completely mystified. He said, "See, this is exactly why I know that God wants me to be a bachelor. I could swear that you were about to cry, but here you are giggling like you need a straight jacket. I'm sitting over here with absolutely no idea how you went from one extreme to the other."

At this Annie went from giggling to full laughter. After about a minute, she settled herself down and took a few deep breaths to regain her composure. She finally looked at Cy and said, "Yes Cy, I want to discuss all of this… stuff, but I think we should include Brian and Charlie, after-all, if I was feeling left out, then I'm sure she was too, and Brian was involved in all of this too. If I'm going to get an accurate picture in my mind about your ether, then I want all the input that I can get." She looked around to see if Sandy was anywhere nearby. When she knew where she was she looked again at Cy and asked, "How long have you been enjoying that view?"

Cy was puzzled at the switch back to Sandy. "I've been coming here for years. Why?"

Annie waved her hand in front of Cy's eyes as though he were blind. She said, "Are you totally oblivious to the fact that she has a thing for you?"

"Nooo, you're nuts!"

"Cy, she just poured me a cup of grinds, she thinks I'm the reason that her swing isn't in your backyard!" And with that Annie started to giggle again.

Cy looked down the diner at Sandy and then back at Annie. First he said, "Nooo." Then he thought for a minute and he began to see Annie's point. He too began to chuckle. He added, "You have nothing to do with why I haven't asked her out."

Annie stopped giggling and turned serious, almost too quickly and said, "Actually, I do." After a brief pause to let Cy's demeanor change she added, "You haven't had anything like a relationship since I introduced you to Lexi. You should either get over her or call her. Geez Cy, how long has it been, eight years? Are you really going to waste your entire life? A big guy like you and what are you afraid of?" There, the cat was out of the bag. She had made her opinion known and hinted at Lexi's marital status as well as the possibility of her being open to a call from Cy.

Cy was slack-jawed at this. He couldn't tell if what he felt was anger or elation. It was his turn to be stunned emotionally. Finally he looked at Annie and asked, "Do you think she'll want to see me?"

Annie smirked and feigning a teeny-bopper look said, "Well gee, do ya want me to pass her a note in study hall?"

Cy shot right back, "Would you? And let me know on the bus home this afternoon?"

Annie just looked across the table and said, "Look, Your name doesn't come up in our conversations, in the same way that her name doesn't come up in your and my conversations. It's too deliberate. I've minded my business and kept out of it. I don't know what would happen if you called her, but I wish you would and get it out of the way. That way maybe both of you will get on with your lives. Look Cy, Dave is gone. Dead or alive I can't have him in my life anymore. If I knew where he was you can bet I wouldn't be waiting around for a miracle to drop him in my lap. My advice to you would be to either call her once and for all, or go for a ride on the swing! But do something! Don't live your life alone."

Cy was incredulous. He had never seen Annie with this set manner before. All he could manage was, "Would you get me her phone number?"

Annie got her cell phone from her purse and punched a few buttons with her thumb.

Cy got his cell phone from his coat pocket and copied the number into his phone in like manner, with his thumb. After he had entered it, he looked at it with a puzzled expression.

Annie asked, "What now?"

Cy just looked at her and asked, "This is a local area code. Where is she living?"

Annie smiled and said, "Why don't you ask her?"

Cy nodded, still staring in disbelief at the number displayed on his cell phone. After a minute he turned his attention back to his cooling breakfast. Mostly he picked at it, eating the eggs and hash, but leaving the English muffins in favor of the wheat toast, which he used to sop up the cheese sauce.

Annie enjoyed watching Cy eat, and carried the conversation while he occupied his mouth. She caught him up on her family, how her parents were. She told him about things at work. She even told him that she was thinking about dating again. But she didn't have anyone in mind yet.

At the mention of her dating, Cy stopped and just looked at her. He said, "You know Annie, I never really thought about you dating again, it's just that you've always been with Dave. I think he would want you to though. He would definitely be jealous, but I know that he would want you to be happy."

Annie's eyes began to fill, but she got a-hold of her self and managed to stem the flow. She said, "Thanks Cy."

Sandy came back to the table and asked, "How was breakfast?"

Cy said, "It was great, thanks. Could I have the check please?"

When Sandy turned and left to get the check with an arm full of dishes, both Annie and Cy watched her sachet away. She returned a minute later with the check, which Cy immediately gave her a ten and a five-dollar bill to cover both the tab and a tip. She said, "Thanks Cy."

Cy said, "You're welcome Sandy, have a good one!"

As they got up to leave the diner, Annie looked at Cy and said, "Let's give her something to watch for a change!"

Cy grinned and said, "Catty, catty, catty!"

With that they put their arms around each other like lust filled lovers and walked out the door. Before the door shut, Annie dropped her arm down and gave Cy's butt cheek a pinch.

She said to Cy, "That was better than coffee grinds!"

That night the phone rang at Annie's house. She answered, "Hello?"

"Hi Annie." The voice on the receiver said.

"Hiya, Lexi..."

CHAPTER NINE

After breakfast with Annie, Cy decided he should get into work after all. His mind had quieted some in regard to the things that were causing him difficulty sleeping. Now, of course, he had something new to ponder: the reality that he may yet be able to have something with Lexi. Of course the very reason that she called it off with him had never left, which was why he had never tried calling her. And now with the subject coming back into the forefront of his life, he was thinking that he would still post-pone calling her until after everything had been hashed out for Annie's sake. He couldn't think of what he would be like if she came back into his life only to leave again, especially if it were for the same reason.

When he came home from work that night he took Morgan out into the backyard with his Frisbee. Morgan loved to chase the disc. He would start out by Cy's side and run across the yard sometimes over two-hundred feet from where Cy had flipped the disc, and catch it in stride. There were even those occasions when he would jump and catch it in midair, just like the wonder-dogs on TV. Cy would usually bring a bottle of water out with him and at some point he would turn the Frisbee over and pour some water into it so Morgan could have a drink. Eventually he would tucker Morgan out and they would go inside. Cy always felt that he needed to give this attention to Morgan, not because he was Dave's dog, but because if he couldn't spend some time with him then he shouldn't have taken him. He was a good dog and deserved the attention.

Cy was going to have to exercise patience now. He had decided not to call Lexi, but the temptation was going to be difficult to resist.

He called Brian. After only the first ring Cy heard the receiver being lifted out of the cradle. A young voice on the other end answered. "Hullo?"

Cy came back, "Hi, is this Mike?"

"Hi Uncle Cy." Mike said. His voice was at the breaking point and had a rasp to it. Sometimes when he got excited it would go from being like a little boy's alto into the tenor that it was bound to fully become.

Cy liked that the boys called him Uncle Cy. It helped to make him feel like family. Over the years he had remained friends with Brian and had become a friend of Charlie's. Just because a friend of yours gets married doesn't mean that you are going to be friends with his wife. In fact, that is usually why so many guys drift away from their friends after marrying. Charlie was good about it though, as she knew how Brian valued his friends. Eventually she didn't have to work at having the guys over and trying to be happy about it. Cy and Dave, Cy especially because Dave was in a relationship, had to work to get into and stay in her good graces. What is difficult here for a single guy, is knowing what things were acceptable as things-to-do-with-with-a-married-man and what things were not. Weekend white water rafting trips with the office crew, which included some single women, were not on the good list. Really, what it came down to was, he had to reassure Charlie that he wasn't trying to undermine their relationship, and that he respected that Charlie came first in Brian's life.

Cy asked, "Is your Dad there Mike?"

Mike said, "Yuh, I'll get him."

"Thanks kiddo." Cy answered.

Brian must have been right there by the phone because almost immediately after Cy thanked Mike, Brian came on the line. "Hey Cy, how're you?"

"Holding my own Brian, how about you?"

"Man I haven't been holding my own in years! So I guess I'm doing better than you are!"

Cy just shook his head and said, "Dude, you are one sick puppy. Hey Brian, I talked with Annie today. She seems like she's ready to tie up some loose ends and make some frayed knots. She wants to talk, and she really wants to include you and Charlie. Is there any time that's best to get together?"

Brian said, "How about you let me get back to you on that. I'll see what's going on with Chuck. I'm sure we can pull something together." Chuck was Brian's pet name for Charlie. She hated it and only barely tolerated it from Brian. He for the most part seemed to only call her that when he wanted to tease her, which was most of the time. Brian asked, "How is Annie these days?"

Cy said, "You know, she's really looking good. She still has a lot of pain in her eyes, but that's to be expected.

And probably outside of a small circle of friends that pain wouldn't be all that evident."

"Well, that's good. I've been meaning to call her, so this will be a good chance to see her and catch up. Having the boys really puts a crimp in the ole' social life."

"Yeah, but their worth sacrificing a social life for. Are they keeping out of trouble?"

"Oh yeah, they're still young though, it's the teenage years that I'm worried about. They are both very strong willed."

"Well look, give me a call when you know what's good for you guys and hopefully we can all get together soon and open up this can of worms."

Brian said, "You got it. I'll try and get back to you by tomorrow night."

"Okay."

"Later."

"Later."

Brian had never had an encounter with the ether. Not like Cy or Dave at least. He did, however have the distinction of seeing both Cy's at Annie and Dave's wedding. When Cy #2 left the head table to make room for Cy#1, he saw Brian by the bar and headed straight for him. He looked at Brian and told him, "Bri, don't ask, just let me get behind you." He let Cy duck behind him and followed Cy's gaze back out to the head table where he saw the other Cy approach Dave's seat. He spun around in time to watch Cy fade before his eyes as the two remerged. Later, when Brian and Cy talked and Cy recounted to Brian what had happened, Brian didn't need any convincing to believe it. David Copperfield couldn't have done a better disappearing act. From that time on Brian was always curious and interested in what Cy and Dave would share about the ether. He had even made a believer, albeit a skeptical one, out of Charlie. In this case, there was need for a skeptic, it helped to keep the theories honest and at least plausible. If there was such a thing as a plausible theory in regards to the ether.

It was fall, so Brian was out raking leaves an hour later when Charlie came home from work. Mike and Craig were helping, if you could call it help. They would rake up a big pile of leaves and, as all kids in New England did, they would get a running start and jump into the pile. As Charlie pulled into the driveway the boys were jumping up and down brushing leaves and grass clippings off of themselves and searching over their clothes frantically. They had just jumped in when Brian told them that they shouldn't have jumped into that part of the pile because that was the area he had just seen some dog poop in. They were in a panic looking for soiled clothes. Brian was in a panic to keep a straight face.

Charlie got out of her car and crossed the lawn. They embraced and kissed hello as the boys ran up to her.

"Mom, Mom," Mike said, "We're helping Dad! But Dad said we just jumped into dog poop!"

Craig said, "Mommy do I have poop on my back? Mikey said I had poop on my back!"

"No Honey, I don't see any there, just leaves." Charlie looked at Brian and said, "I think I should go back to work."

Brian said, "That's fine, just make supper and give the boys a bath first will you?"

"Then I can go back?"

"Yeah, sure. I'll put the boys to bed for you. I'm good that way."

"You're too good to me!"

"I know, I spoil you rotten."

The boys went back to the pile of leaves and were kicking around in it trying to find the offending offal. They were scattering leaves that had taken the better part of an hour for Brian to gather with all of their help. Brian said, "All right guys, jump break is over, time to get back to raking!"

Craig, who knew where to go for the best chance to get his way, said, "Mommy, do we have to rake again? I want to jump in the leaves some more." As he was pleading with her he was hugging her leg and resting his head against her thigh. He knew who, and he knew how.

"You can jump some more tomorrow, you come inside with me now and get cleaned up." Charlie knew that she had let herself get all wrapped around these boy's fingers, but she was determined to do something about it. So every so often she would surprise them with an answer they least expected and enforce it.

"Ha ha Craigy, you gotta go in!" exclaimed Mike, elated at the prospect of being able to stay out and play a little longer. The elation was short lived.

It was Brian's turn, "You grab a rake Mike. We've got to finish this pile and haul it out back before we go in for supper!"

It wasn't until after nine that evening when the boys were fed, bathed, toothbrushed, story read and properly tucked in, that Brian was able to talk to Charlie. She had managed to beat him to the sofa. Brian knew the rules, the last one to the sofa brought the ice cream. He dug a bowl of double fudge swirl for Charlie and a bowl of strawberry for himself. The double fudge swirl would be better with dry-roasted peanuts so he sprinkled some on and carried the bowls out to the living room for a little Mommy-and-Daddy-time. "Here you go Chuck." Brian quipped. Then he added, "I've been waiting to talk with you."

"Yeah, I know. What did Cy want?"

Brian looked at his wife with a puzzled look and asked, "How did you know Cy called?

"You've had that 'How-do-I-approach-her-with-this-look' on your face all evening. You usually get that look when Cy calls."

Brian looked at Charlie and just shook his head. "I've never been able to hide anything from you. You know what I get you for your birthday and for Christmas long before I do.

"Cy called about Annie actually. She's ready to talk about all of the things that happened."

Charlie took a spoonful of ice cream and kept the spoon in her mouth pensively. After a few moments of consideration she withdrew the spoon and looked at Brian and said, "What makes you think that she's going to believe any of that stuff any more than I do?"

At first the remark stung Brian, but not for long. Charlie had always made her feelings known when it came to this invisible, intangible whispering wind that had been spooking these guys since they were boys. She had tolerated and indulged them their fantasy about the ether, before Dave's death, but now it didn't seem right to her. It didn't seem right to drag it all up for Annie, in the name of helping her to cope. It didn't seem right that grown men should get together as friends and spend hours talking about these experiences that best fit under the category of paranormal. That was too much like watching Ghostbusters. It was a funny movie, but you didn't want it playing over and over again in your living room.

Brian said, "Listen Babe, let's just once sit and spend some time with Cy and Annie and get it all out so if nothing else we can put it all away."

Charlie took another mouthful of ice cream and relented. "Alright, but really Brian, I don't want to see you going nuts with this again."

"No worries sweet cheeks, now what do you say we go make a little brother or sister for Mike and Craig?"

"Yeah, you do remember that we're both fixed, don't you?"

Brian grinned and said, "That doesn't mean that we shouldn't give it a good ole' college try!"

Charlie smirked, "We didn't go to college, remember?"

Brain feigning exasperation said, "Hey, am I the only one in this thing or what?"

Charlie said, "Oh, alright, if we must." Then with the back of her hand on her forehead she quoted Dickens, "'Tis a far, far better thing that I do than I have ever done before."

Brian nodded and added, "Wait 'til were upstairs!"

CHAPTER TEN

The rain was starting to come down steady now and Ezra decided she had better get back to the cabin before she got caught in a downpour. It wouldn't really matter much, she was already wet, but everybody knew that only witches stayed out in the rain. Ezra didn't want to be accused of being a witch. She gathered the potatoes that she had been digging into her basket and headed toward the break in the stonewall that would lead to the homestead. Father would be expecting her soon anyway because it was starting to get late in the day.

At the stonewall there was a big chestnut tree which still bore some leaves that the autumn hadn't claimed. Even in the waning light with the cloud cover and the drizzle, the deep oranges and light reds were enough to slow Ezra's stride. She loved the sight of that tree and had already told her father that if he had any thoughts of using it to build an addition onto the cabin that she would run away. Her father was always talking about that big old chestnut tree and how much house he could get out of it. Ezra suspected that it was mostly to get her riled up some.

That was when she noticed the odd sounds that seemed to be coming from the forest, or better put, the odd silence. Being raised in the wilderness in a relatively untamed new world with savage Indians running around, a girl learned quick, or too late, of the sounds in the forest. She felt the hair on the nape of her neck rise up on end with the goose bumps. There was an all over tingling as she became acutely aware of her surroundings. The air felt as if it were alive, charged with some kind of energy. She looked in every direction and saw no one, but she knew that somehow her senses were being tricked…she was sure that there was someone or something there. There was a whispering in the treetops, it was just a little too soft for her to make out, but she could hear it. The drizzling stopped. The air became and iridescent orange under the chestnut tree. Ezra was sure that a witch had caught her and was placing a spell upon her.

She picked up her pace and hurried along. The chestnut tree would have to wait for another time to be admired. She was hurrying along through the woods when a pine cone dropped alongside her feet. She had no way of knowing that it had fallen from a pine tree on that very spot three hundred years later, as it was falling to the ground where three boys slept. As Ezra looked at the pine cone she was completely dumbstruck. It was standing on end and spinning rapidly. Finally it went over on its side and dropped, coming to rest wedged between two stones near Ezra's feet. There wasn't a pine tree in the cluster of trees in which she stood. There wasn't a pine tree anywhere near where she was. There was nobody about who could have thrown the pine cone at her. Certainly this was witchcraft!

She screamed and ran the rest of the way to the barn where she found her father. "Father! Father!" she called.

Her father looked at her and said, "Peace child, where hath thou been, and why art thou so troubled?"

Ezra was so frightened she was having trouble talking, even with her Father's arms holding her safe. "Father, 'twas a witch! For certain 'twas witchcraft!"

Ezra's father clapped his hand over her mouth and held it there. He looked at her and said, "Hush child, thou ought not speak of such. Thou knowest the penalty. Doth thou wish to be burnt at the steak?"

Ezra shuddered. She knew better than to speak out loud about anything that might get a finger pointed at her, but she was so overcome by the sight of that pinecone just popping out of nowhere and spinning like a toy top on the orange chestnut leaves that covered the ground. She didn't trust herself to not speak of it. She worried that that very distrust of her own self was a sign of being a witch. She didn't know if witches were different than other people on the outside or not. For all she knew she was a witch.

Pinecones don't just pop out of thin air and spin at your feet.

Everything turned black.

When Ezra came to she was in her own bed with her Mother and sisters looking over her. Mary-Beth and Jo looked frightened. They had never seen anyone who had fainted before. To think it was their own sister was more than they were ready to cope with. At seven and ten there was still a great deal in the world for them to see. All three of the girls took their lessons from their Mother. They were learning their ABC's and 123's with all of the discipline of young scholars in the finest schools in Boston, or even London. It wasn't likely that it would count for much. If one of the girls went out into the world and wanted to further their education they would be rigorously tested, probably more astringently than if they had gone to one of the fancy school houses off of the farm. It was Ezra who would be most likely to want to spread her wings and fly when she was older. She was already thirteen and by all accounts ready for marriage. If her father didn't start taking an active interest in finding her a husband soon she would run the risk of being a maid at eighteen and becoming a spinster. Young men here in the wilds of the Massachusetts Bay Colony were not growing on trees. There were three brothers born into this family alone, however, fate had been cruel. Boys didn't seem to be as hardy as girls when they first arrived. One had been stillborn. He would have been Ezra's older brother. There were twin boys between Ezra and Mary-Beth. They died, one of them, Joshua, at three weeks, the other, Samuel, lived for eight months and died in the middle of the winter. Father had to find a safe place to keep his little body until the ground thawed and he could be buried with his brothers in the spring. All of the girls were thriving though. Perhaps one day there would be a boy that would survive. Father needed some help on the farm and an heir that he could pass it along to. It didn't seem fair to the girls that they couldn't own property. The King didn't allow it. But he was all the way off in London town and what did he know about living here on their farm anyway?

Father. Where was Father?

Ezra looked around the cabin for the first time as she was awakening.

Mary-Beth said, "Mother, she stirs."

Ezra's mother came to her bedside. She was very large now, almost ready to have another child. The unspoken hope of it being a boy was heavy in the family and had been for months. She carried a damp cloth with her to wipe at Ezra's forehead. She said, "Child, what has troubled you so that you should faint?"

Ezra looked up at her and, remembering her father's admonition, said, "Mother, I cannot speak of it. Where is Father?"

Mother's forehead wrinkled making two very deep worry lines between her eyebrows and answered, "He hath gone to scout the forest for savages. Child you have seen savages before and thou hast not fainted, there was more tonight. Pray, tell me."

Ezra was torn. She wanted to tell her mother but she couldn't disobey her father. She said, "Father hath told me to speak naught of it."

Mother's discerning gaze softened. She comforted her daughter and did not pursue the matter any further.

It was three days before Ezra was able to return the stonewall and the chestnut tree. The leaves had all fallen, save for a few hangers on that held tenaciously to their perch. The winds and rain would soon attend to these. Ezra back traced her footsteps to where she stood when the pinecone materialized. There was nothing there in the trail. Only fallen leaves. She was turning to go when she saw it, caught between two rocks and mostly covered with leaves. The tip of a pine cone peeked out at her. She looked at it for a long moment, not wanting to believe her eyes. She had nearly convinced herself that she had imagined the entire affair. Now the truth was staring her in the face, confronting her. She was frightened of what this meant. If she had not imagined this pine cone's appearance then perhaps she was a witch after-all.

Ezra knew that she could never let anyone know of this. She reached down trepidaciously and brushed a leaf aside. A newt scurried from under the leaf to the rock and disappeared under it. Ezra was so startled she jumped backward and tripped on a log, falling over. She landed on her bottom and laughed at herself for being frightened by a salamander, of all things! She got her feet back under her and returned to the pine cone. This time she simply and without hesitation reached for it. Her fingers closed about it and she lifted it from under the leaves. Nothing happened. It was just a pine cone. There were no magical pulsations. She felt no different from before she picked it up. She looked around, making sure that she was still alone. Taking the pine cone with her Ezra went through the stonewall to the open field beyond. She made her way along the wall to the unmarked cemetery where her brothers were buried. Deciding that she wanted to never see the pine cone again, she dug a shallow hole in the ground near the unmarked graves, dropped the pine cone in and covered it with earth.

Later that month Ezra acted as a midwife for her mother and helped to deliver a baby brother. He was named Joseph. Joseph was strong. He survived and thrived. He would grow up to marry and have children of his own. Ironically it would be he, not his father that would be remembered in history as the first settler in the Upper Wachusett Valley.

The winter came with bitter cold, then spring with the promise of new life. The cemetery had a new pine sprout growing near it. There were two new graves added to it as well. Ezra and Mary-Beth had not lived out the winter. They had fallen through the ice on the little pond near the cabin while fetching water. Mary-Beth drowned right then. Ezra got frostbitten toes and fingers in her futile attempt to save her sister. She was blue all over for two days. Her extremities looked as though they may heal, and she seemed to be regaining her color. In the middle of the third night, when everyone was asleep, Ezra rose delirious from her bed and walked out of the cabin. It was a clear night with a full moon. The air was frigid, with no moisture in it. Her breath hung before her as she exhaled, then fell downward in front of her. They followed her footprints through the woods on the next day. They stopped at the chestnut tree and went no further. Ezra was nowhere to be found. Her mother's anguish for her was that she had died then, never having gotten warm again. Her grave was empty save Ezra's favorite few belongings. In the grave died the real story of the origin of the pine grove. In the grave lived the unanswered question of the whereabouts of a little girl named Ezra.

These were the last deaths in the family for twenty and three years. It would be Joseph who would dig the next grave, for his father. He would dig it in a new location, far from the little pine grove that he used to play in as a boy. A new place, with a fence and a sign over the gate telling anyone who entered that this was the Wright Family Cemetery.

CHAPTER ELEVEN

Cy sat cross legged on the floor with Morgan lying by his side. The big dog had his head in Cy's lap with the rest of his body flopped on it's side. Cy was opening and closing his finger tips absent mindedly around Morgan's ears. Morgan was enjoying the massage. His eyes were closed and he was completely relaxed. Earlier, Brian's boys had run him ragged chasing his Frisbee in the yard. Now the boys were in bed and Morgan was content to just laze in Cy's lap. They had come in the late afternoon to Brian's house. Brian had inherited the house from his father three years ago. His father was still alive, but had moved to an elderly community where all of his friends were living and actually given the house to Brian to raise his family in. It had been in the family for generations along with the land. There were only one hundred-fifty acres left. There used to be hundreds but the state had taken most of the land from the family about eighty years ago to build a flood control reservoir. The old family homestead was under water now. Brian was determined to keep the remaining property intact.

Annie was sitting in a recliner opposite Cy in the room. She had arrived shortly after he did. The Wrights hosted a cook-out for the first get together to the talk about this business with the ether. So far the conversation had been slow to get started. It was difficult for this group to be together. Dave wasn't there, and his absence was felt by everyone.

None-the-less, the issue needed to be brought to the forefront. So Cy decided to begin. He took a long haul on his beer and asked, "So Annie, what did Dave tell you?"

Annie was a bit surprised, but at the same time, she knew she shouldn't have been. She said, "Well, remember, I already knew about all of the things that happened when you were boys from that time after our walk in the woods. After that, Dave was reluctant to share. It was probably me, I didn't like to talk about this stuff. I still don't, but if there are things about Dave that I should know, then well, I guess that's why we're here."

Cy nodded thoughtfully, he asked, "Did he ever tell you about your wedding day?"

Annie looked shocked. She had creases in her forehead from a scowl that had taken over her face. She said angrily, "Cy, did you bring that thing to my wedding?"

Cy looked hurt. "Annie, I need you to understand, I have no idea what 'that thing' is. I don't control it. I don't know why or how it does what it does. I didn't bring 'It' to your Wedding, 'it' brought itself."

Annie cooled down. She looked at Cy again and said, "I know. I know, Cy that you don't control anything to do with it. I'm sorry. I shouldn't have snapped at you. This thing, what do you call it, the Ether? This has been a difficult thing for me to deal with. Since that first night in the woods that it did whatever it did to Dave, he changed." She took a deep breath and added, "Tell me about my wedding."

At this Brian spoke up, "Annie, this is going to sound very Sci-Fi, but I saw it happen. I saw it and I still have a hard time believing what I saw."

Cy looked at Brian and then back at Annie. It had been years since he had recounted the story, first to Brian and then to Dave, and finally to a skeptical Charlie, who was convinced that the guys were trying to pull one over on her after a few too many beers. He took his time and told Annie about the pea and the napkin; his talk with himself, the return to the wedding, his encounter with Brian and how he dissolved right there in front of him, his memory of being both Cys and remerging into one person. When he had finished he looked at Annie and said, "There's more. Do you want me to take a break or should I continue?"

Annie looked at Brian. She asked, "You saw this?"

Brian simply nodded. Then he said, "Annie, I know how weird this sounds but, I was right there. Cy was right in front of me, we were talking, and yet, I could see him all the way over at the head table. Then the Cy that was right next to me just faded away! I looked over at the head table again and Cy looked right at me, he just stared at me like he had just been slammed in the gut or something. Then I watched you and Dave go back over to the table and talk with him. Dave kept looking down at his plate. After you guys left for your honeymoon I got together with Cy and he told me about his little journey. It sounds fantastical, but I thought seeing Cy in two places at one time was fantastical, not to mention a bit nightmarish, one is bad enough! Yeah Annie, I saw it."

Annie was incredulous to the news of this invasion of her wedding. It was difficult to process. She wanted to get out of there and just forget the entire matter, but she knew that for some reason, she needed to stay. She looked back to Cy and asked, "Alright, what else?"

Cy looked at her and said, "Annie, here's where it starts getting weird."

"STARTS getting weird? Cy it's been nothing BUT weird since all of this began."

Cy's eyes dropped, he looked at the floor and knew that there was going to be an uphill battle. He also knew he had to wage it. Ever since the wedding when he took his little 'quantum leap' he has known. He and Dave's story had to be told and the chips will fall where they fall.

Then as he was about to speak there came a knock at the door.

CHAPTER TWELVE

It was morning. The sun was shining and there were birds singing. The air had a hint of the smells of spring; mountain laurel blossoming, lilac, even fresh ice melt on a lake. A cool, gentle breeze washed Ezra's face and the sound of small waves gently lapping the shore filled her ears as she slowly awoke. She was laying in a break in a stone wall with her face in the dirt. She pulled herself up from the stones and pine needles. There was a pine grove at her back. Just beyond her feet was a beautiful lake. The early morning sun glistened on the waves as it slowly ascended to a more prominent position in the sky.

Ezra had no idea where she was. She rose to her feet. That's when she realized that her fingers and toes were stinging. She had no shoes on, only a thin pair of old threadbare stockings. She remembered her sister falling through the ice and drowning, and how she jumped in to try to help her but not being able to find her in the dark water. Mary-Beth, she was dead. Ezra remembered being ill and having a fever, but she also knew that that had happened in the beginning of April. There had been a foot and a half of snow on the ground. There was no snow now, and the blossoms on the bushes and leaves were beginning to pop from the trees.

Sitting there on a stone in the early morning, Ezra was getting cold. She felt that she should get home, wherever that was. She was beginning to realize that she had no idea where she was. She also knew that she had to get herself out of the open.

Looking around her she saw a trail that seemed to follow the shoreline of the lake through a pine grove. She felt her only option was to make her way through the trees. She removed her stockings and put them into her house-coat pocket. Her feet were callused from being barefoot; there was no need to wear a hole in her socks. Slowly she made her way along the path into the pine trees. The trail was well beaten and smooth.

After only a few minutes she heard a strange noise. A loud droning with the sound of the wind following it. She hid behind a tree for fear of what it might be. This was a strange place, and all Ezra wanted was to be at home with her mother and father. The drone grew to a roar and when she looked toward the sounds origin she saw something bright red and shiny move past the end of the trail ahead, something that moved faster than anything she had ever seen. The sun shone so intensely upon it and flashed its rays back down the path onto Ezra's face. The creature continued on. It must not have seen her and it moved away with the same roar that it had approached with, and the wind still following behind.

What is this place? Ezra thought with a start that she must have been taken by the witches; taken from her world into theirs. These beasts that roar so were strange and surely must be dangerous. Even the wind follows them as if bewitched and caught in a spell. She would have to survive using her wits. She knew how to live off the land, she and her family have been doing so all of her life. She would go back farther into the woods than she was when she awoke, far from the loud creature that commands the wind. With that she turned and ran, silently and as swiftly as her bare feet would carry her into the forest. When she had been running for ten minutes she came to a place where the path opened up, widening and making Ezra feel exposed. She slowed her pace and gave herself time to look around and be more aware of her surroundings. Finally she noticed a path up to the right of the trail. It was a small footpath and it offered more cover, she went into the path. It wound uphill and was covered with pine needles and soggy leaves. The sun was slowly getting higher in the sky and it was getting warmer. Ezra took her house-coat off and folded it over her arm. She continued onward up the hill. A pile of stones off to her left caught her eye. She slowly made her way over to it from the trail. What she saw made her catch her breath. It wasn't a pile, rather it was a hole, a hole lined with stones, as a cellar. It was about five feet deep, so when she was inside of it she could just barely see out. She felt safe here, and decided she would make a lean-to. She would need shelter, it would be temporary, only until she could find someone that she knew. This place was old, there was moss on the stones and everything inside was falling in. It was likely that there weren't many indians around, perhaps the witches had run them off, or cast a spell to keep them away.

 She set herself to the tasks that she needed to get done. She started by gathering fallen logs. Because she didn't even have a knife, she would have to rely on nature to give her what she needed. When she had enough to build a small wall, she chose the northern most corner of the cellar so her little hut would have southern exposure. Ezra spent the rest of the morning and a good part of the afternoon building her walls. She neither heard nor saw anyone throughout the day. In the corner she had chosen she found a piece of broken glass. It was a peculiar green and very thick and irregularly shaped. The word 'Mason' was written in bas-relief across part of the glass. There was one edge that was very sharp. If she was careful she could use this as a knife. When the sun was starting to go down she realized that she hadn't eaten all day. Her stomach was rumbling fiercely as she had worked up a powerful appetite. Father had taught her to build a snare to catch a rabbit. Now that she had a makeshift knife she could fashion a snare easily. She could use strips of cloth from her clothing in place of rawhide, at least until she had caught a rabbit or two for food and hide. She worked into the evening and through twilight and was forced to stop only when it was too dark to see. Ezra would sleep on an empty stomach that night. Tomorrow, tomorrow she would build a snare and eat rabbit by midday. If she could build a fire, that is.

The sun had been up for about two hours. Ezra was about to climb out of her shelter to go set the trap that she had just finished building. There was a noise in the forest. She could hear footfalls crunching the leaves in and among the trees. Someone was approaching from up the hill. She felt trapped in the cellar hole, but she knew she couldn't climb out without being seen. She picked up a pine bough that she had broken the day before and held it over her head. Carefully, and with all of the stealth she could manage she made her way to the uphill side of the hole. With the pine branch over her head she slowly raised herself up and looked up toward where the sound was coming from. There were two very curiously dressed people, a man and a woman walking and talking idly down the trail. They were older, perhaps forty, and plump. Ezra was startled by the sight of them. They were as no one she had ever seen. She could make out their talk, but even that was odd. It was english, but not like any form of english she had ever heard. These must be witches. The problem was that they didn't look evil. Witches, as everybody knows, are evil. Ezra was able to make out part of what was said, but she couldn't make any sense of it. Really it was the joviality that made her think that these people weren't witches.

Just then Ezra's foot slipped on the rock that she was perched on and she fell back with the pine bough in her hand. When she landed she let out an 'Ooff' as the leaves under her crackled. She no sooner recovered from the fall when she heard the sound of running through the leaves. The couple came to the edge of the hole and looked down inside. They had a genuine look of concern on their faces.

The woman asked, "Are you alright dear?"

Ezra was afraid to answer. She knew this language was slightly different from her own and she was afraid to expose herself as from another land. She remained silent.

The old man climbed down into the cellar hole. He approached Ezra slowly. He was calm and was making no sudden moves. "Did you hit your head dear?"

His wife asked from above, "Do you think she needs to go to the hospital?"

He looked at Ezra more appraisingly now. He could see no open wounds and no real sign of injury. "No, I don't think so, I think she's probably healthier than anyone there. I don't know how long she's been running around in these woods. Hungry I'd bet."

Ezra was watching the man's eyes carefully. At the word hungry she involuntarily raised her head.

"Yes, she got that word alright." He was smiling now. "How about we get you some food?" Then looking down at her clothing, "And maybe something a little less worn to wear." He reached his hand toward her, outstretched and palm up, empty.

Ezra reached up and placed her fingers in the palm of his hand.

They had climbed out of the cellar hole and were on the trail out of the woods. After a half hour they passed into a clearing and there on the other side was something that Ezra had never seen before. It was like a wagon, only it was all metal and bright shiny steel. There was glass all around it at the top of it. The wheels were short and solid in the middle with no spokes, and instead of a steel band around a wooden wheel frame there was a black material the likes of which Ezra had never seen. This wagon was like what she had seen the previous morning roaring past the trail and with the wind at its back. Only that one was red and this one was blue. What kind of magic was in this machination? She was frightened by the sight of it, but she managed to bravely continue on with the kindly old couple. It was their lack of fear that bolstered her confidence. She could see that this was a machine after all and not a beast as she had thought the morning before.

The woman went to the end of the machine, she produced a small steel key and inserted it into a small hole. She turned it and the entire back opened up exposing a large compartment. She reached in and pulled a paper package out.

The old man said, "Kristina, is that all we have for her? A branola bar?"

Kristina looked at her husband and said, "I think her spine is wearing a hole in the back of her navel, we'll give her more when we get home, but for now she needs something to hold her over." She approached Ezra and opened the wrapper. She held it out to her and said, "Go ahead dear, eat this, it's all we have right now but we can get you something better once we get you home. We don't live far, only twenty miles or so."

Ezra took the branola bar and tasted it. She had never tasted anything so delicious in her life. There were nuts, and fruit and honey, it reminded her of the suet cakes that she had made with her mother, only better. Her mother. She must be worried silly. And her mother would want her to show her good manners. She looked at Kristina and said, "Thank you."

Kristina said, "Did you hear that Tony? She can talk."

Kristina and Tony took Ezra to the local authorities, by way of a local thrift shop for clothes and a nearby diner for a good full meal. Every time they climbed into the car Ezra was apprehensive, but she complied. They traveled at such speeds that Ezra never would have believed possible.

The roads were covered with something hard and blue that made them very smooth and easy to traverse. There was so much for Ezra to get used to. The most difficult was that she could never go back home. This hardly seemed fair to Ezra, but she had seen hardships before and knew that you had to work through them if you were to survive.

She was placed in a home for runaway girls in a nearby town. While she wouldn't speak, except to say 'please' and 'thank you,' the judge in the local court decided that she must be a runaway. Fingerprints yielded no results. She was photographed and age regression technology was used to attempt identifying her with older missing persons photos. There was no success.

Tony and Kristina visited every day. Still Ezra spoke very little. She would tell no-one her name. Ezra was interviewed regularly by a court appointed psychologist. They would sit and talk at length about things that Ezra could not understand, nor could she grasp the reasons to talk about them. No matter how they tried they could not manipulate Ezra into revealing anything about her past or where she came from. One afternoon while visiting with Kristina and Tony she asked, "Can I come and live with you?"

That was all the encouragement they needed. Within six months the legal guardianship was approved. It took three more months for the adoption to become final.

CHAPTER THIRTEEN

Charlie got up to answer the door. There was more than just a little surprise on her face as she recognized the woman standing in the autumn air. Charlie took her coat and led her to the rear of the house where everyone else was, anxious to see the looks on their faces.

Cy sat and stared from the floor. He wasn't sure if he could get up, but he decided he had better try. The sight of Lexi was a shock. Her hair was flaxen and long still. She still had her figure, indeed she hadn't changed noticeably since she left, eight years ago. Now he couldn't take his eyes from her. He slowly rose as she made her way around to him. He hugged her and said, "Hi Lexi, you're still as beautiful as ever."

She smiled and said, "Hey you, thanks. You're looking good too, where'd all your hair go?"

Cy blushed.

"Who's this guy?" Lexi asked as she was scratching Morgan's ears.

"Ah, Lexi, meet Morgan, Morgan, Lexi." Cy made a hand signal and Morgan sat and reached up with his paw.

Lexi took his paw and gave it a shake and praised him for being so clever.

There was a great deal of curiosity in the room regarding this surprise visit. The timing was odd as well. Lexi could sense this, especially since all eyes were on her. She said, "Brian, Charlie, I am sorry to barge in tonight. It's no accident that I came here on this night."

Space was made for the Lexi in the room. When everyone was seated Lexi said, "Last week I called Annie. In our conversation she mentioned that all of you would be getting together tonight. I didn't tell Annie that I wanted to come because I wasn't sure I could make it happen." Lexi took a deep breath, and slowly surveyed the room. She said, "I think that the only people in the world who may possibly believe what I am here to say are here in this room right now. My mom and dad, have wanted me to tell them something for many years now. Tonight I am going to give you the answer, I'll figure out a way to tell them another time." She paused, took a deep breath, the first of many and said, "My name is Ezra Wright."

Brian actually did a double take at Lexi with a puzzled expression.

"Brian, I'm not sure how to explain this to you. I am a distant relative, ha, yeah, a very distant relative. Oh, God this is going to sound weird."

Cy looking at Lexi said, "We're running a special on weird tonight. Chances are what you have to say may fit right in. Then again…"

Lexi said, "Cy, I'm so sorry I bolted all those years ago. What was happening here then was too reminiscent of what happened to me when I was a little girl. But I had blocked all of that and only knew how frightened I was by it. I couldn't face it, not then." She turned then to everyone else in the room, "I was found in the woods not far from here actually, by my Mom and Dad. I was becoming wild and beginning to starve. My parents came across me in a cellar hole about two miles from here. I've gone back. I found it again and have visited it several times over the years. I'm fairly certain that it was my actual father's root cellar."

Lexi took a deep breath and began. "I was born in Bedford, MA in August of 1694." She paused at this to gauge the reaction. When she saw that no one had moved, in fact, saw that their interest seemed to pique, she was mildly surprised. She continued, "My father had been a whaling man. When I was born he decided to give up the sea and take up farming so he could be with his children as they grew up. We moved to the center of what was then the Massachusetts Bay Colony. There were land grants in those days, given to men who were willing to work farms. My father got six hundred acres granted to him if he remained on the farm for five years. Otherwise it reverted to the colony. He and my mother moved here and began building their farm. I don't remember any of that, I only know about it because my mother told me." She paused to think and breathe. Lexi, or Ezra, noticed that not a movement had been made. She knew she had made the right decision to come tonight. "When I was thirteen, in 1707, I was digging potatoes in a field my father had cleared when it began to rain. I started to hurry home, it was nearly sunset anyway. I ran through the field to a break in the stone wall where an old chestnut tree stood. I continued down the trail until I was compelled to stop. I saw an apparition, no it was more than that. What I saw was a pinecone hanging in mid air and spinning very rapidly." At that she noticed everyone looking at each other, so she stopped, feeling self-conscious.

Cy said, "No, don't stop, you don't understand. We were just talking about something very similar. I'll tell you after, but please, go on."

Lexi looked at Cy, then took another one of those deep breaths and continued, "I was very frightened, we believed that there were witches in those days, and I thought that there was a witch casting a spell trying to possess my soul. Anyway, I was frozen in my tracks as I watched this pinecone spin in midair. When finally it fell, I ran to my father. Some days later I came back and found the pinecone and took it from that place. I buried it not far from there; there's a pine grove there now. I have no doubt Cy that it's the same pine grove that you, Brian and Dave were sleeping in all those years ago as boys when you first encountered the phenomenon that you are all here discussing tonight."

Cy said, "The grove out by the stone wall near the lake?"

Lexi sighed and said, "Yes, oddly enough, I think that I planted it with a pine cone that came from its own future. Well, anyway, it was a few months later when my little sister and I had an accident getting water at the stream. She went through the ice and drowned. I tried to catch her and pull her back from under the ice, but I was too late. In the process I got soaked through. In those days if that happened you were one step away from dead. I managed to get back to the cabin. My mother got me to the fireplace and my father ran to try to find Mary-Beth. I went into a delirium and from that into a fever. It was three nights later I think when I got up in the night and took a walk. I woke up on a spring morning in the break in the stone wall. The next day was when my new parents found me in the cellar hole. Three hundred years in one nights sleep, how's that for a Rip Van Winkle? That was just five years before I met all of you." Lexi was fighting tears now, "I don't even know if my father ever found my little sister's body or not."

Brian was staring intently at his Aunt. He said, "Actually, he did." Lexi looked up at him. Brian continued, "I've taken an interest in genealogy, I've had the benefit of a previous ancestor that had the same interest and he made some fairly compelling recordings. He wrote about your father and mother coming to the Upper Pequot region of the Massachusetts Bay Colony as you've told us. He also gave an account of Mary-Beth Wright's drowning, and Ezra Wright's disappearance. It was speculated that Ezra was kidnapped by hostile Indians. Her body was never found."

For a moment no one spoke. There was a lot of new and unexpected information to digest.

It was Charlie who broke the silence. She said, "What if we take a break, you know refresh drinks, potty breaks. Then if there's more to talk about, we can pick it up fresh."

As though motion were the only acknowledgment needed, everyone started to rise and stretch their legs. Even Morgan jumped to his feet and stretched out as dogs do.

Cy asked, "Lexi, do you want a cola?"

"Sure." She answered.

He started to go, then turned back to her and said, "Don't you even think of leaving!"

Lexi smiled and said, "I promise I'll be right here when you come back."

Cy turned and went to the kitchen.

Annie hadn't moved. She was still sitting in the recliner. She had a very pensive expression.

Lexi said, "Hi Annie."

Annie looked up at her. Morgan had come to Annie for a little petting. His big head and right paw were in Annie's lap. Annie's hand was absently stroking the top of his head. His eyes were closed and he was obviously enjoying the attention from his previous mistress. Finally Annie asked, "Did Cy ever tell you about how we got Morgan?"

Of all the things that Annie could have asked her at that moment Lexi had never thought of that one. "No, Annie, he didn't"

Annie said, "Hmm, well I guess it was during the dark years after you left, so he wouldn't have had occasion to tell you." She looked down at Morgan now, then with both hands she lifted his head up toward hers and bent a little closer to him. She held him like this and stared into his eyes as she spoke to Lexi. "They came home with this adorable puppy during that following summer, said they had 'found him in the woods'. I didn't believe them… he was too well cared for and well fed. He didn't even have fleas! Who finds puppies in the woods? Now it seems people can find kids in the woods too. Where do you come from Lexi? Where does Morgan come from? I guess this means I have to rethink where Dave is too!" Without waiting for a reply Annie got up and went out.

Cy came back in time to see Annie going out the door. He approached Lexi cautiously, realizing that they had just had some kind of exchange. He sidled up to her, handed Lexi her cola and asked, "Is there something I should know about here? Or is that between you two?"

Lexi said, "Cy, none of this is going to be easy, for anyone involved." She sipped her cola and asked, "Do you at least understand why I walked away all of those years ago?"

"Yes, but don't you ever do that again. I've missed you" He had said it. Now Cy knew the full weight of his vulnerability.

Lexi said, "Cy, I haven't allowed myself the luxury of having any kind of relationship with anyone, before or since you. When we met I was starting to accept what the shrinks were feeding me about my childhood being a façade that I had built up to protect myself from traumatic memories. My parents were very supportive of that line of reason. I still haven't told them about all of this. When we were at Brian and Charlie's house that night and you and Dave started talking about this 'breeze' and the trees and the whisperings, it brought it all back. I was sure that I was going to need to go back to therapy. Instead I started to research the Wright ancestral tree. I found my brother and my father. Brian is a direct descendant of my brother, the little boy that I acted as midwife to my mother for. She named him Joseph. Do you understand Cy? All of this means that I've come home."

Her words hung out there like the moon hangs in the sky. They were untouchable but undeniable. Somewhere along the line the room had started to refill. Annie had even come back inside. Brian was still holding back from Lexi, not quite sure what she was about. With everything that they had encountered he could accept unbelievable, but this was a bit closer to home. She was claiming to be a long lost Aunt. Now he began to have a greater appreciation for his wife. She hadn't seen any of the things that the others or even he had seen, but he was asking her to believe it. Now he was on the other end of it. He didn't like it. That didn't take it away. Brian resolved that there would have to be more conversation with his Aunt Ezra.

Annie was on the other side of the room now. She looked at Cy and said, "Cy, before Lexi arrived, you said something about things starting to get weird?"

Cy had forgotten that he was about to talk more about Dave, Brian and his research. He said, "Well, the three of us were looking aggressively into this after your wedding. Annie, I'm not sure how to say this, but I think there might have been a connection."

Annie sat staring. After some thought, she asked, "Are you saying this, Ether, had something to do with Dave's disappearance?"

Cy looked back, trying to get the courage to say the words. "Yes, with Dave's, disappearance."

Annie was getting very agitated now. She stood, her fists were clenched. She looked at Cy then at Brian, then back at Cy and asked, "What are you saying?"

Cy looked at Brian.

Brian said, "Annie, we think there's a possibility that Dave is… caught, out there somewhere."

Annie was incredulous. She looked at Brian and asked, "How can you say that, Brian?"

Brian said, "If we believe Lexi is Ezra Wright then we should accept the possibility that Dave is somewhere or rather some-when out there waiting and hoping and trying to come home."

Annie stood and walked out.

CHAPTER FOURTEEN

Lexi sat with her legs pulled up on the sofa. Cy was getting her a cup of tea. He had turned on the stereo and was playing a CD called, 'Greatest Hits of 1750'. Lexi thought he was clever when he pointed out that the music may be a bit new wave for her, but she should give it a chance. What she really thought was how adorable it was that he was being serious. She had followed him back to his house from Brian's in her own car. The discussion had gone downhill rapidly after Brian mentioned Dave's disappearing as opposed to his death. Part of it was because of Lexi. She realized now that her timing was both good and bad. Good for a time when sharing the truth was so conducive, bad for Annie. She had had enough trouble coping with the loss of her husband, to listen to people tell her that he had disappeared as opposed to died, and that he may even be alive, well that was more than she could take. As soon as Brian pointed out that 'if we believe Lexi is Ezra Wright then we should accept the possibility that Dave is somewhere or rather some-when out there waiting and hoping to come home,' Annie walked out.

Cy felt that Annie would cool down, and if not, then she would at least cope while they were trying to find a way to bring Dave back; if he could be brought back. But there was the problem of where and when he went, did he go forward or backward. If back, then when. If forward, he may have gone way ahead like Ezra, or just a few years. He may come walking in at any time. There were too many possibilities. Who could blame Annie for walking. The whole prospect is preposterous. And yet, here was Lexi.

Cy came in with her tea, placed it in front of her and returned to the kitchen for his cup. When he placed his cup on the coffee table in front of her he looked at the sofa beside her and around at the rest of his furniture. Now that she was here with him, with the circumstances being what they are he wasn't quite sure how he ought to proceed. He finally decided no guts no glory and sat himself on the sofa, a safe eight to ten inches away from her. He asked her, "So, what do you prefer to be called, Ezra or Lexi?"

She smiled and looked downward. "Well, I've been one about as long as I've been the other. Just keep it Lexi and it will be fine."

Cy said, "Alright, Lexi it is then. I want to ask you a question. Why did you stay away for so long?"

Lexi said, "Look Cy, I was so unsure of myself then. I've come to understand who I am now. I also know that I can never tell certain people unless I want to be committed. As time went by, and you didn't call, I realized I was on my own. I couldn't go back to my parents. They would have wanted me to return to the therapist that I went to when I was an adolescent. I had actually told him about my childhood. He determined that it was an elaborate fantasy that I had created in order to escape a traumatic childhood experience. Ironically the greatest trauma I had suffered was being taken from what he thought was a fantasy and flung forward in time three hundred years to his time. There's no explaining that to a shrink and not being committed! It took me a while to do some research and find the historical background on the area, but I found my family. Not all of the information that Brian has, but enough to confirm for myself that I hadn't been making it all up in my head. I grew tired of hanging out there alone. I decided that I would return to the very people who would be able to grasp what had been my fate."

"I didn't call because this Ether never let me alone," Cy said. "It continually kept coming into my life. I respected you not wanting anything to do with it and realized that for as long as it was a part of my life, I couldn't pursue you." Cy reached his hand over to Lexi's face and touched her cheek with his fingertips. She responded by inclining her head toward his fingers. He said, "I wanted to call. God knows, I've been a mess about it. Then every time I got to thinking it would be a good time to try and get on with my life, something else would happen. It's been two years since Dave, and the last ethereal outbreak. All I wanted to do was get through tonight with Annie and I was going to call you. Really, she gave me your phone number just last week. Hey, where do you live anyway?"

She just grinned and said, "Here, in town, for the last two years."

Cy straightened in disbelief, "What? How could that be?"

"Well, I don't get out much." She reached up with her hand and took hold of his. They sat and looked at each other for a moment. Cy leaned toward her. Their lips touched, his fingers still caressing her face. After only a few seconds she broke the kiss and said, "Cy, I have to tell you something."

Cy backed away only a few inches and said, "You aren't going to tell me you're married."

"No."

"You aren't going to tell me you're engaged."

"No."

"And you aren't going to tell me you're a Nun."

"No, no, listen to me." Lexi was laughing now. "Cy, I want to go back."

Cy backed up a little further now. His eyebrows were knitted and he was trying to grasp what she meant.

"I want to go back home. I don't belong here."

"That's Ezra talking."

She said, "Perhaps, but I think it's more than that." She turned thoughtful and asked, "what did you have to tell Annie about tonight that it warranted a group meeting?"

"Well, there were some encounters that I felt she had a right to know. I didn't want her to have to run from one of us to another trying to get straight answers, so I arranged for all of us to be together. I had to tell her about the uninvited guest at her wedding. And Brian and my suspicion that Dave is still alive, just in another time. I couldn't do that without moral support."

What uninvited guest?"

Cy told Lexi about the pea and his own experience with time travel.

She said, "So she was already wound up, even before I arrived."

Cy said, "You could say that."

"And, that explains why my story was so readily accepted, even by Brian, I was worried that he would think that I was trying to take him for money or something. What about Charlie?"

"She is for the most part skeptical. I don't know if what you had to add to all of this made her more or less skeptical. I would like to convince her, if for no other reason so she doesn't think I'm a mad man. Cy got up and went to a bookcase across the room. He came back with a candle. He placed the candle on the coffee table and lit it. He then went to the entrance where the light switch was and turned down the lights. He said, "Can't we just have one night together? I've waited for you for nearly eight years now. I don't want to talk about different worlds, spinning objects and time travel. I just want to be here with you now. I don't care if all we do is sit here and stare at each other all night. I've bought and paid for at least that with the last eight years. Please?"

Lexi was moved. She was also frightened. If he knew what she had learned in those eight years… that would have to be for another time, the truth was, she felt the same way.

The Ether would wait.

The next morning while Lexi was showering, Cy prepared breakfast. He scrambled some eggs and chopped up some potatoes with green peppers and onions. There were some fresh fruits in the fridge, and so he even made a fruit cocktail. Lexi came down from the bath wearing one of Cy's old robes. He said, "You actually make that robe look good. How did you sleep?"

Lexi smiled and said, "Thank you, and quite well, thanks."

Cy served up the breakfast he had been working on. He poured the coffee and placed the creamer and various sweeteners on the table for her to choose from. As a finishing touch he placed a candle in the center of the table and lit it. He said, "We don't need the light, but..." He stopped, realizing he didn't need to explain. He looked at Lexi, she was straight from the shower, her hair wrapped in a towel, no make up and wearing his old robe. He couldn't believe how beautiful she was. He remembered she had said that she wanted to go home, so he said, "Lexi, you can't go home. Even if there was a way to control this thing, you would be a grown woman where a child had been. It's likely you would also be accused of being a witch. I mean, you would have to turn back the clock on yourself before you stepped into the way-back machine, and hope that the settings were accurate. We just don't have that control over this thing. We don't even know the time or place that it will manifest next."

Lexi thought for a minute and said, "I know."

Cy said, "Well, I'm glad we have that taken care of."

Lexi said, "No Cy, I mean that I know. I know when the next manifestation will be."

Cy looked at her. "Excuse me?"

She smiled, glad that she was getting the point across, "I said, 'I know when the next manifestation will be'"

Cy looked at her for a moment, then took a sip of his coffee and asked, "How do you know?"

Lexi said, "I've been doing research, remember? I started looking into my family tree, like I said, to prove to myself that I wasn't nuts. Cy, I noticed something pretty incredible.

There were other incidents of people disappearing. So I recorded the names and dates. That's when I saw the pattern. Cy, Dave went missing in early October, right?"

Cy nodded.

"I was taken in April. But Cy, I saw the pinecone spinning around in October. Early October. What month were Annie and Dave married in?"

"October."

"October, that's right. You and Dave experienced touches in August and in December, right?"

Cy nodded, he was very intent on what Lexi was telling him.

"But nothing more happened at those times, only touches. Here's my theory. In April and in October the Ether eddies. The eddy acts like a whirlpool in water, only it's in the air. It catches anything that may come across its position. The pinecone that I saw was still in an eddy. The pea was caught in an eddy. You got sucked in when you threw the napkin on the pea and took a hold of it. How long you're in the eddy determines how far you move through time. When you moved backward that one day it was because you got out of the eddy, you freed yourself from it most likely by letting go of the napkin. I was in it for a longer period of time because I was unconscious. Perhaps I turned in my sleep and that was all that was needed to release me."

Cy asked, "Do you remember which direction the pinecone was spinning?"

Lexi said, "When you see something like that it gets burned into your memory. The pinecone was spinning clockwise. Why?"

"Well, that's the direction that the pea was spinning, and I went backward in time. I wonder if the April eddy spins counter clockwise."

"Do you think the direction reverses?"

Cy said, "I don't know, but it would fit with your theory and would help to build on it. It would imply an ebb and flow, almost a tidal behavior to the ether. I went backward in time in October, you went forward in April. I've never seen an eddy in April, have you?"

"No, but to be honest I wouldn't know where to look, specifically."

"Right, even if you know what day, you would have to know exactly where to look, and then you would need to be careful not to get caught in it." Cy looked at Lexi, somewhat startled and said, "Unless you were planning to jump right in."

She just looked back at him. The towel on her head was starting to droop to one side. She reached up and unwound it from her hair and shook her hair out letting it fall down her back. She lay the towel across her lap and took a sip of her coffee. The eggs were getting cold on her plate, so she took a few bites before they became unsavory.

The realization that Lexi was planning to seek out an ethereal eddy and intentionally throw her self into it was unnerving to Cy. He watched her for a moment as she ate her eggs. She was calm. She seemed lucid. How was he going to convince her of the impracticality, not to mention the danger, of what she intended to do? He asked, "You aren't really planning to do this, are you?"

Lexi grew somber, "Cy, I don't belong here. I was never supposed to be in this time. I've spent the second half of my life trying to understand my place in your time." She reached across the table and took his hand, "Baby, don't make this any harder than it already is. I know how you feel, and I feel the same. It's not about what you or I want though, don't you see? It's about what needs to be restored. Wouldn't you bring Dave back if you could?"

"Of course I would, Lexi, but what's that got to do with…" His voice trailed off. He knew what her point was. He didn't like it, but he got it. Cy asked, "When is the next manifestation?"

Lexi held his hand tight. She looked intently at him. "In two days." She answered. The look on his face told her that he would help. She continued, "I need to take you to the library."

This was an unexpected turn. Cy asked, "Why the library?"

"I think you would be better off just going and letting me show you. You won't be disappointed."

CHAPTER FIFTEEN

Lexi led Cy down through the stacks in the library to the periodicals. She brought him to the newspaper section. "All newspapers over three years old here are preserved on microfiche." She thumbed her way through the file and chose a film. Looking at Cy she said, "I hope you're ready for this."

They went to the viewer and she placed the fiche on the plate. She switched the light on and the view screen lit up. First across and then down, Lexi went almost directly to an article about a Sheldon man who had been killed in action in 1916 during World War One. There was a photo of him. Cy was in shock by what he saw. It was his friend, Dave.

Lexi asked, "Is this for certain Dave?"

Cy looked at her, then back at the photo. It was old. The paper had to have been fifty years old when photographed for the microfiche. The name was different, he was listed as David Brooks. Cy studied the face in the photo carefully. When they were eight, the three of them had been playing hide-and-go-seek in the neighborhood. Dave was hiding in a tree about ten feet from the ground. Brian was 'it' and he found Dave up the tree. Dave raced to get down the tree so he could get to the goal, but fell instead. He hit his head, more pointedly his right cheek against a branch on the way to the ground. The rough bark opened a cut just to the side of his eye. When it healed there was always a noticeable scar. That scar was staring Cy in the face now from a 1916 edition of The Sheldon News. "That's definitely him." Cy said, "We need to show this to Annie."

Lexi said, "Wait, Cy, we need to talk about that first." She sat back in her chair. "We don't know if there is anything we can do about this. Do you think it's necessary to torture Annie with this information? She already believes Dave to be dead. This just confirms it. The other thing to consider is the age."

Cy looked back at the screen and scanned down through the obituary. It said he was thirty-six at the time he was killed. Dave had been only twenty-four when he disappeared. "This says he was thirty-six, he was there for twelve years when he was killed in World War One. He traveled back to nineteen-oh-four." He looked back at Lexi, "Without any real way of controlling this thing we don't have a chance of knowing when we will arrive."

"Or if we'll arrive together." Lexi added.

"Right," Cy said, "A few seconds in an eddy could mean a day, a week, month or even a year. I guess we'll just have to get really close together, hold each other tight and move in synch. I could think of worse things." Cy grinned.

Lexi blushed, understanding his meaning. She said, "Well, that should keep us together, now we just have to figure out how long to stay in."

They sat thinking for a few moments. The prospect of getting into the ethereal eddy weighed heavily on both of them.

Cy said, "Listen, I was in for maybe three seconds, I traveled back about eight hours. We can't proceed with anything more than assumption here. If we extrapolate that out, nine seconds would move you a full day. Dave went back to 1904, that's ninety-nine years..." Cy started calculating the times out on a scrap of paper, finally he said, "We would have to hold onto one another for three days and eighteen hours."

Lexi drew a deep breath, she said, "Cy, I love you but I don't think I could hug you for that long." She looked at his figures on the sheet of paper that he was using and said, "According to those calculations I was unconscious for about twelve days. That can't be right. I'm not saying you did the math wrong I just don't think that this scaling of the timeframes can be right."

Cy asked, "Is there anything else that you wanted to show me here?"

"No, this article is the most provocative thing I found. There are other things, but nothing about Dave and nothing that I can't just relate to you."

"Good," said Cy, "Let's get out of here."

As they drove back to Cy's house, Lexi had a revelation. "Cy," she said, "the eddies, they aren't a daily phenomenon!"

Cy shrugged, "So?"

Lexi said, "Don't you see? You were calculating on a daily basis, as though you could get out any time. The eddies only occur every two years!"

Cy pulled the truck over to the curb. He held the brake and turned in his seat. He reached across to Lexi and took her face in his hands, leaning across the seat he kissed her. He backed away and said, "Beauty and brains! No wonder I love you!"

Lexi just held his hands and his gaze, she said, "I love you too, Cy, I just don't know what is going to happen with all of this. You understand, don't you?"

Cy said, "Better than anyone else on Earth."

They drove back to Cy's house, Cy went over his calculations out loud as they rode. Lexi wrote them down and used a pocket calculator to punch out the math. When they had finished and gone over the math twice, Cy said, "So that's it then, seven minutes and twenty-five and a half seconds to Dave." Cy pulled his truck into his drive-way. He asked Lexi, "Do you think you can hug me for seven and a half minutes?"

She looked at Cy coyly, smiled and said, "I could manage."

They sat and thought about what they were preparing to attempt. Cy asked, "You didn't happen to see any pictures or articles about you or I in those newspapers did you?"

Lexi said, "No, only Dave."

Cy thought out loud, "I wonder how we should take that?"

"What do you mean?"

"Well, his story is there, does that mean that we can't change it? Does the absence of our photos anywhere in our past mean that we didn't get there, or were we just careful not to be photographed?

Lexi thought for a moment and said, "So now that we know that we are looking for something, if we go back successfully and leave something for us to find in this present, we should be able to find it somehow now."

Cy smiled, he said, "Did you read any of the advertisements in the paper?"

"No, why?"

"Let's write an ad to place in the paper after we arrive. We should be able to find it in the library archive as soon as we compose it. That assumes of course that we are successful in arriving." Cy took a notepad from his glove box and a pen from his pocket. He thought for a moment, then began to write. When he finished he handed the slip of paper to Lexi. He asked, "What do you think?"

Lexi looked at the ad. It said 'Dave, meet us at the campsite next Saturday night, friends for ether.'

Cy said, "We can run it for three days, then we'll have plenty of time to get established and get a feel for the neighborhood." He restarted the truck and they returned to the library. They hurried down the stairs to the archive room and got the micro-fiche slides out.

Lexi began going through the newspapers starting in 1903, October, just to be safe. She scanned through the April 1904, then October 1904. She let out a loud gasp and reached out clutching Cy's arm. There in the middle of the personal notices column was the advertisement that Cy had written. The only difference was that the editor must have thought he was fixing a typo, it was changed to read 'friends forever.' Lexi quickly scanned forward to the next day's paper and read the ad again. She said, "Look, you went back and set him straight."

Cy was sitting and just staring now. The full magnitude of what they were about to do was beginning to set in.

They sat in silence for a few moments as Cy contemplated. When he had thought it through he decided to let Lexi know what he was thinking. He turned to her and asked, "Lexi, I've thought this through and I want to ask you something. Lexi, will you marry me? Will you marry me tomorrow?"

She looked back at Cy. She was probably more surprised at her lack of surprise than by the proposition he was making. Then she was ultimately surprised when she heard her own voice respond without further hesitation, "Yes, or today if possible."

It was quiet in the archives as they consummated the proposal with a long kiss. They then left for the city hall to get a marriage license.

The wedding took place the next day. Brian and Charlie witnessed the civil ceremony. Lexi became Mrs. Cyrus Hill at two O'clock in the afternoon on October fourth. Time was short, there was enough time only for dinner with Brian and Charlie, Cy hadn't even told his family. They went to a local restaurant, The Scupper, for a seafood dinner. This was when they told Brian and Charlie about their plans.

Lexi began, "In the archive section of the Library you'll find old newspapers saved on microfiche. Look for the August 7, 1916 edition of The Sheldon News. Read the obituaries. Cy and I both feel that telling Annie what you find there would be a mistake."

Cy added, "We are going to try and fix this thing, set the time lines to rights. If we are successful then it's possible that Dave will never have disappeared. If what we are doing is wrong then we may only make it worse. We only know that we need to try. And we wanted someone here to at least know where we were, even though if they told anyone they would probably get committed to the Looney bin!"

Brian looked at them as though they were insane. He said, "What are you two planning?"

Cy said, "We're going to go after Dave first, then we're going to try and get Lexi, or should I say Ezra, back home."

"You guys are crazy to even try." Brian said, "Even if you are able to find Dave, and even if you are able to get him back here, and to push it a little further, even if you are able to go back to Ezra's time, you have to remember that you, Lexi, are older now than when you left. This isn't the way to return you to your time, at least not if you want to have your childhood back."

Cy said, "I disagree Brian. If we go back to a time before Ezra got caught in the eddy and prevent her from being caught in it she will have her life again. I'll return here when I'm sure she is safe in her parents cabin." Cy paused and looked at Lexi. "When we stop Ezra from being scooped into the eddy Lexi should cease to exist. I'll be left alone and I'll know exactly where the eddy will be opening to take me home."

Charlie asked, "I don't understand one thing, if you are going to try to alter the time line and change the current reality, then why did you guys get married?"

Lexi answered, "Charlie, I am an early eighteenth century girl living in the early twenty-first century. I still have my values from childhood instilled in me from that time. I couldn't be with Cy the way I wanted to be, unless we were married. If all of this fails then the poor guy is stuck with me, but if we are successful, then we had something out of time, something that we otherwise wouldn't have had.

It's selfish of me. I may cease to exist, but until then, I wanted to have something, someone, to hold tight to."

A tear welled in Charlie's eye, she said, "I guess I can understand that well enough."

Brian said, "Well, you never know what the alternate time line holds."

Cy said, "Brutha, I think this IS the alternate time line!"

CHAPTER SIXTEEN

There was a pain in the middle of his back that felt as though he were laying on a rock. As he rolled over he realized that he was indeed, laying on a rock. Every joint in his body ached as he tried to orient himself to where he was and how he had come to be there. His clothes were drenched through from rain. His feet were soaked and freezing in his shoes. Every part of his body felt soggy.

Dave sat up and looked around. It was dark. Somehow he had passed out and had remained unconscious through the late afternoon, sunset, and a major weather change. There were some strange things in the air; like the smell of cow manure. There was even the sound of cattle lowing in the night that just put the finishing touches on his disorientation.

He had no idea where he was, he had no memory of being anywhere near a farm, but knew he had to find shelter and warmth soon or risk hypothermia. He struggled to his feet and started to walk in the direction of the cattle. His sneakers were squishing with every step he took. He saw a light in the distance, across the field from where he found himself. Stumbling along, Dave found it difficult to walk on his cold feet. They hurt bad from the cold and wet. It only exacerbated matters when he stepped in a cow plop every few feet. At least some of them were warm. He took it as a good sign that he could feel warmth in his feet at all. Annie was going to pitch a fit. He could hear her now, grilling him as to how he managed to get himself so filthy dirty, all covered in cow manure, out until all hours of the night doing who knows what and on and on. He really longed to hear her voice right now, her interrogation would be a most welcome alternative to his current circumstances.

Dave started to realize that something was wrong. This was no place that was recognizable to him. How had he gotten so far from home? Why didn't he remember? Surely he would have remembered walking a great distance like this. He hadn't been drinking, just out hiking in the woods with Morgan, taking in some fresh air and the foliage. It was beautiful this year, especially down by the lake.

As he neared the light he came to a post and rail fence. He lifted his leg and put it through the rails, leaned down and followed through with his body and stepped out on the other side. The manure was different over here. 'Yup,' he thought, 'The manure is always browner on the other side.' He chuckled to himself under his breath. When he straightened up he got a clear view of the barn that he had been making his way toward. The rain had lifted some and a light fog was blowing around in the night. A horse nickered in the darkness from somewhere near the barn. Dave feared he knew exactly where: from under the shed roof on the far end of the barn. This was Brian's family barn. He had played here as a boy. He was married here just a year and a half ago. This was waterfront, not a pasture. Understanding was coming to Dave, slowly at first, then with lightning speed. He was getting dizzy, growing faint and feared he would pass out. He began to remember the afternoon, how he had hiked in the woods with Morgan running through the brush. He recalled sitting at the water's edge as the sun was nearing the horizon. Morgan was laying on the moss just to his left. He had been so relaxed he began to doze off. Now he began to understand what Alice had felt like when she took her trip down the rabbit hole and into wonderland.

Just then a hand clamped down on his shoulder. He spun away from the hand gripping his shoulder and looked at who it was.

"Dave," Cy said, "Dave relax, look at me."

Dave looked at Cy, then saw Lexi standing behind him. He said, "Ooohhh, what's going on here? What's happening Cy? You had better not tell me what I think you're gonna tell me!"

Cy grinned, he said, "Don't worry Dave, You just took a little spin, that's all. We'll get you back to Annie before she knows you're even gone."

But it was too much, Dave passed out.

Lexi stepped up along side Cy and looked down at Dave.

Cy said, "Well at least he can't get any dirtier than he was, laying there in the manure."

Lexi tilted her head, she had a quizzical look on her face. She said, "Do you realize how difficult it is for a girl from the early 18th century to comprehend humor from the early

21st century?" She looked down at Dave and added, "Do you know how absolutely crazy it is to even be asking that question? Seriously?" She looked back at Cy.

Cy was looking intently at her face when she looked at him. He said, "Lexi, there are only a few select people who would think that you aren't crazy asking that question, I'm happy to be one. For now though, we had better get our friend here out of the pile of crap he's landed in and into a hot bath. And we had best be quiet so Zeke doesn't hear and come poking around. He's likely to wonder why my "nephew" here is laying around in the barnyard." Cy squatted down and lightly slapped Dave's face, first one cheek then the other. "Dave, wake up Dave"

Dave's eyes blinked, he opened them and slowly focused on Cy. "Okay, okay stop slappin' me already." Dave propped himself up on his elbows. He looked at Lexi and said, "Lexi?"

Lexi said, "Hi Dave."

Dave looked at Cy and said, "Lucy, you got some 'splainin' to do."

Cy grinned and said, "Well it's like this, you fell in cow manure. So do you feel like getting cleaned up?"

Dave looked at himself as best he could in the light from inside the barn. He could see manure caked on his sneakers and up his legs. He held his hands up and saw there was manure there as well. He said, "I think it would be great to get cleaned up. But if I'm where, or rather when I think I am, Cy when the hell are we?"

Cy said, "Dave, it's alright, we've got it covered. Come on man, we have to get you inside, out of sight, and cleaned up."

Dave got to his feet with Cy's help. They made their way to the back of the barn to where Mr. and Mrs. Hill were currently residing.

Cy heated some water that he had brought in earlier that afternoon as he had done for the last three nights in preparation for Dave's arrival. He poured bucketful after bucketful as it came off of the fire in the fireplace into the metal tub in the middle of the apartment. Lexi sat facing the other direction as Dave sat in the tub washing the manure off and warming himself in the hot water.

Cy said, "This sure makes you realize just how much you take for granted. Heating water for a bath over fire like this and bathing in the middle of the room with no privacy."

Dave said, "You're really not trying to make me feel better, are you?"

"Whaddyamean?" Cy asked.

"Come on Cy, I'm feeling a little vulnerable here. It's time to give me the story."

Cy said, "Okay, but first, realize this, we're changing everything as we go along here. The time line we remember is changing as we speak." He took a deep breath and began, "Lexi came and told us about her origins, she was caught in an eddy too, only for her the trip went into the future, into our time. She came to Brian's two years after you disappeared and related her story to us all. Well, after that night she took me to the library and showed me your obituary."

"My what?!"

"Yeah, I thought you would react like that. It was the second obituary of yours I've read and you're still alive.

Dave the thing is, we left to come here to this time two years after you did. And when we did, we planned our arrival actually to over shoot your arrival by four years. We've been living here working for Dave's great grandfather for all that time, waiting for you to drop in tonight. By my reckoning it's been five years since I've seen you, by your reckoning it was yesterday. Your going missing made the newspaper headlines for better than a week. Every so often a reporter would drag it up again to keep the story alive. A lot of people thought you just ran out on Annie. The people that don't know you thought that. Lexi brought me to the library to show me what her research had yielded and had me read your 1916 obituary. That gave us a target date on your arrival time because it listed your age as thirty-six. We wanted to be sure that there was time in case the info was wrong. That's why we over shot by four years. We knew where you would turn up, it was just a matter of, well, when."

Dave was listening, but was having difficulty accepting what Cy was saying without going into shock. He said, "So you're telling me that this is what, 1904?"

"Yes. Dave the good news is there is a way back. The bad news is, you'll have to wait here for another half year before you can go."

"A half year? I don't understand."

"We spent some time considering the events that we've experienced, and Lexi and I figured out a lot of things. We don't know how it works or why, but we do understand that it does. We also figured out when the ether is going to spin. Dave, you got caught in a time eddy. It was pure chance that you landed at this time, but because we were able to determine how long to stay in the eddy we could target the time that we wanted to go to. This thing is like a naturally occurring time machine."

Dave contemplated what Cy was telling him. "I guess I believed this was all possible, what with that thing at my wedding, but I didn't think it would happen to me, much less happen so abruptly." He looked at Lexi, her back still to him and said, "Lexi, I can only imagine how difficult it was for you when you awoke that morning and found yourself in a different time."

Lexi turned her head to talk over her shoulder and said, "It was pretty frightening Dave. You're lucky to have had a welcome wagon!"

Cy said, "Look, Dave, why don't you just concentrate on warming up right now. We all need to get some sleep. We have to get up at 4:30 A.M., that's only six hours from now. It's going to be a busy day tomorrow for Lexi and me, but tomorrow evening we can go into greater detail and help you make sense of all of this. Zeke knows we're expecting you and is looking forward to another hand for harvesting. You can plan to winter with us; we've saved plenty of money to support the three of us through winter. Then you can go back to Annie. Dude, she'll never even know you were gone. Oh, one more thing, Zeke, he is undoubtedly Brian's great-grandfather. You won't believe the resemblance."

Dave looked at Cy dubiously from his tepid bath. He said, "Gimme a towel will ya."

Cy smiled. He got a towel from a cabinet and gave it to Dave. He said, "You can sleep in the bunk that we set up in the make shift pantry. Lexi and I are going to bed now. Don't sleep walk. If you have to go, the outhouse is around in back of the barn. Make sure you knock first."

Dave was still trying to decide what was real and what was just him coming unspooled. He nodded.

Cy said, "Goodnight Dave, it's good to see you again. Ready for bed Lexi?"

Lexi got up, being careful to keep her back to Dave. She said, "Goodnight Dave."

"Goodnight Lexi, Cy." Dave said. He stood and toweled himself off, then dressed in the clothes that Cy had put out for him. The outfit was more in keeping with the period. He made his way down to the back door of the barn and let himself out. The outhouse was right where Cy had told him. He mused to himself; it was almost exactly where he and Annie had had their first dance as man and wife. When he had availed himself he went back upstairs to the little loft apartment that Cy and Lexi had in the barn. Dave remembered the apartment from childhood. He never thought he would be one of its tenants. He made his way around to the pantry and got into the cot that had been made for him. Within moments sleep overtook him.

Geeze, Dave thought, he does look like Brian. Dave was looking out the window at Zeke as he was driving a team of horses pulling a buckboard wagon. He seemed to be leaving the farm. Cy had told him early in the morning to just stay put today. So Dave stayed low and quiet in the loft. It had given him time to think about the situation he was in and absorb all that Cy and Lexi had told him. They got married. Cy and Lexi were Mr. And Mrs. for four years now. Too much. He had gotten married a year and a half before they had and yet they were married for four years and he was only married for a year and a half. He felt weary. Even though he hadn't done anything all morning his eyelids were heavy. He settled back onto the cot and went back to sleep.

In the late afternoon Cy shook Dave awake. He said, "Come on man, wake up. Zeke wants to meet you. Then we have a lot to talk about."

Dave rose and rubbed his face. He went to the wash basin and splashed cold water on his face. He said, "Cy, I'm starving."

Cy said, "Good, we eat supper with the Wright's, and there's always plenty on the table. They like a good appetite in a man and won't be offended when you go back for seconds. I have to tell you a few things. I told Zeke that you are my nephew, my sister's son. You need to call us Uncle Cy and Aunt Alexis. Listen, hit the outhouse and I'll bring you inside and introduce you."

Dave smirked, he said, "I couldn't have been your cousin? I have to call you Uncle?"

Cy smiled and said, "I didn't think you would mind."

Dave said, "Uncle Jerk!"

When they entered the house, Dave was amazed at how familiar the house was. Over the century some of the furniture had been changed, but he was surprised at how many pieces that he had always thought of as antiques were there in the house now and looked new. Even though he was expecting it he was surprised when Zeke walked into the room.

Cy said, "Mr. Wright this is my nephew, David Brooks. Dave say hello to Mr. Wright."

Dave looked at Cy, surprised yet again, this time by his name change. Then he turned his attention to Zeke.

He said, "Hello sir, it's a pleasure to meet you." He reached out his hand to Zeke to shake.

Zeke's powerful hand engulfed Dave's and gripped it firmly. He said to Dave, "David, it's good to meet you." His eyebrows knitted and he asked, "You aren't too accustomed to manual labor are you David?"

Cy didn't wait, he came right to Dave's rescue and said, "Sir, remember I told you that David has been in school?"

Zeke looked thoughtfully at Cy and said, "Yes, that's right." Then back at Dave and asked, "Accounting isn't it?"

Dave felt relieved, at least he could talk about a profession he knew something about. "Yes, that's right."

Zeke rubbed his beard and said to Dave, "Perhaps you could be of service to me more than just in the fields. I have some problems with the State, they want to take my land."

Dave realized then that his arrival was just previous to the land grab by the state for the creation of jobs building flood control dams and reservoirs. He said, "Eminent domain."

Zeke nodded saying, "Yes, that's what they are calling it. It seems to me a crime though."

Dave said, "After harvest if you would like, I can do some research into this and see if there is anything that can be done."

Zeke looked at him and said. "Son, I may impose upon you sooner than that if only because there may not be a farm after the harvest otherwise."

Dave said, "I'll be happy to look into this first thing in the morning Sir."

Later that evening, after all of the chores were completed Cy and Dave stood out by the corral at the rear of the barn, out of earshot of anyone. Cy asked, "Do you think you can do anything about it?"

Dave said, "I don't know for certain Cy, the laws are different now than in our own time. I read about all of this in Brian's family history and I remember him talking about the things he was uncovering about the politics of the dam site. This event was a real thorn in the family side. They almost lost the whole farm, not to the land grab but because of the economic impact it had on the farm business. Once the bulk of the land went under water there weren't crops enough to sustain the family. They didn't know any other way of life. It wasn't until after World War II that they started the business that Brian still runs in our time. The thing is, I don't know off hand what if anything can be done to stop it. And the other thing is, would stopping it be bad for the timeline?"

Cy thought about it for a moment and said, "I don't know Dave, for all we know we've done all of this before, and really screwed it up worse and lost the farm, now we have a chance to fix it. Look, see what you can find out. If it's do-able in under six months then I say, do it!"

Dave thought for a moment and asked, "So two questions, first, why Brooks and second, why six months?"

Cy said, "Well, Brooks is the name on your obituary printed twelve years from now. We're going to try to make that not happen. Lexi and I determined that the eddy spins twice every two years, once in the fall moving backward in time and once in the spring moving forward in time. It's fall, we have to winter until spring, then we can send you home."

"Me? Not us?"

Cy saddened at this, "No, Lexi wants to go home, to her time. She wants to live the life she was born to live."

Dave said, "Maybe she is living the life she was born to live."

"Since I told her about what happened to me at your wedding she is convinced that she can return to her time and life. To tell you the truth Dave, I agree that she can do it, but it's breaking my heart."

Dave said, "Well, if what you've figured out holds true, you should have another year and a half together here."

"And a few years perhaps more when we arrive. We plan on shooting for an overlap to be early like we did when we came here to find you."

Dave asked, "What'll you do after she's restored?"

Cy said, "Well there really won't be much keeping me there so, I can just jump into the eddy that brought her to our time in the first place."

After a long silence Dave said, "That should just about set things to rights then shouldn't it?"

"Yeah, except for my heart. But I suppose in the vast configuration of things, my heart is a mighty small thing. I'll live. Besides, maybe when I get back home, I'll just forget."

The sun had long since set. There was a chill wind blowing across the field that was penetrating the fabric of the coats the men were wearing. In the distance the cattle were lowing as the moon, in its early first quarter, rose with ease from the horizon as though it were breaking the bonds of gravity and loosing itself from the earth.

CHAPTER SEVENTEEN

The waiting room was unheated. The air was dank and musty with the sweet smell of plaster and freshly painted walls. This was the new Sheldon City Hall. As with any institutional building of its era it was painted with oil and lead based paint. The color was a sickly green that did not compliment the architecture of the building. Why the people of this time had to paint all of their public buildings in this fashion; two tones of puke green, dark puke on the bottom and light puke on the top, Dave would never understand. The chairs were utilitarian with no cushions on the seats. Dave's backside was getting numb. The U.S. had only been a country for a hundred-twenty nine years and Sheldon had only been incorporated as a city eight months ago but already they had perfected some of the typical and essential bureaucratic maneuvers required of any city. There were no telephones, but they knew how to play the call forward game, only in this game you were forwarded and not your phone connection. It seemed much like an Ayne Rand novel Dave had read in college, "Atlas Shrugged." As the story line developed more and more people were unwilling to commit to any decision or even discuss issues for fear of being implicated or accused as a decision maker and thereby have to be responsible for any problems coming from the decision. Such was the case now for Dave when it came to the Wright farm. In fact some folks seemed downright fearful at the mere mention of Zeke Wright and his acreage.

What Dave was able to find out so far was that there had been a series of floods down river from the Wright farm on the Lawrence River. Calling the Lawrence a river was like calling a newborn calf a raging bull. The fact was they were building their dam too far upstream from where the problem was. There were several tributaries that joined the Lawrence after it passed through the Wright farm. They were prone to seasonal flooding, more so than the Lawrence. Damming the Lawrence at the Wright farm would not solve the problem.

This prompted Dave to look in a different direction, namely, to follow the money. He had obtained topographical maps of the communities that followed the Lawrence downstream. Then he had visited those communities and investigated the ownership of the land along the river. There were three other sites that were proposed by the state. All three of them made more sense than the Sheldon proposal, but there was one that made perfect sense. About fifteen miles to the east in a town called Peterston three rivers converged in a broad valley. This was the valley that was regularly flooding in the spring. It was also a valley that was very panoramic with a thirty room manse built upon it owned by a very wealthy man, Mr. Avery McKinnon.

Dave had learned from Zeke that McKinnon was a prominent man in state politics. He was a State Representative and was eyeing the legislature with eventual hopes for the governorship. He was one of Massachusetts' darlings who wielded too much power and influence in the state. Some things are the same no matter when you are.

Much of the information Dave had gathered from Zeke seemed innocuous enough on its own, but by simply putting it all together as Dave had, it showed the nefarious plot that now threatened the Wright farm. Now it was a matter of filing injunctions and an epic David and Goliath battle to save the farm. Dave wasn't hopeful. Zeke on the other hand had placed all of his hopes in Dave's ability to litigate the matter. In Zeke's eyes there was no difference between an accountant and a lawyer. Perhaps there was something to Zeke's understanding of things, there was a noticeable difference in the volume of law suits in the hundred years he had traveled back in time. Certain cases involving land titles and many domestic issues were handled by the general public on their own without the involvement of a hired attorney. Still, Dave didn't much like the idea of going to court on his own to fight something that bore such consequences.

So here Dave sat, in the new city hall building waiting for the city clerk's office to let him in and assign him a docket number for the next circuit court hearings in two weeks. They closed at five PM. It was four-fifty now and Dave's thinking he would be stonewalled was being confirmed as he waited in his uncomfortable seat in a fresh puke green paint stinking City Hall waiting room. He missed Annie.

The door opened to the inner office. Dave stood and faced the door. A short man poked his head out like a groundhog looking to see if his shadow was anywhere in sight. When he saw Dave and saw that Dave had seen him he scowled visibly. Dave advanced and said, "Are you Mr. Emerson?"

With obvious agitation the man answered, "It's five o'clock sir there's nothing I can do for you today, you'll have to come back again tomorrow, I recommend at an earlier hour." He was abruptly closing the door on Dave.

Dave stepped forward and quickly placed his foot in the doorway to prevent its closing. He said, "I've been here for an hour and a half sir, waiting to see you. You aren't going to shoo me away so easily."

Emerson looked annoyed. He said, "There's nothing I can do for you, please come back tomorrow." He pushed at the door against Dave's foot.

Dave wasn't going to be pushed out tonight. He had come to the end of his patience and tolerance for being passed around. The deadline for filing for the docket was today and he was determined that he was not leaving without it. He pushed back and easily opened the door against Emerson. He said, "Look here Emerson, I'm tired of being passed around like this from one office to another as though I were some kind of hot potato! Now open up and do your job."

"My office is closed sir, please come back tomorrow!" Emerson was panicking, his face was contorted and anxious.

Dave said, "Your office is open for another ten minutes, you sir have plenty of time to attend to my business."

Emerson said, "Why don't you just comeback tomorrow?"

Dave said, "Because tomorrow is too late, you know that! You know who I am and you know what my business is. Today is the deadline for filing a docket for the next court circuit. I am not leaving until you give me a docket, and neither are you!"

Emerson realized there was nothing he could do. He released the door, went around his desk and sat down. Dave looked at him appraisingly for the first time. He was small in stature, almost demure. He was going bald and had already started lowering his part down toward his ear. The comb-over was held in place by pomade that was popular in this day. He had a thin mustache trimmed to the top of his upper lip. It seemed like a caterpillar stuck there for the purpose of warming his lip. To Dave it seemed more like it was painted on than grown naturally. Emerson was the classic' picked on kid' that grew up and found himself in a position of somewhat limited authority. This authority was the only power he wielded in his life. He was abusive toward those he wielded it over. Dave knew however that now, confronted with no alternative, Emerson had to do his job.

Dave placed the writ on Emerson's desk and said, "here is the writ, please, issue my client's docket."

Emerson looked at Dave over his thick round glasses and pursed his lips on the right side. He looked at the document and asked, "Is everything in order in this writ?"

Dave said, "Yes all of the necessary documents are here, in triplicate, all signed, everything is in order, the docket, please."

Emerson looked the paperwork over. There was nothing he could do but issue the docket. With the resignation of a pall bearer he proceeded to write and stamp the docket slip. He placed it on top of the writ that Dave had prepared keeping his copy for the court records. He said, "I hope you're satisfied Mr. Brooks."

Dave stood and picked up his writ and the docket slip. He said, "Thank you Mr. Emerson." He turned and walked out triumphantly. Now all was set for his first step. He had to prove that there had been collusion and a conspiracy by McKinnon to reposition the dam away from his property farther up the valley. Theoretically this should be easy, but the reality was that Dave didn't know for sure what he was going to do when push came to shove. At the same time he had to acknowledge to himself that he had come along pretty well so far.

As he walked outdoors into the brisk fall air he set his face toward the south side of Sheldon and the seven mile walk back to the farm. Lexi had asked him to pick up some ground beef at the butcher shop along his way home if he was early enough. He would have just enough time if he hurried. The shop closed at six PM and was two miles to the south, along the way to the Wright farm. He picked up his feet and made tracks.

CHAPTER EIGHTEEN

The air was brisk as Dave made his way toward the railroad tracks that he would use as a short-cut to the Wright farm. He had just left the butcher shop with a paper package filled with three pounds of ground beef wrapped up and bagged. He braced against the stiff breeze as he walked. The wind was coming from the east, which may have indicated an incoming Nor'easter, but without the six-o'clock news to help him, the fact was, it was evident that he could not read the weather signs. There were definitely clouds building in the sky and the air smelled humid. He quickened his pace. As Dave made his way to the tracks he came across something that he hadn't expected. In the woods along both sides of the tracks there were huts built in the underbrush. There were hoboes living in them. This was something that Dave was fascinated by. As a kid he had dreamed and romanticized life as a hobo. He loved his train set and always wondered what life would be like hopping cars and riding the rails. He had to admit, as intrigued as he was by the hoboes he was glad to have a warm place to sleep tonight and the knowledge that he would be sleeping on a full stomach.

On the north side of the tracks there was a ruckus being raised in the brush. One of the hoboes emerged behind a small scraggly creature that wasn't even knee high. Its fur was covered with dirt and grease. It barked, revealing itself as a dog. Dave crouched down as the whelp ran straight to him. As Dave caught the pup up in his arms he looked at the hobo for the first time and saw that he was carrying a long knife in his hand.

The hobo stopped running and said, "Thanks stranger, I thought I was going hungry tonight."

Dave was horrified realizing that this puppy was to be supper for the hungry man. He looked down at the dog and then back at the hobo and asked, "How much do you want for the dog mister?"

"Want for him? I want to eat boy, give me the dog." The hobo could see Dave's youthfulness and he was immediately taking a dominant stance.

Dave knew he couldn't win in a fight, and that if he wasn't careful this man and his desperate friends in the brush would clean him out and take the puppy for chow as well. He held up the bag from the butcher shop and said "Look mister, here's a couple of pounds of ground beef, its more meat than you'll get off this mange, you take it and let me keep the mutt." The hobo looked unconvinced. Dave held the ground beef out to the hobo and said, "It's like this, I want the pup for my kid, see? This meat is all I've got and my wife is going to have a stroke when she sees the dog and no meat. The meat is worth more than the mutt, but it's yours. You take the meat, and me and the dog, we take a walk. See?"

The hobo looked at the bag in Dave's hand and decided it would likely be a long time before he had ground beef again. He also knew he didn't want john law or the railroad dicks busting up the village because he got greedy. Besides, fleece the punk and let him go, maybe he'll come back another day with more meat. He grabbed the ground beef from Dave and made for the tree line.

After paying the bum Dave heard the long howl of a distant train whistle as it was approaching Sheldon from the east, most likely Boston. He wanted very much to get through this section of tracks and out onto the roadways again so he picked up his pace and strode at a quick pace the remaining half mile to the next roadway intersection. At the road he turned south for the last four miles to the farm. Dave felt he could relax a bit and there would be no more trouble from 'hobo haven.' He reached into his coat pocket and withdrew a quarter of an egg sandwich that he didn't finish at lunch that day. It was wrapped in an old linen sandwich wrap. He didn't have to work too hard to unwrap it, just shook it loose really and fed it in pieces to the puppy. The dog ate the sandwich with a feverish appetite and licked Dave's fingers clean of any offensive crumbs or remaining traces that humans cannot detect. Then he lifted his head and started to lick Dave's face. That was when Dave looked at the dog's face closely for the first time. There was a white stripe that ran down the snout and did a peculiar jog out to the left then continued down to the black wet nose. Dave thought out loud, "Huh, just like…Morgan's?" Dave started to examine the puppy closer. He was dirty, flea bit, quite scrawny, but there was less and less doubt in his mind, this puppy, almost supper to a hobo, was his own Morgan. A tear fell from his eye as Dave held his dear pet close to him and he felt Annie's absence all the more profoundly. There was a certain comfort knowing that if in fact this was his Morgan, which Dave was convinced of, that one hundred years from now this very dog after traveling through the ethereal eddy was laying on his back in Annie's lap getting his belly rubbed. Dave, carrying the dog still, flipped him over onto his back and cradled him in his arms and rubbed his belly. Most dogs didn't like to be held this way for fear of falling, Morgan always tolerated it, actually seemed to enjoy it, as he was right now in Dave's arms.

When he arrived home the snow had already piled up six inches. Dave had found himself wishing that he had worn overshoe boots. If he had had to stay out much longer there was the possibility he would lose some toes. It took all of fifteen seconds to bring Cy and Lexi to the same conclusion regarding Morgan. The greatest concern was Zeke, who because of what Dave was doing for him, ought to be very tolerant about a pet.

They heated up some water for Dave to bathe with and when he finished Lexi and Cy gave Morgan a bath. Morgan was like most dogs, he didn't much like baths, but he behaved well because he did love the praise. After his bath, Morgan went straight to the fireplace. He was wet and shivering, the heat from the fire was causing the dampness in his fur to evaporate in a visible mist rising off of his clean coat. All of his markings were visible now providing more confirmation about the dog's identity.

Dave needed to go in and give Zeke an update. It was good news he was bringing him. But because Dave was so inexperienced with this he didn't like the idea of raising the hopes of this family. Being from the future had its perks and foibles; while you did know the outcome of some things, the whole business of changing the timeline bore with it a great weight of responsibility.

CHAPTER NINETEEN

Zeke listened intently as Dave reported the status of his case to him. He passed the paperwork over to Zeke and discussed all of the findings with him. He wanted Zeke to understand completely the line of strategy in fighting this case. In the event that he couldn't get a hearing before his trip into the future in the spring, Dave felt Zeke should be prepared to fight this battle on his own.

From this court, if the judge felt it was warranted, the next step was to the Massachusetts Environmental Planning Commission, Waterways Division. These were the boys that planned eventually to take possession of the farm through eminent domain. Unless, of course Dave and Zeke could prove to the commission that the dam site in Sheldon was folly. Unfortunately this wasn't a case of showing rational men that a course of action may reap disastrous results, it was instead forcing politically influenced men to accept accountability for a mistake they had yet to make so they wouldn't make it. Politicians and policy makers don't typically live bound by the same game rules they institute.

Dave knew that his only hope was to force them into a position that should a flood occur in Peterston's Lawrence River Valley after the dam was built in Sheldon that they would be to blame for the improper dam site. Especially when Avery McKinnon came looking for someone to blame. As Dave was growing up his Dad taught him not to bring a problem to him without also bringing a solution. In this manner, Dave was bringing a solution to the commission. The three Peterston tributaries that were ultimately the flood causing rivers ran down the sides of the valley ridges and passed through natural areas that formed basins. Three smaller dams could be constructed to capture flood waters at these locations for less than it would cost to build the Sheldon site. The land is already the property of the state, and is uninhabited by people. These flood control basins would serve to protect McKinnon's land. The small ponds that would result form the dams would serve to support aquatic and wetland wildlife. Good for fishing and hunting. Less societal impact coupled with a positive environmental impact. Win win.

Dinner was on the table. Zeke's wife, Olive, had put out a beef stew, all the children and the Hills had gathered. Zeke and Dave joined the families at the table. Supper was served by Olive and the eldest daughter, Adele. Adele was 17 years old and was exhibiting all of the signs of a girl with a crush. It did not go unnoticed by the object of her affection, and as a result, Dave felt increasingly uncomfortable around her. He did the very best not to encourage her, short of being rude he tried not to acknowledge her. What Dave didn't understand was that in this time, It would have been rude to acknowledge her without her father's permission to court her. Then whether she liked him or not he could call on her and she would have to abide by her father's wishes. Time changed many things in the upcoming century.

Dave decided to help ease the situation a bit. He looked to Lexi and said, "Aunt Lexi, I meant to tell you, I received a letter from Annie, she wanted me to remember her to you."

Lexi looked confused at first, then played along, "Really David, how is she?"

Dave answered, "She is unhappy to learn that her fiancé would be wintering here instead of closer to home. She said to tell you that you and Uncle Cy should release me from your tyrannical grip and allow me to come home."

Lexi said, "Cy, do I have a tyrannical grip?"

Cy looked at his wife and said, "My dear, no Ceasar in all of roman history had such a hold as you."

Lexi looked to Zeke and said, "Mr. Wright, I do believe the snow isn't the only thing that is getting deep around here."

With that laughter erupted around the table. Even young Adele found amusement in this banter and began to take her sights off of Dave.

After the meal, when they were all enjoying a cup of Olive's coffee, Dave said to Zeke, "Mr. Wright, I wanted to tell you about Morgan." Zeke turned and was listening. Dave continued, "I was walking home from Sheldon this afternoon and I encountered a hobo on the railroad tracks. He was chasing down a golden retriever pup with a knife. I spoiled his dinner. I hope my keeping a dog isn't a problem for you."

Zeke looked at him thoughtfully for a moment, then said, "I should have told you to stay away from the railroad track short-cut. There are too many unsavory men down through there. You were lucky to escape with the dog, and anything else that you had with you. If you keep the dog or not is of no consequence to me." Zeke looked around the table and seemed to be thinking about something. His gaze lingered for bit longer on Lexi, then continued to Dave. There was something pensive in his behavior this evening. Whatever it was he decided to let it go by for another time. Instead, he said, "Well good people, I believe I am going to turn in. Olive, would you agree it's bedtime?"

Olive who was very quiet ordinarily and rarely spoke said, "Yes Ezekiel, I think it's time."

Able to take a hint, Cy, Lexi and Dave rose and began to pull on their coats.

Lexi said, "Olive, you really must share your stew recipe with me, it was quite delicious."

Olive replied, "Thank you, Lexi, There is a great deal I should like to share with you, please come in tomorrow and we will have a lovely visit while the men clear the snow."

"After breakfast then?"

"Yes, That will be fine."

"Very well, until then goodnight. Goodnight, everyone." Lexi said as she stepped through the door into the front vestibule.

The men followed Lexi out into the waiting storm. The wind was whipping the snow into their faces as they made their way across the barn yard to the apartment in the back. Lexi went straight to the out house before going in for the night. As was customary with them, Lexi would go first with Cy standing by as Dave would go to the shed entrance and wait. Cy went next as Lexi made her way across the yard, she was visibly upset as she approached Dave.

Dave asked her, "Is there something wrong?"

Lexi said, "We'll talk upstairs, after."

Dave agreed and crossed the yard for his turn in the privy.

Later, upstairs in the apartment, Lexi had heated some water for tea. She poured three cups and sat at the table. She said, "I've been noticing Olive staring at me for weeks now. I'm not sure what is going on but she definitely wants to talk about more than stew tomorrow morning."

Cy said, "I agree, and did you see the look Zeke was giving us all after supper? Something is up."

Dave said, "Guys, there is a possibility that we may have overlooked here. What if we aren't the only ones on this farm who have had physical experience with the ether?"

There was a moment of quiet as they each considered this.

Lexi said, "Zeke paused when his eyes met mine at the table tonight. I get the feeling Dave is right, we aren't the only travelers here."

There were cattle in the barn downstairs and even though there were walls separating them from the beasts, their lowing could still be heard through the floor. The newest addition to the household wasn't used to the cow sounds and would look curiously at the floor whenever a moo could be heard. Dave was amused by this and would grin each time the pup cocked his head to one side then the other as he was trying to determine what the sounds were. Dave said, "I should probably bring Morgan outside to go before bed.

Maybe stop by the cow stalls along the way so he can see who's making all that noise."

Cy looked at Lexi and said, "What do you think sweetheart, shall we hit the hay?"

"I think so," said Lexi, "Whatever Olive has to say, we will find out in the morning. Until then I think it would be best to get a good night sleep."

Dave said, "I'll probably walk down to the gate with Morgan, so I'll be about forty-five minutes or so. I want him to have every opportunity to go so he makes it through the night." He got up and pulled his coat on. At the door he bent and pulled on his overshoes and called, "Morgan, come!"

Immediately, as though he had been responding to the name and command all of his short life, the pup bounded across the room and was hopping up and down at Dave's feet.

Cy said smiling, "Well that's definitely Morgan. Goodnight Dave."

"Goodnight Dave." Lexi said as Dave and Morgan went through the door.

"Goodnight you two, see you in the morning." Dave said as he turned with Morgan at his feet.

They went quietly down the stairs to the rear of the barn. There was a kerosene hurricane lamp at the bottom of the stairs that Dave occasionally took with him on these strolls, he flipped down the lever that opened the globe at the bottom near the wick. He took a box of matches out of his pocket and very carefully lit one. The last thing he wanted was to be the man remembered for burning down the Wright barn with his friends asleep in it. Once it was lit and safely adjusted, Dave bent and lifted the puppy into his arms. He carried him to a stall where three cows stood chewing their cud in the night. He held the lantern aloft and illuminated the cattle for Morgan to see. Of course they wouldn't low while he was standing there wanting to give the pup a lesson. That was alright, there would be plenty of time to teach Morgan about cattle. Lowering the lantern Dave turned toward the rear of the barn. He got to the door and put Morgan down, he re-hung the lantern while he pulled his collar up and tied his scarf about his neck. Once he felt he was ready he took the lantern off of the hook and opened the door. The wind immediately pushed against him and challenged him as he stepped into the night air. Morgan bounded out past him and began at once to frolic in the snow. In his short life, today had brought his first experience with snow. He seemed to enjoy it. Dave was smiling under his scarf as he watched Morgan bouncing about trying to catch snow in his mouth as the wind whipped it past him.

They made their way out to the road that went from the farm to the town road. It was much darker in this time Dave thought as he strolled along the road. There were no overwhelming city lights rising in the horizon of the night sky. He missed Annie, and wanted to get back to her desperately, yet he knew he was going to have a difficult time leaving this time. Things were so much simpler in this time. He could understand also Lexi wanting to go back to her own time. If it's this peaceful in this time it must be next to paradise in her own, that is, once you got past the Indian problem and the fifty mile trek to the nearest general store. Well perhaps frontier life was a bit extreme, but life in this era was pleasant enough.

Dave picked up a stick on the side of the road and tossed it down the road. Morgan was off, a retriever couldn't resist chasing after a stick or anything thrown for them. Morgan chased after the stick and instinctively brought it back to Dave. So they began what was to become their evening ritual. Dave tried at least three or four nights a week to stay out of the apartment in the evenings. He wanted to give Lexi and Cy time to be alone as husband and wife. His presence in the apartment was certainly causing some inhibition in that area, he knew that, so he tried to give them some time alone every night. There was a loft at the front of the barn that Dave was thinking about asking Zeke if he could convert into another apartment. It wouldn't take much in materials or time, especially if all he did was to build a room for sleeping in. If he slept there he thought Cy and Lexi would still welcome him at the other times of day. He wanted some privacy so he was sure they did as well. He would ask Zeke in the morning as they were clearing the road.

The snow was about eight inches deep now. Morgan was up to his belly in the fluffy white stuff. He didn't seem to notice or mind at all as he chased the stick Dave threw for him. Dave could feel the chill in his feet though, and he was beginning to realize that this was going to be a much more severe winter than he was used to. It was only October 22nd and they were having a nor'easter. On the next throw he turned and threw the stick back toward the farm, abandoning his push toward the town road.

When Dave opened the back door to the barn he stepped in and immediately felt the relief of shelter. Morgan had found a sufficient spot to do his business while he was chasing around the stick on the road. Dave decided to scout the forward loft to see if it was habitable. While he was crossing the barn with Morgan, one of the cows lowed.

Morgan turned quickly and looked inquisitively at the offending bovine. He had his lesson after all. When this happened Dave's gaze fell on the space directly under the apartment. There were walls partitioning it off from the rest of the barn already. This was also the leeward side of the nor'easters. Maybe this would be the better scenario to ask Zeke about. He decided to investigate further.

The room was small compared to the enclosed loft above. There were no kitchen facilities, but all that was needed these days was a ewer and basin for washing. It wouldn't take much to make the room livable and even downright cozy. He didn't mind dirt floors. The chimney that went up through the apartment passed through here on its way. This would be a preferred alternative to Lexi's pantry.

Dave would ask Zeke about the space in the morning.

CHAPTER TWENTY

Brian and Charlie were discussing the possible effects of Cy and Lexi's trip back in time. There seemed to be a bit of difficulty in reaching a common ground concerning whether what they were doing was the right thing or not. The argument was rendered moot by the fact that there were too many possible paradoxical paradigms. It was much like looking at a piece of artwork that was by its nature a labor in surrealism and optical illusion. Stairways leading upward to a floor seemingly suspended upside-down instead of a ceiling, shapes that seemed to bend laws of nature. The ability to come up with any kind of venture as to the effects of Cy and Lexi's little trip were a bit like a dog chasing its own tail. How could they tell if something had changed when after all, it would be incorporated into the present reality and seen by them as a historical reality. They decided that as long as they could remember the couple, their wedding and their leap back, and they were still together, then nothing too bad or hugely significant could have happened. If something did change though, they knew they would not remember anything of this reality. This gave them cause to celebrate every evening that they had together as though it were their last. Because after all, there was a possibility that it was.

Besides, there was plenty else to keep them busy. Operating a family farm took a great deal of time and energy. The Wright Dairy bar was a full time job in itself. Brian and Charlie had met there years before when she was hired by Brian's Mom to work a summer. Now Charlie was married to Brian and managed the production, packaging and sale of all fifteen flavors of ice cream sold at the bar every summer. Brian managed the bed and breakfast that operated in the main house. They lived in an apartment that had been built in the barn a century before. Business was good, and they were planning to expand the loft apartment into a much larger space. Perhaps even fill that space with children one day. Brian didn't want to have kids until after they were able to buy the other half of the farm from his cousin Tara. Tara Brooks was as much a legal heir to the farm as Brian as the result of his Great-grandfather leaving the property to a son and a daughter instead of choosing one of them alone to be the sole heir. It was understandable that the farm went to both, Tara's Grandfather had saved the farm from a land grab by the state. If not for him the farm would all be underwater now. After he successfully lobbied the state and won his case he returned to Sheldon and married Adele Wright. Adele's father, Ezekiel, could not deny half of the estate to them. He dedicated the estate to be cohabitated and operated by both families. Now for the first time since, one of the two heir lines was uninterested in maintaining their half of the farm and had agreed to sell to the other. All Brian and Charlie needed to do was raise enough to buy out fifty percent of the value of the property. The bank would only lend them four hundred fifty thousand toward that end. The property was worth 1.3 million. They had fifty thousand set aside leaving them one hundred fifty short. The problem that kept them back was that every year the real estate value of the property went up, which made them further behind than the year before, even if they managed to put away a significant amount. Brian was working some investments with a five year plan sponsored by the bank. They agreed that if he kept the money invested and was able to keep up a profit from the farm, in five years they would write him the mortgage. He would believe it when he saw it.

CHAPTER TWENTY ONE

Lexi entered the kitchen with a certain amount of trepidation. She was unsure of what would come of the conversation with Olive. She and Cy had talked about this in bed when it became apparent that neither of them were falling asleep any time soon. The possibilities were numerous, ranging from Olive wanting to talk recipes, to the Wright family being fully aware of the ether and the eddies and all that they brought. How much was known and by whom? The only recourse at this time was for Lexi to simply go and see what was on Olive's mind.

Zeke and the other men were out with the horse teams plowing the roadway. They would be gone for three hours or more clearing the fourteen inches of snow that had fallen. The sun was breaking the horizon on a downy white world. There was snow on the tree limbs, the fence rails and on every horizontal surface that nature could affix it. Lexi thought of the Thomas Kincaid candles and calendars that were popular in the late twentieth century. Ironically they had depicted this era. The sun was reddish this morning.

The hues and the angles created a truly breathtaking effect as the morning got underway.

Olive greeted Lexi, "Good morning Lexi, please come in and take your coat off. Would you like tea?"

"Yes please, Olive, that would be very nice."

Olive poured the hot water over a tea bag in a cup for Lexi. Then she poured her own. It was like any tea party that all girls play at when they are young. She said, "I've taken the liberty of writing down the recipe for my beef stew, as you've asked." She turned and replaced the teapot on the woodstove and then produced the recipe from her apron pocket. She handed it to Lexi and said, "Here it is."

Lexi said, "Thank you, Olive, that was very kind of you to take the time."

"You are most welcome, Lexi. There is something else that I wished to speak with you about. Something a bit more, well, intriguing than beef stew."

Lexi thought to herself, "Here it comes." But she said, "What is it Olive?"

Olive asked, "Lexi, are you prone to sleepwalking?"

Lexi said, "My, what an unexpected question. Olive have I been parading about in the barn yard in my sleep shirt?

Olive said, "No Ezra, but I think you've been out for a stroll before that turned into taking a spin. Ezekiel and I both think you might have a bit of a story to tell." She calmly sipped her tea as Lexi felt herself being caught at her deception.

Lexi said, "Oh, dear."

"Yes... oh, dear. Please don't be distressed. When Ezekiel and I saw you for the first time we knew there was something afoot. You see, you could be his mother. You and she bear such a great resemblance that we knew it was more than a coincidence. Ezekiel had done some genealogy and had found the tombstone placed in your memory in the family graveyard. He was always very curious about what became of you. That was many years ago. When you and Cyrus showed up we were surprised but not shocked. You see, we know about the spinners. We know about how they move things and even people through them. We know about them because I came through one of them myself.

Lexi looked at Olive, she was a very attractive woman, about forty to forty-five. She was slight of build, almost pixie like, long blond hair with blue eyes. There was something about her that she thought was familiar but wasn't quite sure. With all that was happening surrounding the ether Lexi wasn't surprised by anything anymore. She asked, "You know who I really am, now you tell me… what's your real name, and when are you from?"

Olive smiled demurely, she said, "My name is Deirdra Evans. I'm from the year 2183. I was visiting cousins in the country with my family when I was nineteen years old. We were staying at a bed and breakfast here in Sheldon, here at this farm. I had been out on the nature trail enjoying a hike. I returned to the corral area and I stumbled on a stone and evidently fell headlong into a spinner. I woke up on the ground in this time twenty-four years ago. The corral was fenced in even then and fortunately for me, there were only goats in it. When I stood and looked around I thought I was going mad. Horse drawn carriages, people on horseback, cows all over the place. The lake over beyond the pasture seemed to have disappeared. I gradually came to accept that something very fantastic, had happened to me. The Wrights took me in. Ezekiel was only a few years older than I was and it was only a matter of time before he and I found love. He had already seen some of the spinners and knew where to avoid. When I confided in him that I wasn't from this time, he didn't think I was crazy, instead he seemed to immediately know that I had been dropped here by a spinner. When you and your husband arrived here it was like his mother had been resurrected. Ezekiel took out the tin type of her so we could see her image again to be sure that we weren't imagining." Olive stopped for a moment to catch her breath. Then she said, "So, that is a brief version of my story, now you tell me yours."

Lexi said, "Wouldn't it be better to wait until your husband is in so I don't need to repeat it?"

Olive agreed, "Perhaps, but please, there are some things that I want to know. Who is David Brooks?"

Lexi said, "Dave is one of Cy's childhood friends. He went missing from his home two years before we came here." Lexi smiled and continued, "You see, I found his obituary in a 1916 edition of The Sheldon News. We were able to calculate when he arrived here. We intentionally overshot our arrival in order to prepare for his. Our trip was intentional, we knew his wasn't."

Olive said, "So the two of you came here from the future to help a friend get back home."

Lexi said, "Yes, and it's my intention to go back home as well."

Olive stared at the floor for what seemed a long time. Then she looked back up at Lexi and said, "I never realized that the spinners could be controlled. I always thought it was a one way trip. Would you excuse me please?"

"Certainly" Lexi said. "I'll watch for the men. But first Olive, you need to realize that it's not really that they can be controlled, but rather predicted. With the recognition of a few certain rules, you can use them."

Olive was grasping this for the first time. She nodded to Lexi and left the room with a sullen look on her face.

It was almost an hour later before the men returned from the chore of snow removal. As they entered the back door of the house and removed their heavy coats, Lexi went to the el of the house to the room that Olive had retreated to, to tell Olive that they had returned. When she came to the room she saw Olive inside sitting in a rocker. She was gently rocking herself as she looked out over the meadow from the bedroom window. The sun was reflected blindingly from the fresh snow and illuminated the room as though there were a super nova right outside the window.

Olive didn't turn to see who had just arrived at the door, she knew Lexi would come for her when the men returned. She said, "It's days like this that I sure miss sunglasses!"

Lexi smiled and said, "There are a lot of things from the future that are good that I miss."

"But this is a good life." Olive said. She said it with the tone of voice that suggested that she was actually trying to convince her self as opposed to making a statement. "Lexi, why are you trying to go back? You're married, you're much older than you were when you went through the spinner. What can you do back in the 1700's?"

Lexi said, "How about we just go to the kitchen, the men are back and I think it's time for the whole of us to talk."

Olive looked at her now. She rose and they both went back to the kitchen.

When they came to the kitchen Lexi went straight to Zeke and put her arms about him in embrace and said, "Hello Great nephew."

Zeke held her like a wounded kitten in his arms and said, "So then it's true ...Aunt Ezra." He looked over Lexi's shoulder at Cy and said, So I should call you Uncle?"

Cy looked surprised at this and said, "Well, I'm about a hundred years younger than you, so I think you should go on calling me Cy."

Then Zeke released Lexi. He looked at Dave and said, "I've not puzzled you out yet. How do you fit into all of this?"

Dave said, "I just went for a walk with my dog here." He gestured at Morgan and added, "Of course he was much bigger then."

Cy said, "Lexi and I came to find Dave. He disappeared almost two years before we arrived at your door. Lexi found his obituary in a newspaper printed in 1916. We were able to plot his approximate time of arrival and we overshot to give ourselves time to get established. We hope to send him back to his wife."

Zeke looked at Dave and said, "You? You're married?"

Dave said, "For almost two years. That's why I discouraged Adele."

"What are your real names?" Zeke asked.

Cy said, "You know that Lexi is Ezra, My name is Cyrus Hill, as I've introduced myself."

Dave said, "My name is Dave Boudreau. Cy surprised me when he introduced me as Brooks."

Cy said, 'That was the name that you had in your obituary, I've no idea why."

Zeke said, "I can tell you why, Boudreau's an Acadian name. Acadians weren't very popular around here for the last hundred years or so since the exile from Nova Scotia. Either change your name and try to assimilate or you don't get work. There's still those who think we're better off without them."

Dave said, "That must be why then, when I came here and arrived alone, I probably found that out the hard way and changed my name." He looked at Cy and added, "When you and Lexi came here to meet me this time, you changed it for me. I wonder if this is the second time here for me or if I've been looping around over and over again."

Lexi said, "There is a school of thought that is popular in the late 1990's and early twenty-first century that is building on Einstein's principles and the need for a Grand Unified Theory. The theory is explained by comparing the universe with foam, they call it Quantum Foam. This foam exists at the sub-atomic level and is thought to be between the components of the atoms. I don't mean the electrons and protons and neutrons, I mean the smaller particles, quarks. The theory allows for infinite possibilities all playing themselves out within infinite universes. Maybe you are looping around Dave, then again, maybe you're just one of a million, million Dave's falling down the same old ethereal eddy." Lexi noticed that the room was silent and all eyes were on her. She suddenly felt very self conscious.

Zeke said, "Aunt Ezra, how is it that you would come to learn of these things?"

Lexi answered, "Soon women will go to college to learn more than how to keep a house."

Olive said, "That is most definitely true." She looked about the room as she talked, "In my time scientists are very actively pursuing time travel, by means of attempting to open wormholes and access the quantum foam that you are talking about Lexi, or Aunt Ezra if you prefer, these scientists would be elated to get their hands on the Wright Farm Phenomenon."

Zeke was looking down at the floor, he was shaking his head, obviously disconcerted over his lack of understanding of what he was hearing. He shook his head and said, "Something must be done." With that he rose and said, "There is work to be done, after all, this is a farm." And he strode out the door.

CHAPTER TWENTY TWO

Annie rolled over. She was in the state of sleep just before coming fully awake. Still mostly asleep, but beginning to gain awareness of her surroundings. She could sense his presence by her side in bed and she rolled over to snuggle up to him for warmth. It was a Saturday morning made for sleeping in. Annie wanted to enjoy her Saturday privilege for as long as she could. Being seven months pregnant with their first child she knew that soon there would be no more sleeping in unless Brian got up to take care of the baby so she could sleep, and even that would have it's limits, because she planned to nurse. For now it was wonderful for her to simply savor the moment and anticipate the baby to come.

Two hours later they both emerged from their late morning recharge and rose from bed. They performed their bathroom dance with precision brought about by five years of marriage, who moved where and when which sink in the large custom vanity belonged to whom, toilets, toothbrushes, hairbrushes, clothing and rendezvous in the kitchen for yet another breakfast ritual.

Up until two years ago their childhood friend Dave was a semi-regular guest at Saturday morning breakfast. Then he disappeared from the face of the planet. Missing person reports and investigations took up the time and thoughts of all in the vicinity, especially those who were close to him. And more recently, the curious disappearance of Cy Hill and his girlfriend Alex Iachovelli. They went missing at the same time of year, almost to the day of when Dave disappeared. It was curious, and it had the local law enforcement officials considering calling in the F.B.I.. That was three weeks ago, and there was still no sign of them. The local paper was turning tabloid by raising the question of possible alien abduction.

Annie figured they took off and eloped. They were probably in Hawaii on an extended honeymoon. They'll turn up and everyone will feel stupid for raising such a fuss about it in the first place. Brian agreed with his wife. He was better pals with Cy while growing up. Cy was prone to falling head over heels and this was exactly the kind of thing he would do if the right girl came along. This Alex seemed to be the same kind of romantic fool for love that Cy was. Brian figured that that made her the type alright.

All was well in Sheldon, as time after time marched on.

CHAPTER TWENTY THREE

Dave was sitting in the crowded court room that was built above the police station in Sheldon. The air was growing stagnant. His docket was set to be heard today, Wednesday December 5, 1906. Dave had plenty of time to ponder his visit to this time as he waited his turn before the judge. He had been here now for two months and two days, since October 3rd. There was no telling if what he was doing was the right thing or if it would have farther reaching consequences than he and Cy could perceive. For now at least it was something to keep him occupied other than winter farm work, which he decidedly did not have an affinity for. Dave had determined that he didn't care much for farm life at all.

He and Cy had completed the room under the loft where Cy and Ezra lived. Since the meeting two weeks earlier Zeke had taken to calling Lexi Ezra, so it came to follow that the rest of the household did as well, except for Cy, who loved his Lexi and could only think of her as Lexi. Dave would call her either or, when he was alone in she and Cy's presence he called her Lexi and when they were in the house at supper he would call her Ezra for Zeke's sake. The poor boy had been hit hard with the reality of the ether and all of the time travelers living about him. He had children with Olive and so he wasn't concerned that she would try to escape back to her own time, but of course he still wondered about if there were no children, would she stay or want to leave him. Dave thought that was the question that was burning deep inside Zeke.

A gavel rapped hard on the judge's bench as he declared the current case to be in recess as the court went to lunch. Everybody rose and the judge left the courtroom for an hour. Dave realized then that in his anxiety over going to court this morning he didn't take the pre packed lunch that Lexi had made for him the night before. Hunger had snuck up on him over the course of the morning like a cat stalking a mouse. Now it was tossing him about in midair and batting him back down again, he was definitely fighting low blood sugar. He needed to get to a diner. Recess was one hour. There would be ample time to go around the corner to the greasy spoon that he had tried out a few weeks ago. It was called The Sun Riser. When Dave had tried it he had come for breakfast. This visit, he hoped for a sandwich and a cola.

Dave took a seat at the diner bar instead of occupying an entire table and crowding out would be patrons unnecessarily.

A pretty waitress came to him, gave him a menu and asked, "Did you want something to drink, honey?"

Dave smiled and said, "Yes, I'll have a cola please." He watched her walk away and thought how familiar she was. Then he turned his attention to the menu.

After a few minutes the waitress returned with his cola and asked, "Have you decided?"

"Yes," Dave said, "I'll have the roast beef sandwich please." He watched her as she wrote his order on a slip of paper. She turned and walked to the window that divided the area behind the bar from the grill and put the paper on a clip suspended from a wire strung across the top of the window. She called out "Order up" to the grill cook on the other side and made her way down to the other end of the diner to attend to another customer. It was in her smile. He saw her smile at another customer, and when she did, he knew. Somehow, this woman was a relative of his. Whether he was a descendent of hers or a great grand nephew, he wasn't sure, but there was a link here. He wouldn't say anything, for obvious reasons, but he was a little more at ease now, knowing that he had a link here to this time as well, a familial link.

Dave tried not to stare at the waitress every time she passed, he was naturally curious but he also wanted to remain cautious. He listened and heard the grill cook call her Helen. Dave's great grandmother's name was Helen. The sandwich he was eating seemed to disappear before him as his break time from the courtroom dwindled. Isn't that the way it goes, when you want something to last it flies by. Helen seemed to be spending a lot of time at the other end of the bar talking to someone. He listened but couldn't understand what they were saying. Then he realized they were speaking French. He dropped two one dollar bills on the bar and weighed them down with his cola glass. As he was walking toward the door he caught a glimpse of the man she was talking to. He was a big burley man, about six one or two with a massive chest and arms. Dave was convinced this was his great grandfather. If he heard the name Henri before he got to the door he would be certain. He crossed to the coat rack and took his coat off of the hook. He thought he was moving in slow motion as he tried to make his exit last. Finally he heard it. Helen called him by name, Henri, plain as day. Dave smiled and with his court brief under his arm, left the Sun Riser and his great grandparents to their destinies.

In the courtroom the atmosphere was freshened by the absence of people during the lunch hour. The bailiff had also opened a window to let some air circulate. Dave found a better seat than the one he had during the morning session. Many people didn't return in the afternoon because they had seen all they had come to see. That suited Dave just fine, as far as he was concerned the fewer people in the room when he had to stand before the judge and orate the better.

It was one o'clock and the judge emerged from his chambers to the sound of the bailiff hollering "All rise, the Honorable Eustace C. Hartrum presiding, Massachusetts Eighth Circuit Court, Central Worcester County District. Draw nigh and be heard all ye who have business here!"

The judge rapped his gavel on the bench and called, "Order!" He looked around at the seats in the courtroom and quickly determined that the principals in the case being held before lunch were present. He asked, "Are we ready to proceed?"

And so the afternoon dragged on. Dave sat and listened to the way the lawyers addressed the judge. This if nothing else was helpful. He had no practical experience in this and his only point of reference was television shows and movies with courtroom scenes from a hundred years from now and, as Dave was learning, there was scarce resemblance between the two. He began taking notes as cases were being called and was, of all things, surprised when the case of Ezekiel Wright vs. the State of Massachusetts was called. At first he sat there waiting for the lawyers to rise, then he realized that the judge was waiting for him!

He rose and said, "David Brooks representing Ezekiel Wright Your Honor."

Zeke took the horse drawn open sleigh into town. Cy sat beside him and they traveled in relative silence anticipating what Dave would have to say. This was the most anxious Cy had ever seen Zeke in the four years he had been working on his farm. They had knocked off early and hitched one of the horses to the sleigh so they could go get Dave from the courtroom. Cy suspected that Zeke wanted to hear the news from Dave without the women around. If he got emotional it was not too likely that Cy and Dave would become afraid, but Olive and the children would.

The only time Zeke spoke was when they came to the railroad crossing and Zeke reigned in the horse. He looked at Cy and asked, "Do you think he'll cut through the railroad again?"

Cy said, "No, he said he had had enough of the hoboes. Stay on the road."

And so Zeke drove the horse on. They were almost into town when they could see Dave's solitary figure strolling toward them. Zeke pulled in the reins and stopped the sleigh with fifteen feet between them and Dave. He sat just looking at Dave, his jaw set, eyes straight and intent. He was ready for the worst.

Dave was happy to disappoint him… the worst would be for another day. He said, "Gentlemen, it is my profound pleasure to inform you that we will have our hearing before the Massachusetts Environmental Commission."

Zeke was staring at Dave, no expression, just staring. As Dave looked at him for a reaction he noticed Zeke's lips quivering. This was a day and age when men did not cry, and Zeke was a man of his time. He said finally, "Get in the sleigh, let's get on home."

Dave climbed in and decided to leave Zeke to his moment. He settled into the back seat and drew a blanket that was there for passengers up onto his lap. The night was cool, even though the day had been warm enough to melt some of the snow that had fallen in the last few days. The horse turned his face toward home and picked up her cant with the promise of a comfortable stable and hay and water awaiting her at her destination.

Cy turned from the front seat and looked at Dave sitting in the back. He tilted his head toward Zeke with a knowing look and a slight grin, he said, "So Dave, what do you think of Brian's great grandfather?"

Dave said, "Well in some ways he is so like him, but in others they are worlds apart."

Zeke asked, "Who is this Brian?"

Cy said, "Your great grandson. In our time, the three of us are best friends. There weren't many occasions that we weren't all together."

Zeke slowed the horse and let her pull at her own speed, he took his eyes off the road ahead and let the horse take them. He said, "So, you boys knew me long before I knew you."

Dave said, "We knew the historical you. You were a man who lived long ago in our past, but we didn't know you. You can be proud of your descendants, they're good people."

Zeke turned even further from the road and looked full at Dave, he said, "I may have entirely different descendants and an entirely different future, indeed an entirely different present, if Aunt Ezra goes back to the 1700's. My Olive is thinking, I fear, of going back to her time as well."

Cy said, "I agree, I think all of our times are changing." He looked right at Zeke and said, "In the span from your time to ours, scientists understanding of the nature of the universe has evolved, things that weren't even thought of in this time are taught in high school as basic science to teenage students. Olive probably has a greater understanding of the space/time mechanics that brought her here than we do, since she comes from our future as well, she just didn't have the investigative resources we did to put together the pieces of the puzzle. Somewhere along the timeline something went askew. I'm beginning to believe that we all have to make love sacrifices in order to restore order." He looked at Dave, then back at Zeke and said, "Once Lexi is restored as Ezra, this present will be different, there will be people born who aren't here today. With Dave back where he belongs, and once I get back to where I belong, the only one who will be a wildcard will be Olive, or Deirdre." He looked at Dave, "Who Annie is or for that matter whether Annie is, is something that we won't learn until we return to our own time." Cy turned back toward the front and looked at the road ahead as they approached the farm road. He said, "I know already that I won't have my Lexi. Gentlemen, I wish I could offer you both the same level of certainty with a better outcome, but I'm not in charge of this thing. We're all of us caught up in it and stand to loose as much as we stand to gain."

The horse came to a halt in front of the gate at the end of the farm road. Cy hopped down from his perch and walked up to it. He unlatched the hasp and swung the gate inward to let the sleigh pass through. After it was far enough inside Cy closed it and secured the hasp. The sole reason for the gate was to keep livestock in that may get loose from the barnyard. He trod up to the sleigh and swung himself back into his seat.

Zeke snapped the reins to urge the horse back into motion and said, "Walk on."

The rest of the ride to the barn was in silence. Nobody was really in the celebratory mood that would be expected in light of Dave's victory. Dave felt ambiguous about his day in court. He was somewhat unfulfilled because he hadn't been able as yet to tell anyone about it, and what Cy said about the restoration of people to timelines was troubling for obvious reasons.

CHAPTER TWENTY FOUR

It was October 9th, 2188. Dr. William Craig, Hawk to his associates and friends, was standing on the deck of a specially designed space platform preparing for the firing of his brainchild; The Quantum Particle Accelerator. This was years in the making. Paid for by university grants, industrial interests, and a few lives of little or no consequence to Hawk.

The countdown to acceleration had begun three hours ago and was finally nearing T-zero, when history would be made, and remade where Hawk felt the need for reinvention.

The platform was constructed of structural aluminum, light weight and strong, the construction material of choice in space. The air pocket was maintained by a projected energy field that was also capable of streaming breathable air into the bubble it created. This allowed Hawk to stand otherwise unprotected in the vacuum of space and stand directly aside his accelerator device at this time. The anti-graviton emitter was programmed to follow Hawk's every move and keep him enveloped in atmosphere. So he could go anywhere around his device securely tethered to the platform.

Haley Orson was in the control room handling the last details of the firing program and countdown. She was competent as well as beautiful. The fact that she was hopelessly in love with Hawk, lent to her trustworthiness in his eyes. One minute remained, 58... 57... the switches inside the quantum generator began to switch to the closed position. 51... 50... batteries started the generators spinning. Their outputs calibrated precisely by Hawk personally to assure symmetric pulses, 42...41... the platform adjusted to maintain its target position. Hawk admired the sleekness of the machinery's design. He looked at the control booth where Haley gave the thumbs up. He backed from the accelerator so he could take in the entire specter of it and its firing. 22...21... the injectors began their rotation, 14...13... gyros spun in their place holding the accelerator on target, 8...7... the generator reached maximum revolutions, quanta were beginning to pour forth from the generators. 2...1...0 the accelerator fired and propelled the quanta into the fabric of spacetime.

Three and a half seconds passed and there was no data feedback from the firing sequence. The stream was set to fire for one minute. They had anticipated a one second delay in feedback. At five seconds there was a distortion, it was difficult to discern at first, by the seventh second Hawk could see it very plainly. Stars and planets that were visible from their position above the earth were seemingly moving into a fundibuliform in the target zone. As the ninth second ticked by, the surge in the distortion took on a new characteristic. It almost appeared to be coming at them.

Hawk looked toward the control booth and saw Haley screaming frantically. He realized that the distortion was moving like a wave, the center of it coming directly at their position. Spacetime had been pushed to it's gravitational utmost and was pushing back.

The eleventh second. The distortion wave hit the station full force. The platform was torn loose and pushed up at right angles from its original position. The integrity of the hull of the control booth compartment was breeched sucking the atmosphere from the inside, killing everyone within seconds. Hawk was tossed upward into the full brunt of the wave. The accelerator was still firing, as it turned, the streams trajectory crossed Hawk's position, severing him in two. The stream had a cauterizing effect on his torso, amazingly stemming all blood flow. His torso was adrift and he was still alive, for the moment. Unfortunately the anti-graviton beam was damaged in the turbulence of the wave. Hawk's air pocket was dissipating into space. When the platform twisted it tore the generator's back plate from its body. The rear side of the generator was emitting anti-quanta in a stream at 180 degrees to the quanta stream. When the accelerator settled on its new target trajectory, it was at right angles to the wave center which was currently moving away in the opposite direction. The distortion was rippling away from the center, much like waves on the surface of water when a pebble is dropped into it. The wave crests were pierced at their intervals by the quantum and anti quantum streams. The distortion moved away and back again very quickly. Because of the initial pressure of the stream, and the collision with the station, there was a hole in the spacetime fabric at the very center of the wave, which allowed the remnant of the station to remain unaffected by the oscillations of the wave there after. The accelerator stream timer did not cut out at one minute but continued to fire. The solar panel that powered the generator was sure to guarantee a quanta anti-quanta stream indefinitely.

Hawks body was never recovered.

The accelerator project had no survivors. All of the data calculated and recorded, the predictions and outcomes were on the station, adrift in space. Surfing on the ethereal waves with the two halves of Hawk's body it's only companion.

CHAPTER TWENTY FIVE

Olive was sitting at her sewing table darning a pair of socks for her oldest son. Theo was growing rapidly and his toes were literally pushing out through the ends of the socks. Her fingers had become deft in the art of sewing, indeed there were times she surprised herself at how well she did the tasks and chores around the farm. She hated the farm life. She did love Ezekiel, but the truth was she missed her family, and her time. Until the conversation with Lexi a few weeks ago she had never given any thought to the possibility of returning to her own time. Now she knew that it was possible and she was in torment over whether or not she could possibly leave. She listened with great interest when Cy recounted his story of traveling back eight hours into his own past and encountering himself. The part that most intrigued her was when the two Cys rectified their own quantum anomaly and remerged into one being. The memory of the event, from both Cys lived in the remaining Cy. She also realized that his timing was accidental, that had he remained in the eddy, as he liked to call it, much longer, he would have gone back much farther in time, years. She had a decision to make. In many ways it was heartbreaking to stay here, it would also be heartbreaking to leave and return home.

She got up from her table and went to the kitchen. They would all be home soon, and hungry. If Dave came with bad news Ezekiel likely wouldn't eat, but he wasn't the only face to feed on the farm. Darning socks and KP duty seemed to be all there was for Deirdra. She knew more of life when she was twelve than she did now. Her resolve to remain in this time was wavering. She took the large pot out from under the counter top and put it in the sink basin under the well pump head. On the up stroke the pump handle let out a squeal that would bring the pigs to dinner. Ezekiel was supposed to oil it but had been preoccupied, so she just ignored the noise and pressed down on the handle. It took two empty strokes and on the third, water gushed out of the sluice at the top of the pump. It took her seven pumps to get the pot filled three quarters of the way. Olive picked up the pot and brought it over to the stove. She took a mitt off of the shelf beside the stove and put her right hand into it. Opening the stove door, she saw that the burning coals were looking mighty weak. Theo was supposed to have banked them before he went to milk the cows. The embers would have to be nursed back to life with kindling before she could stoke a good fire. She left the pot on the stove, at least it would start to warm, and she went out to the woodshed for kindling. The kindling box was all but empty; she would have to split some from some smaller logs. Ben is supposed to do this chore. She was always getting after the boys for not doing their chores. She hefted the hatchet and knelt next to the splitting stump.

Choosing a small log she aligned her swing and struck at the log. A good kindling chip fell from the side of the log.

Olive was pleased. Deirdra missed her food replicater. Olive didn't mind picking up her son's slack. Deirdra wanted to go on a cruise. Olive didn't mind fixing her son's socks. Deirdra wanted to go to Walmart and Bob's Stores and get some new clothes for her family. Olive was content living as a farmer's wife. Deirdra wished she had never gone for Ice Cream while visiting her Great Aunt Annie whose husband went missing some sixty five years before. Olive/Deirdra was beginning to suffer an identity crisis.

Lexi arrived early to help with dinner preparations. She let herself in and found Olive in the kitchen sitting at the table with an armful of kindling. She said, "Olive? Are you alright?"

Olive said, "The fire is out." Her eyes were red from crying, she said, "I have to make a new fire and I really don't want to."

Lexi said, "Is that all? So we'll call out for pizza, or maybe Chinese, what do you feel like tonight?

Olive looked at Lexi at first with disbelief, then she laughed while she cried. She said, "I don't know what I want to do. If I want to go back to my own time or if I want to stay here with my husband and children." She seemed to have been knocked out of her funk. She rose and made for the stove with a clear head. She expertly placed shredded papers into the stove and piled kindling on top. Then she got the flint out of the cupboard and began making sparks over the pile. A few sparks caught on the paper and began to burn the edges. She blew on them and little flames began to flare up. She fanned the flames from outside of the fire box being careful not to put them out. As the fire grew she added kindling and was eventually able, after about five minutes of nursing the fire, to add some stove length logs. When the fire was finally going to her satisfaction she closed the door and turned down the dampers to slow the burn. Now finally she could begin supper. Theo and Ben would be spoken to.

As Olive was tending the fire Lexi had begun peeling potatoes. The preparation of the evening's meal was only a pretense for conversation between Olive and Lexi. Now it would allow Ezra and Deirdra to get to know one another. Since the confrontation two weeks ago Lexi had been coming in early at every opportunity to help for just that reason. She knew what Olive had gone through and how difficult it was to maintain her sanity. The effect of being taken from your own time and hurled into another time was an intrusion into your life to say the least. It was one thing to be aware as Cy had been and deliberately make the journey, but to be in one time at one moment and another time a moment later was akin to rape or at the very least molestation. Their presence when Dave arrived helped him to make the transition. This poor girl had no one to orient her, as Lexi had no welcoming committee. She had adjusted, but until now there had been no one to affirm that what she had experienced was real and not just a figment of her imagination. Even though Zeke and Olive had put together who she was shortly after her own arrival four years previous, they hadn't confronted her until now, making conversation about the eddies or the spinners or whatever you wanted to call them nonexistent.

There was also the question of whether she ought to be convinced to take the next eddy back to her own time. Dave, Cy and Lexi had been debating just that for the last few days.

It was decided that Lexi should at least prepare Olive for that possibility. Then when the topic was ultimately reached and the decisions had to be made, everyone concerned would know the full impact of their actions.

The whole matter was an emotional quagmire. Zeke and Olive, Cy and Lexi, and who could say what Dave would find when he returned to seek out Annie. Would Brian and Charlie still find each other? There was more to consider than who would be with whom. The question of just how far reaching forward and backward in time the ethereal eddies extended. Who else had been picked up and deposited indiscriminately out of time? What would their absence mean in their own time? What would their presence mean in their new surroundings?

Generally this group had come to the conclusion that there was little if anything that could be done to correct all of the other theoretical trips through time. All they had control over were their own destinies. This meant they had to do what they thought was right. At some point soon Zeke and Olive would have to become involved in those conversations.

Lexi looked up at Olive and asked, "So tell me something, Deirdra, do you ever think of returning?"

Olive said, "I think we should stay with Olive, if the children should hear and ask what is meant by that name there would be trouble in the house. Yes Lexi, I've thought of it every day since I arrived here. It's only since I've come to know that it's possible that I've given it serious consideration. The truth is I don't think I could do it. If I returned and remerged with my younger self as you told me Cy has done and you intend to do, what becomes of my children? Wouldn't I be killing them? If they simply cease to exist and my memory from this time contains them, I will carry them in my heart and mind for the rest of my life and I'll have the knowledge that my selfish desire to go back caused them to no longer have life. Lexi, I couldn't live with myself. No mother could. I think you know that and that's why you've not had children."

A single tear was rolling down Lexi's cheek. Indeed she did know what Olive meant. And that was the reason she and Cy hadn't had children. She also knew that there was another possibility that may eliminate any decision on Olive's part. Restoring herself alone might be sufficient to return equity to the ethereal balance. If hers was the first time violation, perhaps her return to her rightful place in time would preclude the periodic appearances of the eddies. There was only one way to find this out, and if it wasn't enough then Cy would have to come back here and kidnap Olive and return her to her time. Every time he stepped into an eddy he ran the risk of being himself, marooned. She admired his courage in the face of the task that destiny placed at his feet. She worried for his life. She worried for her heart. She simply said to Olive, "You are right Olive, I cannot offer any argument other than to say that returning may not be a choice for you. If timelines return to stasis, you may simply never come from the future."

Olive said, "Then I would have no knowledge of my life lived here, or of my children. I could live with that Lexi, I could live with that."

Supper was served on time in spite of the fire's going out in the stove. Theo suffered the indignation of being scolded for having forgotten to tend to the stove but he wasn't disciplined because ultimately he was doing his father's milking chores. Ben would pick up the task of milking for the remainder of the week for his indiscretion. The children were excused to their rooms to do their lessons. The women began to see to clearing the table and washing dishes.

Zeke said, "I think that instead of doing the house chores right away this evening we should all have a talk."

Cy said, "That seems like a very good idea."

Everyone sat back in the seats they were eating in moments before. There was some unease at the table as everyone felt unsure of who should begin.

Cy decided to begin by asking a question. He said, "Olive, or Deirdra, what do you remember from school that you can tell us about quantum mechanics?"

Olive looked almost bewildered that she was being addressed. She had lived over two decades in this time and had grown somewhat accustomed to being a second class citizen. She looked at Zeke for his consent, and when he nodded she said, "It's been twenty five years since I sat in a classroom Cy. I'll try to answer any questions you ask about this phenomenon, but I don't know how much help I'll be."

Cy asked, "Do you know what it is that we're dealing with?"

Olive said, "I know that there was supposed to be an experiment, involving quantum particle acceleration using a satellite and the vacuum of space. It was set to take place in 2188."

"Quantum particle acceleration, what was the expected outcome of their experimentation?" Cy asked.

"They were hoping to open a wormhole." Olive said. "The scientific community was polarized over the matter.

Some felt that it would be the greatest achievement of mankind, others believed, and it seems perhaps they were right, that instead of a wormhole they would be opening a can of quanta worms." Olive chuckled at the quip, "I can't believe I remember that."

Cy looked at Lexi and said, "Evidently we're dealing with something more than a naturally occurring anomaly. Does this shed any light on the research you did?"

Lexi said, "Well, yes actually, but you already know about it. The two year intervals that we used to calculate how long to remain inside the eddy to get here. I think they're ripples."

"Ripples, you mean like, in the fabric of time?"

"Ripples in the ether; the quantum foam that exists at the sub atomic level." Lexi said.

Olive said, "If the accelerator failed to do what they had hoped it would do, perhaps the actual outcome was to open access points to the ethereal plane. If you think of the time continuum as a perfectly straight line that we in nature are obliged to commute upon in a single direction, and picture it hovering directly over the perfectly flat surface of the ethereal lake, then you drop a pebble into the lake, the ripples would rise and intersect with the time continuum at predictable intervals. Mini wormholes are opening up at regular intervals when the surface of the ether intersects with the accelerated quanta particles."

Cy said, "So they fired this accelerator into space, that acted like the pebble in Lake Ether, the eddies or spinners, are actually mini wormholes that opened up as a result. Why here at this particular point on the planet? And why are we able to go in both directions when like you said, naturally we are obligated to travel through time in one direction only?"

Olive said, "First you have to realize that a quantum accelerator is in the physical world, and subject to the laws of physics like anything else. In this case, Newton's third law, 'For every action there is an equal and opposite reaction.' The accelerator fired in both directions along time's line. The ripples are moving outward along the line, in both directions starting from the moment of the event. The accelerator must have been aimed in such a fashion that it intersected the Earth's orbit. Twice in a year, every other year, the Earth, the accelerated quanta, and the ethereal ripples converge, this is when the spinners are visible and accessible. On one side of our orbit, in the spring, the ripples are intersecting with the quanta that are moving forward. Stepping into a spinner then would move you into the ether, you would be completely unaware of the physical world, in it you would cease to be, until you emerge from it in the future. If you step into an autumnal eddy the ripples are moving in what we perceive to be backward in time." Olive stopped and stared at a point on the table. She said, "I don't believe that I never grasped what had happened before this point, twenty four years after I arrived."

Cy said, "Don't be too hard on yourself, your resources on this are limited. It's not too likely that anyone has asked you the questions that we've asked you tonight either. Sometimes it takes spurs to get the horse to giddyup-n-go"

"Well," she said, "I feel less like a horse and more like an ass!" She got up and began clearing the table. "It's got to be stopped." Was all she said. And she went to work cleaning up from supper.

CHAPTER TWENTY SIX

Brian looked around the barnyard and wondered if things could possibly be any better. There were people coming from all over the state to buy ice cream from him, and it was November. The Campground was booked for the entire next season and all with one day deposits on receipt. He and Andrea were expecting their second child in the spring. Since opening the grounds to campers the farm had gone from being in the red to turning a handsome profit in three short years. Canoe and sailboat rentals for the lake, mountain bike rentals and horseback riding for the trails, and Brian's personal favorite was Andrea's idea, airplane tours and skydiving at the local airport at discounted rates to the patrons of Wright Family Farm Campground, The Wright way to camp!

The Sheldon Zoning Board had been very helpful in putting it all together. They rezoned the whole south side of Sheldon to accommodate the campground. There was foresight in this after all. The tourism alone brought a financial boon to Sheldon at a time when the City needed it most.

When people came to and from the campground the roads were secondary roads to the downtown Sheldon shopping and business district. Summer holidays now were marked with parades. There were bi-weekly concerts on the common with music styles ranging from 30's Jazz, 40's swing and Big Band, 50's doo-wop, 60's love-in and even 70's disco. Anything too new wouldn't attract the nostalgic sentiments of the parents.

There was no more need to operate the Bed and Breakfast. Financially the business was self supportive. Brian could even afford to hire a manager to see to things for him so he and Andrea could travel with the kids while they were little. They talked a lot about that, and ultimately decided against it. The farm had almost been lost once and he was not going to risk losing it again. They could travel all they wanted to in the off season. At least until they started with school.

Still, with all this success, there was something that seemed amiss. Brian couldn't quite put his finger on it. Like something just outside of his field of vision, toying with him and taunting his senses.

Whatever it was, it wasn't going to bring him down, he was on top of the world!

CHAPTER TWENTY SEVEN

Lexi and Cy were laying in bed, she had her head on his chest and his arm was wrapped around her, his hand caressing her shoulder. It was cold in the bedroom but in bed they had each other for warmth. Lexi was more than just a little apprehensive about going back to her own time. She wouldn't tell Cy this, but she knew she was going to miss terribly the warmth of his body and the touch of his hand during these cold New England winter nights. She will miss him for as long as she could remember him. They had been lying like this for about twenty minutes, just warming the bed.

Cy finally said, "I need to have a long talk with Olive."

"About the accelerator program?" Lexi asked.

"Yes, and about the way things are in her time. I'm going to have to go and try to convince them to stop the experiment." Cy said. Not really convinced that he could get the leaders of the program to post pone a frog jumping contest never mind an experiment such as this.

Lexi said, "They'll lock you up. They'll think you're nuts and they'll lock you up."

Cy said, "Maybe, and then again, maybe not. Babe, if there are people from all over the time continuum who have found themselves out of time, then it's possible that they already know that there is something terribly amiss. Even before they fired the accelerator."

Lexi said, "Paradox's are such head scratchers! Nothing can be straight forward or simple with them. Cy what if you are successful and the accelerator doesn't create havoc? The mini worm holes will close and you'll be trapped in 2184."

"Well then the mini worm holes will close and I'll be trapped in 2184. I'll have to make do."

Lexi said, "I was hoping for a different answer."

Cy said, "Most likely I'll live out this time line in that time. However, I also think that when I'm born, if in fact I still am born, that I'll live my life in utter normalcy in my own time. I won't meet you, so I won't throw my life away again…"

Lexi pinched his abdomen and twisted. She said, "Now listen here you, I'm the best thing that ever happened to you!

Cy laughed and said, "Well we'll just have to see about that, won't we!" Their lips met and they held one another tighter. Cy touched her curves gently with his fingertips. Their kiss held fast. Their bodies turned toward one another and soon they were one. They brought the bed and their room up to temperature quickly after that.

The next day was Sunday. After breakfast and the milking, Cy went over to the main house to talk with Olive. He went in through the back door and entered the kitchen. There he found Zeke and Olive sitting and enjoying coffee in a leisurely fashion.

Ct said, "Good morning, mind if I join you?

Zeke said, "Not at all Cyrus, pour yourself a cup of coffee and sit."

Cy poured a cup, and sat at the table. He looked at the couple and said, "I needed to ask some questions of you Olive. Just so you understand my intentions, I'm going to your time, 2184, to try and stop the accelerator experiment." He paused as this information assimilated, then asked, "Olive, when you arrived here did you have any money from your own time?"

Olive said, "Oh, yes I still have everything I came with in a box upstairs." She looked at Zeke then back at Cy and added, "I could go and get those things if you would like."

Cy said, "No, not right now, I wouldn't want the children to see anything that they shouldn't see. It's just that I will need to have currency of the period when I arrive. I actually purchased antique moneys no longer in currency before we came to this time. By today's standards I arrived with a small fortune, much more than we needed to survive. We came here to you because as you know now we needed to intercept Dave. But having period currency and an idea of its value is a great help."

Olive answered, "Money isn't handled in the 2180's as it is in this day and age. Olive held out her hand showing Cy the ring on her pinky finger. This ring has an account access chip imbedded in it. The monetary system is still dollar based. Of course there are more dollars needed for products than today. A gallon of milk when I left was $12.50.

My parents are pretty well off, there's $27,000.00 and change on the chip." She took off the ring, gave it to Cy and said, "Use all you need."

"I'll need it all, and I'll likely need more, but I'll cross that bridge when I get to it. What can you tell me about the location of the project headquarters?"

Olive thought for a minute. She said, "I think they were an outfit called Quantum Dynamics. They were real good about keeping out of the spotlight. They were affiliated with UMass Dartmouth Space Campus and working with them on a grant. When all of the controversy was stirring they would always defer to the college for comment."

Cy said, "Outfits like this usually are. You seldom ever see the real culprits in the news casts. It's always some lackey that takes the fall."

Zeke said, "It sounds to me like some things never change." He regarded his wife's ring on the table in front of Cy for a moment and considered the fortune inside. Then he added, "Cy, are you sure you can stop this experiment?"

Cy said, "No Zeke, to tell you the truth, I don't know whether I'll even get in through the door. But I do know that I have to try."

"And what will become of you, either way?"

"I'm not sure, if I fail, I suppose that I could continue trying. After all, I do know how to use the eddies and get around in time. On the other hand, if I am successful, I'll probably end up living out the rest of my life in that time."

Zeke asked, "Cy, I just don't understand why you feel it's your responsibility. Why are you intent on changing something that you didn't have anything to do with starting?"

Cy stared into his coffee cup. This was a question he needed to give serious consideration to. He was committing himself to a cause that he had very little hope of succeeding in. He thought about lying in bed next to Lexi the night before. It all seemed to make perfect sense then. A man's resolve is a funny thing. How can something seem solid as bedrock one moment and as liquid as lava in the next? When he was telling Lexi about his intentions she was pensive and contemplative; he on the other hand was confident in his course of action and felt unwavering. Now he was having difficulty coming up with one good reason that he could tell Zeke for his plan. He sipped at the dregs in his coffee mug. When he felt he would never have an answer for Zeke he looked at him and said, "Zeke, I don't know quite how to answer that, other than to say that I am compelled beyond reason to do this. I feel it inside more than know it. The need to set to rights this entire aberration done to the time continuum by my own kind is as instinctive to me as a mother protecting her young. Maybe that's it right there, at some level, deep inside, I know I've lost something that I can't bear to have lost. As important as Lexi is to me I'm willing to give her up to her own time for this. She feels it too. Every two years we will continue to be subjected to changes to both, the past and the future. Countless lives along the way will continue to be affected when a family member is lost, when a foundling appears at their home, or when death occurs out of time and away from loved ones and there is no family there to take care of them and see them to their final rest." Cy paused, he realized then and there more than he had ever realized why he had this mission to complete. He also saw in the eyes of Zeke and Olive that he had made some sense to them. He continued, "Your own family has been rent apart and will continue to be so unless this thing is put to rights."

Zeke looked at Cy and said, "Well, it seems you figured out how to answer my question. What do you think will become of all of the people who have been accidental victims of this anomaly?"

Cy shrugged and said, "I really don't know Zeke, they may simply just never be affected, lives may just be lived as they were supposed to have been lived. If there is no disruption, then there should be no way for anyone to leave their own time. On the other hand there may be a simple shutdown of the ethereal eddies. That would leave me and anyone else who is out of time where they are to live out their lives. Aside from those possibilities I don't really have an answer."

Olive said, "There really isn't any certainty with quantum mechanics, as yet it's all theory, conjecture and speculation. But from what I remember about paradox conversations, you're on the right track, Cy."

Cy wasn't particularly encouraged by Olive's agreement. He had hoped that perhaps she could offer more in the way of options. He really didn't want to go to and spend the rest of this life in a strange time. He knew however that he would do whatever was needed to stop the experiment.

CHAPTER TWENTY EIGHT

January came and went. Spring was approaching and so was March 18th, the date that Dave would go before the Environmental Planning Commission to further his quest to keep the Wright Farm intact. It was February 12th 1907 when the letter arrived in the afternoon post. It was addressed to him as representative to Ezekiel Wright, it was from the Massachusetts EPC. Dave was sitting in an old armchair taken from the main house to his small quarters in the back of the barn. There was a fire in the makeshift steel drum stove. His little room was quite cozy especially since he and Cy had added interior boards to both his and Cy and Lexi's rooms and filled the space in between with straw to act as insulation. Zeke was impressed by this new insulation method from the future. The rooms in the back of the barn were at times actually warmer than inside his house.

Dave opened the letter in the privacy of his room without anyone's even having knowledge that he had it. He had just finished reading it for the fifth time and was still in a state of disbelief. He wanted to talk with Cy. Then he could take it in and show Zeke. He wanted Cy to be present when he delivered the news.

Lexi sat at the little sideboard that served as their table regarding the cozy little home they had made for themselves here. She knew she would never be happier in her own time without Cy. She also knew that returning home was the correct thing to do under the circumstances. She needed to live the life she was born to live, and if he survived, so did Cy. It was time to go and help prepare the supper in the main house with Olive. Since everything had come out into the open, Olive and Lexi had become good friends. A woman can tell when another woman is hiding the truth. For four years they had kept their stories from one another. Now that the truth was out they had no secrets, at least from each other, and their friendship had grown. In keeping one another's confidences they had shared their common anguish over whether to return to their own times or not. They each missed their families, but they also loved their husbands. Lexi rose and took her coat from the hook on the wall. She sipped the last of her tea and pulled the coat on over her sweater that Cy had bought her before they came to this time. Having lived in three times and experienced all the different nuances from each, Lexi couldn't decide why she liked this time best. The most compelling reason she could come up with was because she was married to Cy for the entire time she had been here. In truth she found the people of this era to be the harshest of societies. Then again, she wasn't looking forward to returning to the time of the Indians again. Her consolation to that being the research she had done and her acquired knowledge that there were no more raids that would affect her or her family directly. Her greatest concern was not surviving long after returning. If she gave up her life with Cy only to loose her life in the early eighteenth century, she would die with regret. Sadly she didn't know if she would even know it.

Olive was peeling carrots in the kitchen and thinking about Ezekiel's mother. It was because of her that Olive had fallen in love with him. It was also because of her that Olive is the only one that calls him Ezekiel instead of Zeke. His Dad called him Zeke, and it stuck. His mother on the other hand wouldn't have it. She named him Ezekiel and so she would call him Ezekiel. She also helped Deirdra with choosing Olive as her new name. Deirdra hadn't yet told anyone that she had fallen down the rabbit hole. No one knew her real name, or anything about her ordeal at that point. So far as anyone was concerned she was a sad girl who had likely been deserted by her family because she was old enough to fend for herself and food was scarce. Wonderland was a scary place to her. Mrs. Wright was like the Queen of Hearts to a scared Alice. Fortunately this Queen of Hearts didn't turn sociopath, and Alice with her fondness for olives at the dinner table earned the pet name Olive by the kindly matron. By whatever name she had ever been known by, right now she missed Mrs. Wright, right now she missed her own mother.

The back door opened and she could hear feet stomping snow off in the back hall. By the sound she knew Lexi was coming in to help with supper. She put down the peeler and took another log from the pile near the stove. Opening the stove door Olive guided the log and reached for another.

Lexi came into the kitchen. She said, "Hi Olive."

Olive said, "Hi Lexi."

Lexi asked, "What do you want me to start with today?"

"You can draw some water and put a pot on the stove. Then we need onions peeled and chopped."

Lexi went to the well and started pumping the handle to prime it. When the water started down the sluice she placed the pot under the spout and filled it. She lifted it out and carried it to the stove. She said, "Oh, it's nice and warm over here."

Olive said, "Yeah, I made sure Theo banked the coals today. Lexi, I want to ask you something. What would you think if I told you that in spite of every reason I shouldn't be, I'm still thinking about returning to my own time?"

Lexi said, "I wouldn't be surprised. If Cy is successful when he goes to stop the accelerator experiment, none of this will be as it is now. The uncertainty principle applies here in so many ways."

Olive laughed, she said, "When you were born, none of these laws and theories were even dreamed of, yet here you are discussing them with acumen."

Lexi said, "Yes, with a girl who is nearly five hundred years younger than I am."

Olive added, "While we make supper in a farm house in a time that neither of us were ever supposed to be in! And I might add, I am at least twenty years older than you."

They had a good laugh, these two unlikely friends. It was a much needed respite from the tension that had been harbored in their hearts. Both with so much to lose, and yet, the world had so much more to lose if Cy failed. But as it always goes, sacrifices made in a failed endeavor are rarely considered as great as when the endeavor succeeds. In this case however, the sacrifices made if there was success would in all likelihood not even be remembered.

Dave came up the back stairs to the house hoping Olive would be able to tell him where Zeke and Cy were. He stepped into the back entry way and stomped off his boots. Opening the door to the kitchen he found both Olive and Lexi in the middle of preparing supper. He smiled and said, "Hey girls, do either of you know where Zeke and Cy are working today?"

Olive said, "I think they're out in the west pasture. Is something wrong?"

Dave said, "No, it'll wait. I'll be in my room, see you at supper." And with that he smiled sincerely and turned to leave.

Lexi said, "Perhaps Olive doesn't know you well enough David Boudreau, but I do. What's with the Cheshire cat grin?"

Dave let another grin escape him and said, "What grin?" and he left the kitchen. He didn't feel that telling Lexi and Olive would be wrong, but Zeke is from this time, and even though Olive is his wife it would be inappropriate to tell her before telling him. What a difference a century makes. What makes it worse is that Olive would feel it's even more archaic than he would.

Supper would come soon enough. Right now he had a letter to compose.

Supper had arrived. Zeke and Cy were back in from the fields and the horses were tucked into their stables with their blankets and oats. Dave entered the kitchen and looked directly at Zeke and asked, "Zeke, can I see you in private please, before we eat?"

Zeke looked back at Dave with a quizzical expression in his face and said, "Sure, let's step into the parlor." He looked around the table, let his gaze rest upon Olive and added, "Don't wait."

They went to the hall and into the parlor. Zeke lit the wick on the oil lamp that was mounted on the wall as they entered the room. He looked at Dave and asked, "Alright David, What is it?"

Dave produced the letter and handed it to Zeke. He said, "This came today in the afternoon post. It's a letter from J. Richard Elliott, Esq., Zeke, he's McKinnon's lawyer!"

Zeke immediately realized the ramifications of what Dave was telling him about the origins of the letter. He turned from Dave and slowly moved to an armchair that was halfway across the room. The chair was an old wing-back with a high backrest. It was upholstered in leather with thick cushioning in the seat. When Zeke sat in it there were squeaks and groans that were reminiscent of a cow pasture on a flatulent night. Once seated and quiet, he said, "Go ahead Dave, tell me what's in that letter."

Dave smiled, he said, "Zeke, it's a letter of thanks! They are thanking us for pointing out that the damming here in Sheldon would have been folly. McKinnon has fired the planners that advised him to push for a far upstream dam. He realized that they were just telling him what he wanted to hear. When he looked for himself at the topography he could see that the three smaller dams were the best solution.

Now he has turned his political influence toward that end instead of your farm."

Zeke was turned even further away from Dave at this point. Dave was trying to get around to in front of him when he realized that Zeke didn't want him there. Zeke didn't want Dave to see him cry.

Dave said, "I've prepared a letter in response to Elliott's letter. I'll leave it here with his letter to you. If you approve of it I'll bring it in to town and send it on the mid morning post."

Zeke said, "Dave, I don't know how to thank you. Would you please tell Olive that I will be in to eat in just a few moments."

Dave left Zeke sitting there with the hard won victory letters in his hands. He didn't have the heart to tell Zeke that with Cy stopping the experiment in the future it was anybody's guess as to whether or not the amended timeline would turn out the same. For now it was just a matter of wait and see. For now, the feeling of elation was as savory as the pot roast being eaten in the kitchen.

CHAPTER TWENTY NINE

To his associates he was known simply as the Hawk. That was his self appointed nickname. More a tribute to his life's hero Prof. Stephen Hawking from the twentieth and twenty first centuries than anything directly related to his name. Hawk, or Will Craig, had two years until the launch of his life long dream. The quantum particle accelerator stood before him on the factory floor. In its present state it was unimpressive. To most anyone who didn't understand the configuration of the machinery it was nothing but a pile of gizmos and gadgetry that could have been put together as a prop for a sci-fi movie. To Hawk, it was a beautiful baby, his brain child, readying for a glorious birth in outer space where it would make its first utterance and change all time. Hawk's own sweet child, and baby would go on to make Daddy immortal.

Until a mere forty years ago atomic acceleration was the limit of particle accelerators. Then Richard Fish, PhD arrived on the scene. He was Hawks astrophysiology professor and eventually his mentor. He revolutionized and energized the scientific community by infusing some much needed albeit somewhat radical new ideas. By accelerating a string of quanta in single file, Fish postulated, an opening could be incised into the fabric of spacetime and be held open to allow controlled human time travel; a man made worm hole if you will, without the black hole and its nasty gravitational fields to make people all compressed. Hawk was rapt by the very words that the good professor uttered. He took up the cause that Fish had begun, and made it his own. The idiots that disagreed with them believed the opening rent by the accelerator would reap catastrophic results. The only catastrophe would be in not allowing the accelerator to be tested, and used.

The accelerator before him was based on designs that Fish and Hawk had drafted before Fish's tragic death three years ago. Hawk had to complete the designs himself but that was no real problem. He had long surpassed his teacher's own abilities and if anything, Fish had been weighing him down with tedious cautions. In fact, Fish had seemed to be back pedaling, and had begun to sound an awful lot like the skeptics that dissuaded quantum acceleration theory. Fish was even voicing the opinion that many more years of mathematical proofing should be done before attempting to fire the string of quanta. He was beginning to advocate shelving the project altogether.

Fish's death was untimely to all who knew him, even to Hawk, except when it came to the project. If only he had retired, he wouldn't have had to be... terminated.

Hawk had procured funding for the project through research grants at several educational institutions. He would in all likelihood be in a great deal of trouble if and when they came to realize that the research he had done was complete years ago when Professor Fish was still living. All the monies were put into the quantum particle accelerator before him now. Once completed, his next step would be to get it transported to the space station. He could arrange for the college to handle that. With a high power transceiver acting as a remote control he would only need to have the accelerator deployed in a geosynchronous orbit directly over his native Sheldon Massachusetts home.

His parents had passed away years ago and since his only sister had fallen to her death from a tree that she and young Will had been playing in, Hawk had inherited the home. He could activate from there while vacationing after having completed the vast amount of research that, coincidently enough, he was able to procure from the good Professor Fish's files; all unpublished theorems that Fish had been good enough to commit into writing on his computer. It is after all, reasoned Hawk, only plagiarism if it was previously published. So long as Hawk was in possession of the hard chip that was the heart of Fish's computer then he was in sole possession of Fish's final work, rather, Hawk's work now.

For the time being the construction of the accelerator was enough to occupy most of the kindly scientist's time. Since the disappearance of his intern, Steven, he had needed to train a new assistant. Haley was a beautiful girl, and academically qualified, but it was becoming apparent to Hawk that she was falling in love with him. She could not be blamed for this, after-all, Hawk was handsome, intelligent and wealthy. What woman wouldn't want to catch him? Unfortunately, Hawk didn't wish to be caught. This made for a distraction, which he didn't need. He would have to consider this later, for now there was work to be done. He lifted a quantum field generator from the floor using an anti-grav hoist. Navigating the hoist into position was tricky. The placement of the generator required precision. The tolerances were very high here, +/– 0.00015". Initial fitting was nothing so critical, but still required great care considering the sensitivity of the equipment. Hawk was very concerned about the launch causing sensitive adjustments to go out of calibration. He would have to be certain to recalibrate post launch, before deployment. In the weightless environment of space there should be no real difficulty to perform this task. Hawk would have to see to this himself.

Hawk was bewildered by the ignorance of the general population; the fact that there seemed to be no one who could grasp the genius of his project or even recognize the importance of it. Once fired, the accelerator would send a stream of electrons and a stream of positrons on a collision course that would rock history. The matter/antimatter collision would open a permanent and easily controlled singularity. As long as the stream continued uninterrupted the singularity would remain open. Because singularities reach in both directions along the timeline, they exist through all time. The greatest problem was how to make the passage large enough to allow a human being to pass. Fish was good enough to help out here, although Hawk suspected that Fish had picked the answer from his own superior mind. It was simple enough really, they needed only to apply spin. Spin didn't open a conduit that a person would enter into, rather it would draw the individual into the string. It added a gravitational element that would allow a passenger to 'hitch a ride' and use it as a passage from one time to another. The fact that humanity's worst specimens could be dealt with before they became a threat, well, that alone should have convinced those simpletons. He knew better than them how much they needed this. That was why he could allow no errors or obstacles to threaten the accelerator's launch, deployment and firing.

The screws that would hold the field generator in place were snugged, the anti-grav hoist could be freed and stowed. He flicked the release switch and drew the hoist away from the generator. Pressing the auto store button he let go of the unit and watched as it floated above his head and drifted across the room and docked itself for recharge. Hawk enjoyed watching this. He loved the time that he lived in. Turning back to the generator he applied the tuning fork to the harmonic frequency adjustments for calibrations. It was essential upon firing that the frequencies were calibrated exactingly if a usable string were to be generated.

Homicide Detective Frank Plante had been involved in many kinds of investigations. Thirty five years a cop, the last twenty a detective in homicide. His experience told him one thing was evident, there was a sociopath on the loose. This particular perpetrator had been around for decades. It was only because Plante was going through unsolved cases from his past that he began to see a connection in the cases before him on his desk. Perhaps 'connection' isn't the correct term, relationship might be better.

Over the years, as these deaths occurred and they stood on their own, Plante hadn't given a second thought to the names of relatives of the deceased. Moreover, the deaths all seemed accidental; the files were in homicide only as a formality to satisfy insurance companies. What didn't seem accidental was the fact that they all had a relationship with one Professor William Jonas Craig. The Sheldon police detective didn't like such coincidences. The oldest case involved a little girl, Ione Craig, Little William's older sister. It seemed that Ione fell out of a tree while playing with her little brother. The twenty foot drop was complicated by bouncing off of four branches on the way down. Looking at the photos now and reading the coroner's report from 2160 Plante was struck with a suspicious mood. All of the braches hit her in the head. She didn't even have a broken rib or arm from falling twenty feet. Her little brother was up in the tree crying and inconsolable from the trauma of witnessing his sister's fatal fall.

Eighteen years later while the young PhD. was working on research on the new space platform laboratory, his parents were victims of a freak accident involving an anti-grav transport unit at take off. The transport got off of the ground alright, then instead of climbing to the forward acceleration altitude the lateral stabilizers malfunctioned sending the transport into an uncontrollable spin. The machine skipped along just above the ground, narrowly missing a little girl walking home from school and eventually came to a stop by wrapping itself around a great oak tree that had been on the estate for nearly two hundred years. The tree survived, the couple, it was determined by the coroner, were dead before impact. Estimates of the rate of spin of the vehicle were in the neighborhood of two-hundred to two hundred fifty rpm. The G-forces experienced by the couple were not survivable. Their brains were the consistency of mashed potatoes before the tree stopped the transport on its deadly mission.

Even though that was only one incident there were two victims and so two files, that made three family members of this guy that died under tragic circumstances. He warranted watching for his own safety if not out of suspicion. The fourth file had Plante boggled. Two years ago in 2182, an intern of Craig's, who now liked to be called Hawk, was sent on an errand by the good physicist to the Sheldon estate of his parents to retrieve some documents that were forgotten there on a recent visit. The professor needed them for a class that he was teaching at University of Massachusetts Space Campus. The intern's name was Stephen Bryant. Bryant took his transport down from UMass Space Campus, and went directly to the estate. That much was shown by examining the transport log. Where he went from there is still an open matter. He was never found. The estate was searched with Craig's permission and full cooperation, as always, but turned up nothing. Plante remembered being on the search detail as they looked for Bryant, that was only two years ago. Not only did they search the estate, they went beyond into the Wright Wildlife Preserve, a four hundred-fifty acre preserve set up over a hundred years ago for natural ecological preservation. Public admittance was limited to those who paid a high fee and they were expected to obey strict rules of use. The land was first and foremost for the animals that lived there naturally, humans had plenty of other habitats and were restricted from most parts of the preserve. Airspace over the preserve had to be held to one-hundred fifty feet plus according to state regulations for wildlife preserves. Cadaver detectors didn't work at that distance. It was only with a caretaker for every searcher that they were able to go through the grounds and be satisfied that Bryant or his remains, wasn't there. Plante had the feeling that Bryant was still alive. He couldn't substantiate it, just a feeling.

Another missing person was reported just three months ago. One Deirdra Evans, a young woman of nineteen, who seemed to have simply vanished while enjoying an ice cream at the Wright Dairy Farm. Proximity seemed to be the only relationship here. The Wright property had been divided from its original six hundred acres into three parts. The afore mentioned preserve, the dairy farm which consisted of the old farmhouse and barn on five acres, and the one hundred forty five acre estate bought by Craig's grandparents eighty years ago. They were from Boston. A thirty room manse was constructed on the property and remains to this day in Craig's name. Deirdra Evans was visiting a local relative, one Annie Boudreau, who was Deirdra's great aunt. To say that her aunt Annie was elderly was an understatement; she was on record as the oldest woman in the country. She benefited from the pioneer techniques of nano-technology used originally in the 2040's. The nanites were still inside her, keeping her fit and healthy. Annie was approaching her second full century of life. She looked to be a woman in her forties. Against her aunt's wishes Deirdra went for a walk on the hiking trail that was part of the farm. She was never seen again. The aunt's reasoning for not wanting Deirdra to go hiking was irrational; she believed the woods to be haunted. The only connection to Craig in this case was his proximity. It was known that he was visiting his estate at the time.

Plante's last concern where Craig was concerned was nothing to do with Sheldon. He suspected that somehow Craig was involved with the death of his peer, Prof. Richard Fish. Professor Fish died in his Boston home, alone, of what would seem to be natural causes. He was only fifty four. In a day and age when women live to be almost two hundred years old, how does a man die of natural causes at fifty four?

Plante decided he would have to request information from the Boston P.D. regarding Fish's circumstances. Somehow, Plante knew, these cases were tied to 'Hawk,' but connecting the dots was going to prove difficult. It all came down to degrees of separation.

CHAPTER THIRTY

Dave seated himself in his usual seat at the table. He said, "Olive, Zeke said he'll be along in a few minutes, and to go ahead and start."

Olive asked, "What was all of that about?"

Dave said, "All in Zeke's good time."

Olive let it go, knowing that Dave was just being respectful of Zeke's traditional values. She studied Dave for a moment. She asked, "You and Cy were boyhood friends, right?"

Dave said, "Sure were. That seems like such a long time ago, another life. I really want to get back to my life."

Olive was pensive, but decided the time had come. She said, "You mean your life with my Aunt Annie?"

Dave's jaw went slack. He said, "I guess I shouldn't be surprised, but… You are Annie's niece? How? By whom?"

"Actually Dave, I'm more your niece than Annie's. I'm your great, great niece through your brother Albert. Dave, Annie's alive in my time. She's the oldest human on record. In 2042 she had nano therapy for cancer. It was highly experimental at that time, but is used regularly by my time. The last time I saw her she looked to be in her mid thirties. It was 2183. She was approaching her two hundredth birthday."

Dave's heart was racing. He had never thought such a thing was possible. Indeed when he left in 2005 it wasn't, but thirty seven years later Annie had undergone this miracle. Then he looked at Olive, He said, "You've known this, who I am to you, and to Annie, and all this time this is the first you've said anything. I guess I understand why. Why?"

Olive looked down at first. When finally she looked up she said, "Dave, to me it's family history. You never came back. I still don't know why, but in my timeline's history, you disappeared in 2005 and never returned. Great Aunt Annie never remarried in all those years. A lot of people thought she was crazy. They figured the nanites could fix the body but couldn't save the mind from the effects of aging and senility. She believed the woods were haunted because of something from her youth, something to do with you even before your disappearance. We all know what that's all about, but she doesn't, and neither does the general population."

Cy had come in during the conversation. He sat quietly next to Lexi and took her hand. He looked at Olive and asked, "Are you saying that Annie is still alive in 2183?"

Olive looked at Cy and said, "Yes, she is Cy, and in good health."

Cy looked at Dave and said, "Dude, this is amazing."

Dave said, "Yeah, but Cy, Where am I? You heard, I never came back."

Cy grinned and said, "Well, maybe you decided to come with me instead."

Dave looked at him and said, "You can't be serious. I need to get back to Annie. I can't let her live her life alone like that."

Cy said, "Dave, it may be that when you get back, even if you get back before you leave, you may find the future, our time, to be drastically different from when you left. Annie may not even exist. Or even if she does exist, she may be someone else's wife. There are an infinite number of possibilities. But Dave, the most likely is that you came with me. That would at least explain why Deirdra's time had you never returning through her history."

Dave said, "How can I choose between the woman that I love, and a futile mission?"

Cy said, "I think it becomes less futile with you there helping me. And remember Dave, Annie is there, still loving you. I'm the one who will have to leave the woman I love. And I know I'll never see her again." He gripped Lexi's hand a little tighter under the table.

Zeke came into the kitchen. He took his customary seat at the head of the table. He said, "Good people, I am pleased to inform you all of what Dave here has brought to me. It would seem that Dave spoke loudly enough to be heard by McKinnon down the Lawrence. The dam will not be constructed here. The farm is saved. Dave, again, you have my eternal thanks."

Lexi added, "And mine as well Dave, thank you."

Cy said, "Dave, man, I need you too."

Dave looked down at the table and said, "I guess I'm going to the twenty-second century."

After dinner, the men were retired to the parlor. Zeke was smoking a pipe, Cy and Dave were just sitting, keeping time with him. Dave had let Morgan in and he was curled up by the fireplace enjoying the heat from the fire the way dogs do. He would creep up real close to the flames and pant to keep cool. Then there would be a crack from a pocket of gas in a log and he would jump back. The men were amused by Morgan's fire dance. The dog had already wriggled his way into everyone's hearts.

Cy turned from the entertainment and looked at Zeke and said, "Zeke, I need to ask you a favor."

Zeke said, "I'll be happy to see to Aunt Ezra."

Cy nodded. He wasn't surprised that Zeke had known what he would ask. He said, "It will be in the fall, around the end of the first week of October. We've seen the eddies since we've been here, at about the 8th to 10th of the month. You should be able to find it by the break in the stone wall out beyond the west pasture."

Zeke said, "Ayuh, I know just where to find both of 'em; the spring spinner and the fall spinner. My family's been observin' 'em for some years now. Spring will bring the spinner over in the holding pen. That's no coincidence the pen is there, we keep it empty during every other spring. Hate to lose animals to spinners. Then in the fall, a spinner out at the wall. Seen 'em both several times." Zeke thought for a moment, then continued, "I'll return with her to her time. If I survive one way, I'll take my return spinner. I'll need to know how to tell when to get out of the infernal thing so I don't end up with no dang dinosaurs."

Cy laughed and said, "Well Zeke, it's as easy as counting. You'll want to bring some survival gear. You already know the lay of the land, but the inhabitants will be different; hostile natives, lawless white men out looking to make a name for themselves, such as that. I would recommend bringing a gun if you have one. But remember if it's a new gun, it will stick out like a sore thumb. You may want to go to an antique dealer and find something closer to the period."

Zeke said, "It seems there's a might bit of deception involved in this time travel. We only suspected you and Aunt Ezra because of her resemblance to my mother. Aside from that, now that I think of it, you two fit right in. Now, when Olive, or Deirdra arrived we knew she didn't fit in. Of course we just thought she was from another country with different fashions."

Dave said, "Cy and Lexi were here to help me blend in with the natives. You would have laughed if you had seen me on my first night here Zeke, all covered in cow shit from head to toe, frozen to the bone from the cold. It was a warm fall day when I left and I wasn't dressed for the cold."

Cy laughed and added, "Yeah, we had water drawn and ready to heat to give him a bath. We had no idea where he would flop in. It turned out to be a good thing, when he appeared it was in a steamer!"

Zeke had a good laugh. He said, "I suppose next time I go into town I can wander into the gun shop in the south village. Might be they'll have an old muzzle loader. I have one up in the attic, it belonged to my great grandfather, but it hasn't been fired for forty years or so."

Dave said, "Suppose before you go and spend your money on another old gun we take a look at the old gun you already have. It may be in good condition. Maybe it'll just need a cleaning. We could get some powder and musket balls an' give her a try."

Zeke said, "Maybe you're right, we'll pull her down come spring and see about it. Well gentlemen, Ben Franklin was quoted as saying, 'Early to bed early to rise,' and all that healthy an' wealthy bullshit. I'm about ready to turn in."

Cy said, "Good idea, I only have a few more months with Lexi."

Dave added, "Yeah, come on Morgan, it's you and me again tonight!"

Cy and Zeke laughed.

The morning of April ninth arrived with a bright sun shining in from the southeast, urging spring. It was still too early for crocuses and tulips to be pushing their way up through the ground, but sunshine and a relatively warm southerly wind helped fuel spring fever. By 8:00 A.M. the cattle were milked and turned out to graze. Zeke thought this day as good as any and had gone to the attic and collected the muzzle loader and all of the accessories for it that he had. He had it laid out on a small table in the utility room off of the parlor. There was seldom a reason to have a fire in this fireplace but today there were some logs fully engulfed to warm the room and entertain Morgan as the men inspected the firearm.

Zeke said, "It doesn't seem to be worse for the storage."

Cy said, "Well Zeke you had it in the attic, attics are dry, if you had stowed it in the damp cellar it would probably be nothing but rust by now."

Dave said, "Site down the barrel and see how it looks inside."

Zeke lifted the weapon, drew back the flintlock and locked it open. He turned the butt end up and rested the muzzle on the table. He could only see down a short distance, but what he could see looked clean and uncorroded. He withdrew the cleaning rod from the scabbard and attached a barrel tissue to the end of it. Very carefully he inserted the tissue end of the rod into the barrel and fed it in. The tip reached the bottom and he slowly retrieved it. When it came out there was only a little oily residue on the tissue, no rust as they had feared.

Dave said, "Well Zeke, it would appear you may have saved a few dollars on the purchase of a muzzle loader."

Zeke, said, "You're right. We might as well get to town and buy some powder and shot for her and give her a test."

Cy said, "It might be a good idea to bring it along and let the shop's gunsmith take a look."

"Good idea, plus if there's anything I don't understand about her, he can fill me in."

The three men left the house and went to the barn. There was a buckboard in one of the stalls, Cy and Dave pulled it out while Zeke got the mare, Milly from her corral. By now, both Dave and Cy knew how to hitch a horse to a wagon and with the three of them working together the task was done in what might have been considered a pit crew record, If there had been pit crews then. Milly got up and trotted out of the barn out into the yard. She seemed happy to get her legs moving after the long winter. Zeke didn't want to waste her energy though so he held her to a brisk walk. They rode up through the packed down dirt roads avoiding muddy areas like the plague. Milly even knew enough to watch out for the mud, turning her head toward where the driest part of the road as though to cue Zeke on where to drive her. Day had definitely turned into a thaw; in the midst of a New England winter there were days that would come along and fool you into believing that spring had arrived, only to have you find yourself up to your haunches in the middle of a Nor'easter. New Englanders loved to complain about the abrupt changes in the weather. It was true that year round there was always a changeability that seemed to be unparalleled in the world.

The buckboard came to a rest outside of the gunsmith's shop in the center of Sheldon's south village. The trio climbed down and ambled into the shop. Zeke set his muzzle loader on the counter top and asked the clerk, "Hey there Jimmy, is Ol' Steve out back?"

Jimmy said, "Yes sir, he is, hang on I'll fetch him." He turned from Zeke and disappeared through a door in back of the counter.

A moment later Ol' Steve came up front and looked to see who was looking for him. He recognized Zeke and said, "'lo Zeke, who're yer friends?"

Zeke said, "This here is Cyrus and that'll be David, They're a couple a fellas workin' for me on t' farm."

Ol' Steve said, "Nice t' meet you fellas. Where're you from?"

Dave said, "Down the river a ways, outside of Peterston."

Zeke said, "Steve, this here muzzle loader of mine, I wanted to shake the dust out and show these boys how it fires. Can you take a look afore I do, 'n make sure it don't explode in my face?"

"Sure Zeke." 'Ol Steve took the weapon from Zeke and examined it. He did the same as Zeke had done with the cleaning rod and tissue, he checked the firing mechanisms and said, "Looks like you need a new flint." He reached down and opened a drawer. Reaching in he fished about for a moment and finally withdrew a new flint. He set it aside and expertly removed the old worn down flint and inserted the new one. He set the gun on the counter and said, "You'll be needing some shot and some powder. Do you know how to load and fire this ol' relic?"

Zeke said, "My Gran'Dad showed me when I was a boy. Been a long time though."

Steve reached down and unscrewed the packing rod, he poured a measure of powder into the barrel, packed it, then paper, shot, more packing rod, paper, packing… He finished and took a pinch of powder between his thumb and forefinger and packed it into the primer hole near the flint. "Come on, we'll fire it out back."

They followed Ol' Steve through the back and down the back stairway to the vacant lot in the rear of the building. He handed the gun to Zeke and said, "Over yon is a pile of hay bales I use as targets for gun testing. Go ahead."

Zeke took put the muzzle loader to his shoulder and took aim. He drew back on flint lock and locked it in place. Slowly he squeezed the trigger release and the flint lock sprang forward. The flint on the abrasive metal sent up a small flare of sparks which ignited the primer. The primer sent a puff of smoke from the side of the stock and ignited the packed powder within. There was a thunderous roar as the charge exploded out of the end of the barrel. The shot tore into the bales thirty yards away. The enormous bang startled both Cy and Dave to the point that they both jumped back in recoil from it.

Ol' Steve turned and looked at the pair. He grinned and asked, "So Cyrus, Dave, when did you say the two of you are from?"

Chapter Thirty One

Annie sat in the window looking out at the snow covered lawn. She wondered why she had lived so long. She knew the how; she was just having another bad day pondering the why. There she sat the picture of health at two hundred one years old. She could easily pass for thirty five. She wasn't the only medical marvel; she knew that, there were actually many like her. In fact the number of people over one hundred fifty was growing rapidly. She was the one on record as the oldest human on the planet. Sadly that meant that many eyes were on her for an idea of just to what extent nano technology would benefit the human race. So far, the benefit was evident in the health field, but what about love? She was tired of being alone. Dave had gone from her at such a young age. She never found love again while she was young and by the time she felt ready to move on she couldn't find a man that could ever live up to her expectations. So here she sat, in the ever watchful gaze of the public eye waiting for the very thing the public didn't want to see happen; her death.

Many times over the years she heard the accounts of mysterious local disappearances. She would also hear of people turning up from time to time with no knowledge of where they were or how they got there, disjointed from the time and place they had found themselves in. That was how she felt now; disjointed and set apart.

It took thirty years after Dave's disappearance for her to believe the ether was responsible. She couldn't accept until then, the notion that some swirlie in the middle of the woods was responsible for Dave disappearing. Then Cy and Lexi disappeared and the only clue as to where they were was Brian and Charlie saying that they had gone off looking for Dave. She wouldn't talk to them for decades. All she could feel was hurt at their inconsideration of her feelings. Only after thirty years did she realize that it was they who were being honest and it was she who was ignoring friendship by dismissing them from her life. Annie had humbled herself and gone begging their forgiveness. Brian and Charlie never even gave it a second thought. They embraced her and brought her back into their lives. She was thankful for that. They had another fifteen years before Brian died and three after that when Charlie followed him. They were the best of people and Annie was so happy to have known them.

After her nano procedure she began to show visible signs of age regression. She was nearly sixty-five when she went to her oncologist Dr. Deborah Rickford for her initial treatments. Rickford was the one who asked Annie if she would be interested in Nano-therapy. After her first treatment Annie noticed a difference. The pain went away within twenty-four hours. Her second injection was two weeks later. By then she was feeling better than she had in twenty years.

After the third injection she began to notice things like fine wrinkles disappearing on her face. The arthritis in her knee that had set in during her forties seemed to go away overnight. When she had her next hair appointment, the colorist told her she didn't need to have her hair dyed. She felt it was a miracle. Now, after all these years she wasn't so certain. Unless something could bring her back into life, she wasn't living, she was merely existing.

Detective Plante decided to reopen the cases he had been reviewing that seemed related to Hawk. He was certain there was something there, but just how much would he be able to make stick. He requested and received permission to travel to Boston to interview the detective that handled the Fish case. He boarded his transport and programmed the destination into the auto navigation system. The transport hummed as it lifted from the earth. It rose slowly at first and gradually sped upward to the top of the roofline. Transitioning from upward to forward motion was seamless and the transport began the journey to the east. Frank said out loud, "Disable Voice Command Function, authorization Plante, Detective Frank." A message printed on the transport control screen, 'Voice Command Function disabled.'

With that, Plante reached up with his right hand and tapped the mastoid bone directly behind his right ear. This activated his implanted telecommunication device and it prompted him for a name. Out loud he said, "Annie Boudreau."

In a moment he heard the tone indicating the other party was being paged. After only a few seconds he heard her voice say, "Hello?"

Plante responded, "Mrs. Boudreau, my name is Detective Frank Plante. We met once I believe about five years ago. Do you remember me?"

Annie said, "Yes Detective, I do. How can I help you?"

Plante said, Ma'am I'm reopening several old cases and have found a connection between many of them. Because of this new information, I was wondering if it might be possible for me to stop in and ask you some additional questions? It could be quite helpful Mrs. Boudreau. Is there a time that would suit you?"

Annie said, "Whenever it is convenient to you Detective, I'll be here all day today and tomorrow."

"Thank you Ma'am, I'll try to be there tomorrow morning."

"I'll be here."

"Good day then." Plante tapped behind his ear and disconnected. Mrs. Annie Boudreau was something of an enigma in her own right. He didn't suspect her of anything, but he was certain that she knew more than she had given up. Her own husband had disappeared, over a hundred and sixty years ago, she didn't seem to know anything then either according to police archives. All she would say when Miss Evans disappeared was that she had told her not to go out in those woods. What was happening out in those woods? He would have to tap dance around a bit to extract that from her. This would require some thought.

The transport's deceleration and descent were seamless and smooth. The car hovered at the front steps of the BPD building. Plante pressed the door open button and the curbside door slid out of sight into a pocket in the chassis of the transport. He stepped out of the transport and removed the remote from his coat pocket. He pressed the 'Park' button and immediately the door slid shut and the transport rose straight up along side of the building. At about a hundred and fifty feet it docked at an empty charge station and plugged in for anti-grav recharge. Plante turned and entered the building.

The sergeant at the desk looked at Plante's badge and asked, "Who are you here to see, Detective?"

Plante said, "A Detective Cody, in homicide."

"Sure, hang on." The sergeant touched an icon on his screen, he said, "Detective Cody there's a Detective Plante here from Sheldon, are you expecting him?" After a few seconds he looked back at Plante and said, "Go to SL 3 using those lifts over there," as he gestured toward a bank of elevators, "turn left when you step out and you'll find Detective Cody in the fourth door on the right."

"Thank you, sergeant." Plante said as he turned toward the elevators. He wondered why the homicide detectives in the larger cities always seemed to be relegated to the sub levels. He decided it must have been to keep the detectives closer to the morgues. The elevator quickly descended to SL 3 where Plante stepped out, turned left and counted off four doors. He turned and entered the room. Detective Cody was sitting behind the desk drumming her fingers on the armrest of her chair. She said, "Are you Detective Plante?"

Plante said, "Frank, you Cody?"

"Trish. Your message said you needed any information regarding the death of Dr. Richard Fish?"

Plante said, "That's right. I think his death may be related to some local deaths and missing persons in Sheldon."

Cody looked at Plante, sizing him up. She asked, "Why did you come here? All of the files on this guy can be accessed at your desk back in Sheldon."

Plante nodded. He said, "You're right. I wanted to talk to you directly. When you investigated Fish's death, did you interview a colleague of his, a Dr. William Craig?"

Cody nodded, "Sure. What about him?"

"He's related to several of my open cases over the last twenty plus years; never a direct link, kind of always on the fringe. I first noticed it last week as I was reviewing old files. This guy's name was always there, but never as a suspect. That makes me suspicious."

She said, "Yeah, I see what you mean. I talked with the guy. He wanted to be called Hawk. Real weird. But I didn't go after him because I wasn't investigating for murder. Just a routine follow up on what had all of the earmarks of an accidental death."

Plante nodded and said, "You and me both Trish, he never warranted a second look in any of the cases that I have. Somehow I have the feeling that he should have been the prime suspect several times over."

Cody said, "He wasn't even on my radar as a suspect. The only reason I interviewed him is because he was partnered with Fish on a research grant. They were both insured to the eyeteeth with each other listed as beneficiary. Hawk, or Craig, said it was because if anything should happen to one of them the grant would be rescinded and the other would be out in the cold. So they took out these policies to ensure the other would be able to continue the work they were doing. So far as I know that's exactly what he is using the money for, too; some project that they want to launch into space.

I don't get all that astrick-physiology stuff. Do you know the guy actually has a chalk board and chalk? Real chalk; he has it imported from Argentina. Why would anyone want to use chalk?"

Plante sat in the chair across from Cody. He thought about what she was telling him and didn't like it. In all of the cases where a death was involved there was a relationship to this Hawk. And he somehow benefited from the death. How was it he never roused suspicion? In the missing persons cases the relationship was more oblique, but still there. Plante's gut told him there was more to the guy. "I'm pretty sure they call themselves Theoretical Astro-Physicists." He said absently as he was mulling over his next move. He asked, "Trish, would you be interested in a cooperative investigation into this guy?"

She sat back and asked, "Look, Frank, my files are your files. You need info I'm here for you. But I have a full plate as it is. I'll be glad to work anything on the Fish case, especially if it looks to be escalating to murder but I can't really start working your Sheldon cases with you, my captain would have a coronary episode if she ever caught wind of it."

Plante said, "Sure, sure I understand that, that's really all I was hoping for. Just to keep the Fish file on your front burner for a while longer while I dig a bit deeper on my end. If I can show there is good reason to look deeper into this guy I'll need a second detective with the same suspicion before the Fed files on the guy can be opened to me. I don't want to spook him, I want to learn about him."

Cody nodded, "You show me what you've got on him and if I see what you see, I'll back you up Frank."

"Thanks Trish. I'll let you get back to work." He extended his hand to her, "Nice to meet you, I'll be in touch."

They shook hands and Plante left her office. He was pleased with the way the meeting went. Now he could turn his attention to Annie Boudreau. What was she hiding? He stepped out into the late morning sun and took the remote out of his pocket. He pressed the 'Activate' button and looked up to where the transport had docked itself. The car's running lights switched on as it came to life. It scanned its perimeter and backed out of the docking station, turning at right angles and smoothly began its descent. The transport came to hover just a half meter from Plante. He pressed the door button and it opened for him. He entered and sidled across the cabin to the pilot seat. Plante thought for a moment and finally entered 'UMass Space Campus' into the navigation console. Immediately after receiving the instruction set the transport began its ascent to the traffic lane. As soon as the car reached the east bound traffic lane an 'error' message appeared on his screen. A digitized voice announced aloud what the screen had printed upon it. "UMass Space Campus is at too great an altitude for this transport to achieve without being fitted with an oxygen plenishment system. You must book passage on a high altitude transport carrier." With a sigh of exasperation, he touched the Sheldon Icon. The transport reeled out of the traffic lane and shot upward creating a large "U" loop over traffic and joined the traffic lane heading west. Out loud he said, "I guess I'll have to book passage then."

The onboard computer responded saying, "Please restate the input using preprogrammed commands."

Frank said out loud, "Disable Voice Command Function, authorization Plante, Detective Frank."

A message printed on the screen, 'Voice Command Function disabled.'

Plante sighed. Then it occurred to him, he had already disabled the VCF.

CHAPTER THIRTY TWO

Ol' Steve appeared to be a man in his late seventies. He was missing his left eye, as well as half of his front teeth. The remaining teeth were stained and showing signs of rotting in his head. Matted white hair crowned his head and blended into his grey scraggly beard. His right leg was twisted and gnarled at the knee causing him to walk with a pronounced limp, which he did with his right hand planted just above his right hip for support. He was the local expert in guns, both hand guns and rifles. He seemed to understand how they came apart and went together before even seeing them. A local manufacturer of firearms had tried several times with no success to recruit him to their research and development division. He was quite satisfied running his little gun shop where he fixed and reconditioned hand guns rifles and antique weapons.

He crossed the lot and opened a door that was under the stairway that led to the shop above. He looked back and said to the three men, "Well come on in. And close your mouths before you catch a few flies!"

Zeke, Dave and Cy seemed to realize they had been dumbstruck and looked at each other briefly before they headed for Steve's door. When they stepped inside they were all surprised at the cleanliness of the apartment. They noticed that Steve had removed his boots as he entered and they followed suit. He was at the stove, putting a log in atop the coals. Dave was the last one to enter and so he closed the door behind him. When it shut there was almost a vacuum seal that cut all of the drafts.

Steve said, "I'm making a pot of coffee. You gentlemen can have a seat at the table." He busied himself as they were sitting. He said, "Zeke, I remember when you were born. I know this is your time and where you belong. You two though, you stick out to the eye that knows what to look for. I only have one left, but it knows what to look for. I've found others, like you, like me, so don't worry, you've blended well. Almost too well. So, tell me, who are you and when are you from?"

Dave and Cy looked at each other. Dave gestured to Cy and said, "Go ahead man, it's all you."

Cy said, "I'm Cy Hill and this is Dave Boudreau. We're from 2005. Dave came here accidentally in the fall. I came with my wife four years ago to try to rescue him. We found his obituary in the library archives and were able to figure out what time he arrived, so we overshot to allow for error."

Steve said, "Your wife? So there are three of you from the early twenty-first century here?"

Cy said, "Well, not really, she is actually from 1706. She was caught in an eddy that brought her to 1986 when she was a young girl. So she's an early eighteenth century girl by way of the twenty-first century."

Steve got up and went to the coffee percolator. He brought down four clean mugs from the cupboard and placed them on the sideboard. He poured coffee into all four and placed each on a tray. Then he carried the tray across the room and placed it on the table. He did all of this with his pronounced limp and yet held a certain grace about himself as though he entertained all of the time. He looked at Cy and asked, "What was it that you just said? About an eddy."

Cy said, "The eddies are the vehicles that moved us around in time. Maybe vehicle isn't the right word. Means, phenomenon, however you want to call it. Okay Steve, it's your turn."

Steve just sat there and said, "That bastard was right. It worked. The accelerator actually worked."

Cy said, "A little too well. Who are you Steve?"

Steve answered, "I'm Stephen Bryant. I was a graduate student working on a research project as an intern under Professor William Craig at the UMass Space Campus. In the year 2182 I came down to get some paperwork for Hawk, that's what the professor liked to be called, before I went to his estate I stopped off and got myself an ice cream at the dairy farm next door. That's what becomes of your place Zeke. So I was eating the ice cream and wandering about a bit and I saw this pretty young woman. She was a beauty. I didn't have time to approach her but that didn't mean I couldn't admire her. I went to an open corral and found myself in the wrong place at the right time, and the next thing I knew I'm seeing nothing but white. I thought maybe I was having some kind of seizure so I stood still for as long as I could. Soon I couldn't take it any more and I realized that I wasn't going to pass out, so I stepped forward. That was when I found myself in the middle of your door yard Zeke, only there was no barn there. There were only cattle and cold night air. I could see the lights in your parent's house so I approached and knocked on the door. They took me in that night and put me up. It was 1858. A few years later I found myself in the middle of the civil war. That's how I lost my eye, my teeth and got this nicely twisted leg. I've been making my own since then with this gun shop."

Zeke asked, "Did you say 2182?"

"That's right. Why?"

"My wife came from 2183."

Ol' Steve looked surprised. He said, "Olive? No, really?" And he started to laugh. He said, "Hmm, she must have an ITC."

"A what?" asked Zeke.

"An 'Implanted Telecommunications Chip.' Most people of that day had them implanted when they are very young. I could call her right now and find out. Of course the shock of hearing it here and now might be a bit much. I'll tell you what, when you go home tonight you tell her to give ol' Steve a call. Oh won't that be something." Steve was quite pleased with the prospect of hearing his phone implant again.

Dave said, "Steve, you said you worked on the Quantum Accelerator project with Prof. Craig?"

Steve came back from his reverie and said, "Yes, that's right, why?"

Dave said, "So far as we can tell, that's the reason we're all here."

Steve took a deep breath. He said, "Yes, it would be wouldn't it." He took another sip of his cooling coffee and said, "It seems it worked."

Cy said, "Steve is there any information you can give us about the project?"

Steve said, "All I saw was the building that was going under contract for the construction. The project was still in design and preparation. Materials weren't even ordered because the funding had just been approved. Hawk was still teaching classes."

"Where was the building?" Cy asked.

"Hmm, that's a might difficult to say. After all, you're talking about forty seven years ago. It was off campus, in an old warehouse district in Boston. Ha, it may not be so old right now though. It may not even be built yet. But that's about as close as I can direct you to it. Wait a minute, you sound as though you plan to go to the future."

"We are." said Dave.

"How do you control it?" Steve asked, his voice rising.

"No, not control it, but predict it and use it. We can use the eddies to move back and forth in time."

Steve looked shocked. He said, "It never occurred to me that there was a way back."

Cy said, "Steve, we could use your help. Do you want to go back to your time with us?"

Steve said, "I'll have to think about it. For now, I have to get back up to the shop, can't stay closed up and earn my keep at the same time."

They all took their cue and rose from the table and made their way to the door.

Cy said, "We'll need to get together with you again Steve. Will you think about the project and try to remember any details that would be helpful to us?"

Steve said, "I can do that. Just leave the coffee mugs. I sure will give some thought to the project, but I just might be more helpful to you if I went back then with you. It's a pile to think about. Say Zeke, you never did tell me why you wanted that old muzzle loader working."

Zeke said, "Well Steve, I'm going to 1705 to bring my great aunt home. I'll be in that time for a few years and didn't want to bring a new weapon into that time."

Steve said, "That makes sense."

They went outdoors and made their way up the back stairs into the gun shop. Zeke paid Steve for the shot and powder.

As they were going out the front door Cy looked at Steve and said, "Steve, I'll drop in tomorrow and talk with you some more. There's time to think before you decide, the next eddy leaves in April."

Steve said, "I'll see you tomorrow then."

Olive said, "That disgusting old man that runs the gun shop? You're telling me he comes from my time?"

Zeke found this particularly amusing. He said, "Sure does. He said you could call him if your, what did he call it, ITC I think, if your ITC still works."

Olive sat back in her chair. She self consciously touched the mastoid bone behind her right ear. She tapped once and heard the transmit tone. ITC technology uses a network of broadcasting towers and satellites for global and distance transmissions, but could easily stand alone as a point to point transceiver if the distance wasn't too great; depending on the terrain up to fifteen miles. The center of south village was only three miles away. She decided if she needed to reach him that was one thing, but the novelty alone of calling him wasn't enough to make her go any further. She tapped the same spot again this time twice, and the tone silenced. She said, "Ezekiel, I'm very confused and torn about this whole business."

Zeke nodded and said, "I know that, and so am I, to a point anyway, but I understand why you're troubled."

"A big part of me wants to go back. Aw, I miss my Mom and Dad something terrible. But I'm not a young woman any more. Many people who pioneered or immigrated gave up ever seeing family any more. I sort of pioneered back in time. The thing is, I can't leave you. I can't go back to that time with you, and I can't leave you to go back. That makes me a bit angry and sad. I don't know how better to say my feelings."

Zeke said, "You said 'em just fine sweetheart, just fine." He thought some more and said, "What do you suppose I should do about Aunt Ezra?"

Olive thought for a bit and said, "Well, you could always come back before you leave."

Zeke pondered this for a moment, trying to understand what she was telling him. He said, "Are you trying to tell me I could be here… twice?"

"If by that you're asking if you could be here and out there waiting for this you to leave, then, yes you could. If you come back before you leave then you could come walking in that door anytime now. You could decide right now to do so, and then we would know that everything went alright."

Almost as though on cue, the door handle turned and the door began to open. Both Zeke and Olive jumped from surprise and then turned toward the door in expectation. When Lexi stepped into the back entry they sat back down and stared at her.

Lexi could see by the looks on their faces that she had walked in on something. She asked, "If I came in at a bad time I can come back later."

Olive laughed first, then Zeke, he said, "I can tell you, I was expecting to see myself there! We were talking about how I could already be back from taking you to your own time. Olive told me that I should plan on returning today, now that we've talked about it and are ready for me."

Lexi smiled then said, "But what if the children see you together with yourself?"

Olive said, "Well that explains why you didn't come in just now Dear."

Zeke said, "I've an idea. You call ol' Steve on yer ITC thing and ask him if I can come and stay with him for a time. Tell him I'll explain everything to him and that he should call when I arrive."

Olive grinned at him. She reached up and tapped her mastoid, when she heard the tone she said, "Stephen Bryant," and waited.

After a brief pause there was a response, "Is this Deirdra?" Steve asked.

"Yes, please, call me Olive. Steve, Ezekiel and I have a favor to ask you."

Steve said, "Sure, if it's something I can do."

Olive said, "If Ezekiel shows up there, could he live with you for a while?"

"What do you mean, if he shows up? He just walked through the door, I thought he might have forgotten something from this morning."

Olive said, "Actually, he just got back from bringing his aunt back. The Zeke in your store has been gone for a few years."

Steve said, "I see, well under the circumstances, he can stay with me here until your fella leaves. He just said to me that he'll explain everything to me Olive."

"Thank you Steve, I look forward to meeting you one day soon."

"As do I Olive, Good-bye"

She tapped behind her ear twice to terminate the transmission. With a tear in her eye she looked at Zeke and said, "You're safe!"

CHAPTER THIRTY THREE

Zeke sat in Steve's kitchen. He said, "I'm sure surprised at you Steve, all these years and I never figured you for bein' from the future."

Steve smiled, "Well, Young fella, I had to hide it or risk bein' sent to one of them insanytoriums you folks fancy havin' about fer your social rejects."

Zeke smiled, he had heard ol' Steve talk in his normal manner and knew the show was for his benefit. He said, "Fair enough."

Steve said, "So Zeke, tell me what you've been up to these last few years since I saw you this mornin'."

Zeke began to relate.

It was almost six months to the day after Cy and Dave left in the spring eddy. There was no telling how their trip through the ether was or how they were faring in the future. The focus now was on getting this right and getting Aunt Ezra back to her time and, surviving that, getting back to this time in one piece. This would be a long and arduous task for Zeke.

He would have to fend for himself and Ezra for a half year until the next spring eddy so she could remerge with her younger self. Then he needed to make himself scarce for another eighteen months until the next autumn eddy so he could return to this time. Coming back before he leaves means he would have to do for himself until the day that Olive called Steve and made the arrangement for Zeke to stay with him; that's nearly a year.

The day of departure arrived. The Zeke that had gone and returned came to his departure. This was reassurance on many levels. He knew by seeing himself that he was successful. He also knew that his other self would still be with Olive, taking care of her. He and Ezra approached the corral. They both knew the exact spot to be looking for. What they weren't certain of is the time of day. The decision was to go early in the day and watch for signs, sand swirling or pine needles, leaves even pine cones spinning about. When they were at the spot they stopped. So far there was no reason to think that an eddy was there. Zeke saw what Cy had done and copied him. He bent down and took a handful of sand and tossed it in a broadcast over the area. There it was. Directly in front of them, a single grain of sand suspended on air about ten inches over the ground.

Ezra said, "There's an eddy.

Zeke turned to Olive, he went to her and gave her a hug. She was crying, even though she knew he would be alright, she cried for his ordeal to come. Zeke gave her a long kiss. He said, "That will have to hold me until tonight." He grinned as he looked at his other self. Then without waiting for a response he turned back to Ezra and picked up his gear. He cinched up all of the supplies they were taking onto himself and asked Ezra, "Are you ready?"

She said, "Just one thing," and she went to Olive as well. She embraced her as sisters who would never see one another again. Then she was ready. They went together to a position just to the side of the eddy. Ezra got right up next to Zeke, she said, "Okay so we hug, and step in together. Once we're inside everything will go white, you'll feel disoriented, don't worry, it's normal. I'll count out loud to 38 and we step out. It's that easy."

"In less than a minute we'll be two hundred years ago." Zeke said, and he sighed deeply, "alright, let's do this."

They each took a deep breath, then put their arms around each other. Zeke said, "One, Two, Three…" and they stepped into the eddy disappearing to those who remained behind.

Ezra counted, the inside of the eddy was like being in a white nowhere. There was no sensation of movement, no air moving about them, no light playing or shadows flashing around them. Then Ezra said, "Thirty-eight!" They stepped out of the eddy. They were alone in the middle of the woods.

It was night. Rain was falling about them adding to the chill in the unwelcoming darkness. There were no visible details to give them guidance, only their knowledge of the surrounding terrain. The raindrops were splattering on the leaves that were covering the ground. The air was heavy with the musty smell of autumn when it rained.

Zeke said, "This doesn't seem right to me. There are leaves here, this was a pine grove."

Ezra said, "This becomes a pine grove. This is how it was when I left. I think we did alright."

Zeke said, "Let's get the tarp out and wait out the night."

They removed the tarp from Zeke's pack and, after stumbling to a tree, tied one end up and fashioned a crude lean-to for shelter. They didn't want to start a fire so they had to huddle together for warmth. As it turned out they were fairly close to dawn. Not long after they settled in, the eastern sky started to lighten. When it was light enough to find their way they pulled on their rain gear and stowed the tarp back into Zeke's pack.

They were eighteen months early for their appointment with young Ezra. The plan was to make their way east, toward Boston. There they could find lodging and wait out the months. They had plenty of money to live on. Cy had seen to it before leaving 2005. They had visited numismatic dealers and gone online to E-bay and purchased antique moneys that were used during these two times. For the early 1900's they had gotten 300 dollars of varying denominations in 1902, '03 and '04 bills. When Cy was looking for 1700 dollar bills Lexi had to point out to him that in 1700 the colonies still used British pounds. This period was more difficult to secure, but not impossible. They were able to gather 200£ in period notes at a cost, but it was within Cy's means.

The journey was difficult going. Roadways were little better than cart roads. Because of the rain the mud was everywhere. They walked from sunrise to sunset. Zeke didn't force Ezra to push to her limits. There was plenty of time and they had supplies. They made the Concord settlement in seven days. Just to the west of the township there was an Inn where they were able to secure lodging. They used assumed last names and claimed to be brother and sister. The names they used were Ezekiel and Ezra Henry. They used the story that they were waiting to be joined by additional family from England. They would be remaining for an undetermined amount of time.

The rooms had a stove with only a few cooking utensils; one pot, one pan, a ladle and spatula. To save on expenses Zeke cut wood and hauled it. Eventually Zeke's hunting and fishing became the commodity of choice. He developed proficiency with the muzzle loader and as he learned the forests and rivers around Concord his daily take from the land was considerably more than he and Ezra needed. He could feed them and typically three to five more. If he got a deer they could eat for a week.

With the arrival of March came the time to return to the homestead. They packed their belongings and began the journey upstream along the Lawrence. The snow was melting in the tributaries and all of the rivers were up. Brooks that they had jumped over in the fall were over their banks and a full thirty feet across. They spent a lot of time drying out only to go through it all again when they came upon another tributary. Zeke was able to see first hand why there was a need for flood control in the Pequod Valley. He was also proud of Dave in his ability to recognize the problem as being in the tributaries within the valley and not the Lawrence itself. It took eight days to travel up to Sheldon Village. All along the way Ezra was very careful to track the date so as to be certain not to miss her appointment with herself. When they arrived in the village they took rooms at a stage coach stop. Hot baths were in order. It would probably be the last hot bath that Ezra would have until after her intervening with young Ezra. They only stayed at the coach stop for a few nights.

April 1st arrived. Zeke and Ezra had moved from the coach stop to a pine grove just upstream along the Lawrence from the Wright's land. Ezra was growing nervous. She was also concerned for Zeke. She would return to her girlhood and the care of her family. He would have to go back out into the harsh elements and make his own way for another year and a half.

Starting that night they waited for nightfall and made their way down to the cabin that was the first Wright home. It wasn't much to look at, and it wasn't in the same place as the farmhouse that would eventually become the Wright farm. Zeke realized that Little Ezra must have been out wandering in the darkness for quite a long time in the night and that he would have to get her back to the cabin safely after Aunt Ezra had remerged. He had hoped to go undetected and just disappear afterward, but now he realized he must risk being seen by Ezra's father.

They went to the stone wall that Ezra's Father had been building. She knew the area well, even though it had been many years by her reckoning. They took up a position twenty feet from there and waited. They waited all through the night in vane. Little Ezra didn't come. Ezra was unsure of the correct date, she could remember only that it was shortly after one of her sisters went through the ice on the bank of the Lawrence. They decided to come every night and sleep during the day.

On the fourth night, they met with success. It was around one in the morning, during Ezra's watch. She heard a child whimpering and stumbling through the forest. She shook Zeke and woke him. They listened for a moment and then left their little shelter. Ezra approached her younger self, hoping that instinctively the little girl lost would know that they meant no harm. When Little Ezra saw them she froze in her tracks, staring. There was only the light of a third quarter moon still too low to the horizon to see with. The elder Ezra soothed little Ezra and convinced her to stop crying. She wrapped her blanket over the little girl to warm her. Zeke struck a flint and lit a torch they had readied for this. With the torch lit he turned to the area where they had agreed the eddy would appear and held the torch high. Not being able to make anything out he bent to the ground and scooped up some dirt. He tossed it in a broadcast and then raised the torch again. Ezra saw it first, the pebble that was spinning about, just above the ground. She left the child Ezra standing with the blanket and stepped forward. She stood next to Zeke and looked at him, her eyes thanking him for taking her here. Then without a word she stepped into the eddy and disappeared.

Little Ezra's eyes grew wide as she looked at the grown woman disappear before them. Then she looked at Zeke and there was recognition in them. She said, "Okay Ezekiel, I'm ready to go home now."

Zeke was truly amazed. He had heard Cy's story about Dave's wedding day and the pea in the eddy, but he was still unprepared for seeing it with his own eyes. He went to Little Ezra and picked her up. She was shivering in the blanket, if the eddy didn't get her the cold would have killed her. He said, "Aunt Ezra I think you would have frozen to death if the eddy hadn't caught you." He carried her back to the cabin. When they got there he put her down and she said, "Wait here." She ran inside the outhouse and did what she had gone outside all that time ago to do. When she came out she returned to him and reached out her arms. He knelt before her and they hugged for the last time. Ezra said, "Thank you for everything nephew."

Zeke said, "I'll miss you Aunt Ezra." He kissed her cheek.

She smiled and turned from him walking back to the cabin as though nothing had happened, just a twelve year old girl going potty in the middle of the night.

Zeke left the dooryard, not wanting to be seen by her father if he awoke. He returned to the campsite and had almost fallen asleep when he realized something. Was it simply an oversight? This eddy was a conduit to the future. He hurried to break camp, then ran as quickly as he could with all of his gear to the eddy site. He went directly to the spinner, knowing that if the eddy wasn't spinning he would remain there for two years waiting for the next one. He stepped forward and everything was white nothingness. He was on his way home. He began counting immediately. When he reached thirty six he lunged to escape the eddy's spin. As he came into the world, he nearly threw himself into a tree for all of the thrust he had used to launch himself out of the eddy. He was unhurt. He was back in what seemed to be his own time. He smiled.

Zeke made for the woods. The next day he walked to the south village and bought an edition of The Sheldon News so he could find out the date. April 9th 1905. He was successful in returning before he left. He walked over to ol' Steve's gun shop. When he entered the gun shop Steve was talking to himself, or at least that was how it appeared. Zeke knew that he was talking to Olive. He was home safe.

After the other Zeke and Ezra left in the eddy, Zeke was able to return to the farm and his wife. Steve accompanied him and for the first time was able to meet Olive. They were easy in one another's company and enjoyed talking about the future. Zeke was always fascinated with the stories about automobiles that fly and something called a personal home computer that controlled the entire house and helped organize your whole life. He was most taken by the story of Dave's wife. Nearly two hundred years young and healthy as a thirty year old. Zeke had difficulty envisioning a robot, then he had to picture a robot so small that an entire army of them could be injected into a body and you wouldn't know it to look at them. These little things could keep a person alive and healthy indefinitely.

The funniest thing was hearing ol' Steve, the town gutter mouth, talking with such a refined tone. Zeke realized Stephen Bryant was in all likelihood the most educated man he had ever met. He was educated in technologies so advanced that the government would love to get their hands on him. No wonder he had played the fool for so long. This was a secret that must be kept.

It turned out that both Steve and Olive had those little nanites inside of them. Pretty much anyone born after the year 2050 had them injected shortly after birth. Olive said something about the nanites being programmed not to cross the chorionic barrier. Zeke wasn't too sure what that meant, other than that the children didn't have nanites. He was pretty glad to hear that actually. He was dismayed to realize that Olive would likely outlive him by a few hundred years. There were some things that just couldn't be changed.

CHAPTER THIRTY FOUR

It was 8:30 A.M. when the mail tone sounded in the library at Annie's house. She put down her morning tea and rose from the breakfast nook. Annie took her time, there hadn't been any reason for her to hurry in many years. She sat at the mail screen and said, "Annie Boudreau, open mail." The panel lit up and displayed the first page, a cover page identifying the sender. Annie felt dizzy. She stared at the cover page for a full minute as her mind reeled and tried to get around what she was reading. There had to be some kind of mistake. The person who sent her this transmission had identified his self as Cy Hill. Finally she decided to go to the next page and attempt to figure out who would play such a cruel joke. But the next page was no joke, and she soon knew that the mail was indeed from Cy. It was true, what Brian and Charlie had said to her all those years ago, it was true. Cy had learned how to use the eddies to travel through time.

The letter simply read;

Dear Annie,
So you know that it is truly me who is writing this to you, remember the breakfast we shared at Tee's Diner, the many references to getting Sandy's swing in my back yard, and the night we all talked about the eddy at your wedding. Annie, I am in this time now to try and stop the eddies from causing any further harm. I will come this afternoon at 2:00 to visit you.
See you then.
Cy

P.S., I am bringing a friend that I am sure you will be happy to see.

She read and reread the letter trying to decide what to make of it. She had never told anyone the entire conversation that she and Cy had that morning. She realized it was nearly a century and a half ago, but she did remember well the humor and banter about the waitress. She also remembered the night they had told her about their belief that Dave was still alive somewhere. That was also the night that Lexi had crashed the party and stole the show with her story of coming from three hundred years before. If this letter wasn't from Cy then it was from someone who knew a lot of obscure and ancient history.

2:00 this afternoon, Cy would be here with Lexi no doubt. She must have decided to stay with Cy after all and not go back to 1705. Now they were bouncing about through time like that time lord in the old BBC show, Dr. Who. Here in 2184 to have tea with Annie and talk about old times then, fine she thought, let them come for tea!

Annie pressed the off switch and left the library for the kitchen. She wanted to finish her breakfast. If this was some kind of prank she wouldn't dignify it with a response, if it wasn't, then...

She spent the next few hours going about her morning business acting as though there were nothing out of the ordinary going on. She ordered tea for three to be prepared for Two o'clock complete with cakes and jam. Annie wasn't English, but she enjoyed the opportunity for a tea party none the less. When those details were attended to she went to the shopping center and picked out a new outfit. Unlike most of the people of the day, she didn't take her transport to the shopping center, she walked instead. It was a throw back to her day and age. Years of idleness helped to galvanize the uncommon activity. Most folks thought her eccentric to actually walk instead of use a transport. She owned one and used it on the occasion of going out of town, but for a short excursion, Annie thought it better to get some exercise. It was a twenty minute walk to the center. She completed her purchases and was home before One-Thirty. By One-Fifty she had changed and was receiving her tea and cakes from the food service. She sat almost nervously and waited for the chime at the front door. As though the clock and the chime were set by the same manufacturer, they rang simultaneously. She rose and went to the door. Opening it to the bright afternoon sun she was amazed at the sight of Cy. He had changed, gotten lean, grown a beard and tanned.

Where ever he had been in his travels he had been working harder than he had in their youth. When she saw Dave she fainted straight away.

As Annie was coming to she could hear voices, familiar and somewhat distant. She was unsure why she was unconscious and was trying to remember what was happening. Then she did remember. She sat bolt upright. Her eyes were wide and searching him out. When her gaze fell upon Dave for the first time in nearly one hundred and eighty years she couldn't decide if she was elated or furious. She stood and started to cross the room to him when her knees grew weak again and she thought she might faint all over again, so she paused. Regaining her composure she continued toward Dave. At that moment he saw her coming and rose to intercept her. He moved quickly to her and put his arms around her.

Dave said, "I've got you."

For a brief moment she allowed him to hold her as she tried to sort out what she was going to say. Then she pushed him back and said, "No, no Dave, you don't. Where the hell have you been for the last century and a half and what makes you think you can just pop in here like this after making me live an eternity without you?" Then she turned to Cy and said, "And you... I know you're behind this. Why didn't you just send him to me a hundred eighty years ago? Why did I have to go all this time alone if you could have given him back to me?" She broke into tears; tears of anger and frustration at lost youth.

Cy said, "Annie, trust me. You will have him to live your life with, the very life you've just lived. You'll live it again only with Dave by your side."

Annie's eyes filled with contempt when she looked at Cy now. A lifetime of aloneness welled up in her as she stared at him. She said, "There is NOTHING you can say to me that will give me cause to trust you. Trust you. Right, that IS the most obvious thing that you would ask of me."

Dave said, "Annie, Cy wanted me to just go home to you. He was going to come here to this time alone and hope that I was still alive and able to help him. We knew you were here. Our niece, Deirdra told us you were here still."

When Dave said Deirdra, Annie listened. She turned her fixed stare at Cy to look upon Dave's face.

Dave continued, "And do you remember the young man who disappeared a while ago? His name was Stephen Bryant. He was here running an errand. He remembered you too."

Annie looked away for a moment. She moved to a small divan and sat herself upon it. She felt she was getting light headed again and didn't want to fall too far. She looked at Dave again.

Dave pressed on, "I could have gone back to before I disappeared, but I decided to come here now instead because if we are successful then I won't ever disappear in the first place. Your last century and a half of being alone will not even be a memory. Our chances of making that a reality are much better this way, so much better that I gave up that time with you. I believe we'll have that lifetime, and longer."

Cy said, "Annie, I know you're angry, I don't blame you. I won't even ask you to forgive me. I will ask for your help though. We have a much greater chance of making this happen with you helping than without."

Annie was silent. She wanted to think about what they were saying. She wanted to weigh it all with what she knew from the past. She needed time. That was when the doorbell rang. She said, "I'll get that, you two just stay here." She left the room and made her way to the front door. As she was coming down the hall she could make out the silhouette of a man in the frosted glass of the door. That was the very moment she remembered the detective that had called her the day before and made the appointment to come see her today. Detective Plante as she recalled. Why didn't he come in the morning? She slowed her approach to the door as she realized that there was no way to explain Dave and Cy to this guy. Then again, she realized she didn't need to. It wasn't illegal to have house guests. She would simply tell him she had company and reschedule.

Annie opened the door. She looked at the detective. He appeared as he did four years ago when he came to talk with her about Deirdra. She mused to herself that he may have even been wearing the same coat then as he was wearing now. She said, "Detective Plante, it's good to see you."

Plante said, "Good afternoon Ms. Boudreau. How are you today?"

"I'm well thank you, and yourself?"

"I'm okay thanks. Is this a good time to talk?"

Annie tipped her head to the right side a bit and said, "Well to tell you the truth I had some unexpected company drop in. I'm not sure how long they'll be here. Is there any way we could do this another time?"

Plante said, "Sure, I understand. How about tomorrow morning, say, about 10:00?"

"That will be fine Detective, I am sorry to trouble you."

"Not at all, I'll see you then."

"Goodbye." Annie said pleasantly.

Plante turned and left the doorway. He went directly to his transport at the end of the walkway and slid into his seat. He turned and waved to Annie as the car ascended to traffic altitude and accelerated away.

Annie watched the transport leave her airspace and felt the stress of her company's presence return. She closed the door and went back to the living room where Dave and Cy were waiting. She sat in the arm chair across from the two men and looked at them. They were silent, waiting for her to give them an indication of her demeanor. After a while she said, "How am I supposed to explain to anybody, ANYBODY, your presence. Neither of you exist in this time. You aren't outfitted with ITC's, you aren't even in the National Codec and Census System. You guys are trouble looking for a place to happen."

Dave said, "Look Annie, I know we have a lot of things that are working against us. Please, believe me, all we have to do is stop this Professor Craig and we're back home living the life we were supposed to live."

Annie looked at Dave, her eyes were scrunched up at the acanthus. She knew that name from someplace, but was having difficulty remembering where she had heard it.

Dave said, "I know that look, do you know that guy?"

Annie said, "I know the name, I'm not sure from where." She thought for a few seconds and asked, "What is it about this guy?"

Dave said, "He's the guy that built the device that caused the eddies. It's called a Quantum Particle Accelerator. Sometime in the not too distant future, and we aren't sure when, he's going to fire it. When he does it will form the eddies through the future and the past. If we can stop it from happening, everything will go back to normal, at least we hope it will."

Cy winced.

Annie's eyes flared, "You HOPE it will? You don't even KNOW?" She stood and stormed to the window. She said to herself, more than to anyone, "I can't believe this. This is too bizarre." She looked at Cy and said, "This is too far out there, even for you Hill!"

Cy stood up. He said, "Okay Annie, I know how you feel. I'll leave." Then he looked at Dave and said, "Dave, I'm going back to the room, stay or come, that's up to you." He walked from the room and left the house.

Annie looked at Dave and said, "Why aren't you following him?"

Dave said, "Because I at least owe you the benefit of explanation, for your own knowledge." He got up and went to her, stopping when he could see that she felt he was getting too close. He said, "Annie, I never left you. I went out hiking in the woods with Morgan that afternoon. We were sitting out at the lake by Brian's barn. I must have dozed off, because when I woke up I was laying in a pile of cow manure, flopping about with Cy and Lexi looking at me. Lexi was doing her best not to giggle at me. Cy just smiled and asked me if I wanted a bath. Annie, that was six months ago."

Annie said, "No Dave, that was a hundred and seventy-eight years ago. I know because I counted. First I was the deserted wife. Then I was the widow of a freak disappearance when they declared you legally dead. Then after about thirty years I got sick. I tried the new nano technology and had the little robots injected. Boy, did they do the trick. The next thing I knew everyone wanted to see me, that's all, just SEE me. They were looking at me like I was a freak. For decades the world debated whether or not nanite technology would turn a human into some kind of cyborg. They all looked at me and watched, waiting. There were even lotteries based on my survival. No one wanted to come near me, but they all looked! Finally the looking stopped and people began using the little critters. I'm the oldest human ever. No one looks anymore, not at me anyway, now they look in the obituary page instead, to see if my name is there. I remember all of it because those little shit nanites fixed my brain cells and gave me perfect recall. I can't forget a day in the last hundred seventy years Dave, that's how I know it isn't six months ago! I sat over there in the dinette and had tea six months ago! Swimming around in a pile of shit sounds like a grand old time to me right about now Dave!" Annie's eyes were streaming a flow of tears. Her fists were clenched as her anger coursed through her body. She said, "Dave I got over you about a hundred years ago. I haven't loved anyone since, I don't have the capacity for it." The tension in her body eased and she visibly relaxed. "I don't even love myself. I don't care what you and Cy do, you two can stay in this time if you want or go back, that's up to you. This guy you're looking for, Professor Craig, he teaches at the UMass Space Campus. He has an estate on part of the old Wright farm. I remember when he was a boy, the professor title threw me."

She walked out of the room and was headed down the hall. Dave followed her, not sure what else to do. She went into her bedroom and straight to the nightstand. Dave stayed in the doorway and waited. She opened the top drawer and rummaged around for a few seconds and said, "Here it is." She took out a ½ pound bag of M&M's, turned and sat on the edge of the bed. The bag had already been opened and only needed to be untwisted. She opened it up and devoured a handful right away. While she sat there chewing she looked at Dave, then away again shaking her head.

Dave's eyes were welling up. He was stricken by the sight of her. She was as beautiful as when he saw her last, she appeared to be in her mid thirties. He was filled with guilt for making her live these hundred and seventy-eight years alone; for making her suffer. He said, "Annie, this is all we know to do. These eddies have to be stopped before they begin. If we can do that, everything will be different, the way it was supposed to be. Some things already are. You said this guy grew up on an estate that's on the old Wright farm. Before I was caught in the eddy I was sitting the barn that was by a lake that covered about three hundred acres of the Wright farm. Annie I remember the lake, do you?"

Annie was looking at him with an expression of disbelief. She said, "No, there's never been a lake there Dave, always just the farm. Until Brian's son had to sell some of it off. Then he put the bulk of it into a wildlife conservatory. What lake are you thinking of?"

Dave said, "Look Annie, when I was back in 1905 I worked for Brian's great, great grandfather Ezekiel Wright. I petitioned and won the case to have the three dams built on the Lawrence tributaries down in Peterston. The lake never happened after that, so of course you don't remember it. But you know who did remember it? Deirdra told me about it when she got caught in the eddy. Annie when we got married it was there at the Wright Farm on the lakeside."

Annie shook her head and said, "No, Dave, it was at the Wright Farm but no lakeside. There was never a lake there."

Dave was grinning now. He was realizing something that he wasn't sure how to express to Annie or if he even should. He decided not to and said instead, "Annie look, we really need to shut this guy down. Can you give me anything about him?"

Annie thought for a moment and said, "Well, I always thought it was strange how all of these people in his life were dying around him. But he was never suspected of any wrong doing. His sister died when they were just kids. He was there with her, but because he was just a small boy no one ever thought he had anything to do with it. But I thought it was a bit odd. The two of them climbing a tree and she falls. Dead before she hit the ground for hitting all of those branches on the way down. They said young William was so traumatized that he never even cried."

Dave said, "Well that's not too terribly odd, is it?"

She said, "That alone isn't, but years later when his parents died he didn't cry then either. The thing is, he inherited the estate. His sister would have gotten it if she were still alive but, she fell out of a tree."

"That's a little skimpy though don't you think?"

Annie said, "You know, I don't really know the guy, but I remember that anytime I would see him around town, he was always stone faced. So far as I know, he still is."

Dave thought for a moment. He said, "Well it's not likely that we could prove the murder of his sister, but his parents are more recent. I'll have to talk with Cy about this."

Annie tossed another couple of M&M's into her mouth. She said, "I'm sure I'm going to regret this."

Dave said, "What?"

Annie sighed deeply and said, "Look, go to where ever it is you and Cy are staying and bring him back here. You guys can stay here. We have an appointment tomorrow morning."

CHAPTER THIRTY FIVE

Plante's transport landed and parked itself curbside at Annie Boudreau's house in South Sheldon. He disembarked from the car and stood looking at her house. He was thinking about Trish Cody in Boston. She was a beautiful woman, and he was looking forward to being able to go back and see her again. First he needed something to justify the contact. If this case went bust he would have to simply rely upon his charm. Yeah, right. Plante knew he had all the sophisticated charm of a turnip. He would give it a try if he needed to but he really hoped this interview turned something up instead.

He approached the house and thought that there was something different today. Call it a cop's hunch, but he sensed something extraordinary was about to happen.

The front door opened even as he was stepping onto the front porch. Annie Boudreau stepped into the doorway and was smiling brightly. She said, "Good morning Detective Plante, please come in."

He said, "Good morning, thank you." And he entered the house.

She closed the door and stepped past him saying, "Please come with me Detective, my guests are still here, but I think you'll enjoy meeting them."

She led him through the foyer and down the hall. They passed right through the kitchen and out onto the patio in the back of the house. The patio was covered by an open portico with vines growing over it. By midsummer there would be wild grapes growing from the vines, not edible but they had an aesthetic quality that gave the patio an almost Grecian appearance. There were two men sitting by a dinette table enjoying coffee. Plante had no idea who they were but because of Annie's subtle yet intriguing build up, he was anxious to meet them.

As they approached Dave and Cy rose to their feet. Annie said, "Detective Plante, please allow me to introduce my husband Dave Boudreau and our old friend Cy Hill."

Plante had extended his hand as Annie was beginning the introduction but froze in his tracks as she was stating their names. He was mid-stride with his hand outstretched, his head turned toward Annie and his jaw agape.

She was obviously pleased by the effect this had on Plante. It proved that he had read up about her and was prepared in many ways for this interview. Unfortunately for him, there was no way that he could have prepared for this turn of events. Of course, he may not believe that this was Dave here before him. That would just make the meeting all the more… fun.

Dave was the first to speak. He said, "Good morning, Detective."

Plante snapped back to the moment. "Good morning." And he shook Dave's hand. Then he turned to Cy and shook his hand as well. "Good morning." He said again.

Cy responded, "Good morning Detective."

Annie said, "Please, Detective Plante, sit down and allow me to pour a cup of coffee for you. How do you like it?"

Plante said, "Black, please."

Annie poured the coffee for him.

Plante looked at Dave, he had seen the file photo of him. He showed no sign of aging since the photo was taken. Annie looked older, but Dave did not. And why was this Cy Hill a familiar character to him. He said, "Mr. Boudreau, I was under the impression that you went missing some time ago."

Dave smiled. He looked first at Annie then at the detective. He said, "Yes Detective, that's right. But here I am. Case solved."

Plante smiled. He looked at Annie and said, "Mrs. Boudreau, I value my time more than this. I don't know who these men are, or why you are playing this elaborate charade, but I really wish that if you didn't wish to speak with me you would just say so." He rose to leave.

Annie rose as well. She said, "Detective Plante, I assure you, this is in fact my husband and our friend Cy Hill who went missing just a few years later. Their explanation may seem somewhat fantastical but it is relevant to your visit today. And as fantastic as it is, I vouch for its truthfulness."

Plante stopped. He looked back at Cy, remembering where he had seen his face. It was another old file, but that one had no relevance to Craig. He said to Cy, "Okay, Cy, where's your wife?"

Cy said, "She's home. She wanted to see her parents."

Plante said to Annie, "You expect me to believe that these two guys are the genuine article?"

Annie said, "Detective Plante, I don't expect anything of you, other than you accepting that we are telling you the truth. There are more lives at stake here. More than Helen Craig, or her parents; more than Dr. Fish as well. They are only the beginning."

Plante nearly dropped his coffee mug. He looked at Annie with knitted eyebrows and a scowl on his face.

Dave said, "Oh, no Detective, looking at Annie like that won't get you anywhere."

At that, Plante turned his scowl toward Dave.

Annie said, "Detective Plante, Dr. Craig is working on a device that has long reaching ramifications."

He looked at Annie and said, "I had a feeling you knew more than you ever let on about the guy."

"Until yesterday I only had suspicions about him being overlooked for murdering his parents, then these two showed up for tea. A lot more fell into place afterward."

Plante said, "I want to hear what you have to say. Alone, without your two paid actors here mugging it up for my benefit."

Cy said, "Detective we'll wait in the living room. If you want to talk to us, we'll be happy to cooperate."

He stood and looked at Dave, who stood also. They left the patio and went inside.

Plante looked discerningly at Annie. He asked, "Who are they really?"

Annie sighed and said, "They are my husband, Dave Boudreau and our friend Cy Hill."

Plante said, "Alright, say I believe you, how is it they come to your door after all these years?"

She said, "Detective, this is difficult to explain. After all these years I still have trouble believing it as well. The thing is, with what they told me yesterday, it all fits and sadly, makes sense."

Annie leaned back into her seat and took a deep breath. She looked at the detective and began her story. She recounted the night when Dave was 'touched' in the trails out in the woods. Cy was the only one who had also experienced the ethereal touches. They now thought these touches were actually real time manifestations of someone passing through an eddy. Of course she had to explain an eddy to the best of her knowledge. The eddy at her wedding was the closest she had ever come to one herself but Dave had been caught in one a few years later. She told about Lexi coming from 1705, and wanting to go back. That was what Cy meant when he said she had gone home. At last she told him about Stephen Bryant being in 1907 when Dave and Cy were there. That Bryant's extensive understanding of the project Dr. Craig was working on had brought her husband and Cy here to try to stop him. The project involved a Quantum Particle Accelerator that would rip into the spacetime fabric and create the eddies that Dave and Cy had used to traverse the ether and arrive in this time."

This last part caught Plante's attention. He sat back and looked at Annie for a moment. Then he reached up and tapped his ITC. "Detective Trish Cody." He said. After a moment he heard her voice, "Detective Cody." Plante said, "Trish, this is Frank Plante, how are you today?"

She said, "I'm well Frank, what's up?" Plante said, "Trish do you know the nature or the name of the project that our boy was working on with Fish?"

A moment went by and he heard her say, "Yeah Frank, it's called the QPA Project. Let's see, it says here QPA stands for Quantum Particle Accelerator. They're supposed to fire it in outer space. Why?"

Plante said, "How about I tell you over dinner sometime?"

Cody said, "Business or pleasure?" Plante said, "A little of both, tomorrow night alright?"

She said, "You've got a date! I'll forward my home address to your transport. Pick me up at seven." "I'll be there!" With that he tapped his ITC and smiled in spite of himself.

Annie said, "I'm glad you got a date Detective, now could we get back to our conversation please?"

Plante nodded and said, "Let's get your boys back out here."

Annie rose and went inside. She came back out in under a minute with Dave and Cy behind her. They all sat and looked at Plante, letting him take the lead in the conversation.

Plante said, "Okay, I believe this. God help me, I may be going insane, but I do believe this. The detective in Boston who has the Professor Fish Case told me the name of the project that this Craig is working on, it jibes with what you're telling me Mrs. Boudreau. I'm no theoretical astrophysicist, but I know enough to understand that if what he is working on is completed, it won't matter when you live, it can reach you."

Cy said, "Annie, you do believe what's happening then."

She said, "You aren't off the hook yet mister."

Cy knew she was softening, beginning to forgive him for learning about and talking about the ether. She was finally seeing that he wasn't responsible for Dave's disappearance and she was uniting with him for the first time in all time against the real enemy.

Chapter Thirty Six

Hawk had Plante's transport reprogrammed. It was simple really. His file was to have been sealed. When the seal was opened, even by an officially officious officer of the law, Hawk was notified by an automated ITC message giving the time, date and identity of the offending party. Plante's transport was easily compromised by Hawk, who himself was an ingenious programmer. He broke through the system's simplistic security protocols and went straight to the onboard logs. Hawk implanted a daily directive to transmit all destinations, arrival and departure times and any other information in the onboard computer directly to his mainframe. The transport rebooted itself at the first docking opportunity and put all of the new command lines into effect.

Now Hawk knew where the industrious, do-gooder detective was. His next objective would be to tap Plante's ITC. This was a difficult matter. An ITC is such a personal device that most people are able to feel the device at work. During normal use the user's voice is transmitted from the unit. When the ITC is tapped however there is a slight delay, 0.012 second in the transmission which causes a very subtle feedback. This is a privacy feature installed by the device manufacturer to prevent tapping of ITC's. If Hawk could get around the feedback issue, which he was sure he could, he would be able to hear everything the detective was saying and hearing, 24/7.

For now he would have to content himself with following his moves. If it warranted all of the trouble to hack into the ITC, perhaps he would be better off just eliminating the detective altogether.

For the time being he had more pressing matters to contend with. The subassemblies were nearly completed and ever since that fool Bryant had gone and gotten himself lost, the final preparations were entirely on Hawk's shoulders. It was probably just as well. Any fool who could get lost with the automated transport technology of the day at his fingertips, was too incompetent to be a part of Hawk's team. He would have to bring someone else up to Bryant's position soon though. There was too much for one man to handle without bungling one end or the other. It was a bit like trying to be on both ends of a log that you were trying to lift. For now there was no way to be in two places at one time. For now Hawke pressed his ITC and said, "Haley Orson." Shortly he heard, "This is Haley." He said, "Haley, this is Hawk, would you come to the lab early in the morning please? I have something that I would like to discuss." She said, "Certainly Professor, I mean Hawk, I'll be there at half past eight instead of nine if that is early enough." He said, "That will be splendid, thank you." And he tapped out before she could say anything else. She would be the perfect successor to Bryant. She had some hero worship thing for him, he knew. That was understandable, most women were very attracted to him. Haley would be like putty in his hands. She was also very knowledgeable about the project. Her GPA was only slightly lower than Bryant's. What she may lack in the understanding of quantum mechanics she would make up for in her undying love for him. This would be a good move for the project and it would also free up some of his personal time to track the detective.

Hawk had to change his plan to fire the accelerator remotely. With this detective from Sheldon looking at him he felt he would be better off in the safety of outer space. He also decided he would shift the remaining subassembly effort to the space campus from the south Boston warehouse. There was less likelihood of a search warrant being issued to search the prestigious UMass Space Campus. Hawk wanted to protect the project at all costs. This would also allow him to oversee the construction of the firing platform. Besides, freighting the subassemblies, especially now, when they are small and manageable, wouldn't involve the need for a booster rocket. Freight transports could be used to lift smaller payloads into orbit. That suited Hawk just fine, fewer inquiries.

Sometimes, Hawk marveled at his problem solving genius. He decided to leave the details of the move to Haley Orson. She would be so anxious to please him that there was no possibility that she would foul it up. Oh, he supposed he would have to throw her some kind of romantic overture to placate her lusting for him. He either had to fully and outright reject a woman or woo her with a bit of attention if he was ever to get any work done. Perhaps a bottle of Champaign and some strawberries at 8:30 the next morning would be enough of a dangling of the proverbial carrot in front of her. Yes, the poor girl didn't have a chance, between his rugged good looks and sophisticated demeanor, and a bottle of Moet & Chandon, perhaps 2108 or 9, they were both good years, she would be putty in his hands.

Hawk left the warehouse. He boarded his transport and said aloud, "Acquire link to transport Plante 1."

Within a half minute the transport's computer responded, "Link acquired."

"Display specified log." He said. The log scrolled onto his screen. It was a detailed account of the transports usage since the day before when Hawk had last checked it. It was odd to see that the transport was in the Sheldon Police Maintenance barn. It had been sitting there since last evening. After he had returned from Boston where the transport had docked and rebooted, he went to the Sheldon library. From there he went to a small diner to fill his fat little face. Then back to police headquarters. The next operator to log into the transport was Eugene Sutter, a transport technician with the SPD. The transport was going in for routine maintenance. The only thing that bothered Hawk was that according to the archive logs, maintenance wasn't due for another three hundred hours. Why had the Detective put it in for early scrubbing and seal checks. The computer was awake and operative. He would check the status later. For now Hawk tapped the on screen icon for his space campus quarters. He was tired of the warehouse district and craved a more refined environment. Interestingly enough, he found he also wished for female companionship as well. Perhaps he would have Haley Orson come to his quarters tonight instead of waiting until tomorrow.

The transport rose quickly through the atmosphere. When it reached the troposphere the curvature of the earth was more apparent and Hawk thought, the most beautiful at this altitude. Any lower and it's difficult to distinguish and once you move into orbit the earth just looked like a ball. He said, "Hover." The transport stopped it's ascent and hovered at this altitude, awaiting further input. Hawk just wanted to enjoy the view. He was out of high traffic areas and not in the shipping lanes. So he sat, for five minutes until the O2 alarm sounded. This was his little ritual, the alarm sounds and he knows he has ten minutes of O2 remaining to make the two minute remainder of the journey to the space campus. He was bored. These little games were his only diversion. Finally he said, "Continue to previously designated coordinates." The transport resumed its ascent and within fifteen seconds the space campus was looming ahead. The transport went directly to Hawk's docking bay and docked itself, at which time a surge of O2 refilled the onboard tanks. The docking post rotated and the transport was moved inside of an energy field envelope that contained breathable atmosphere. Hawk opened his door and disembarked from the car. The envelope immediately shifted and surrounded him alone leaving the transport in a vacuum. He had changed into his Velcro slippers before he got out of the transport and now he walked in zero gravity with a well practiced and well poised grace of a nobleman. Most people looked like blue herons walking with the Velcro footwear but Hawk made it look like he was walking on earth. He entered the airlock. When the door behind him closed, air rushed in and pressurized the room. The inner door opened and allowed him to enter his quarters. He tapped his ITC and said,

"Send message." Then tapped again to begin dictating the message, "Haley Orson, This is Hawk. I found I was able to return to space campus earlier than expected. If you are able to come to my quarters at anytime during the remainder of the day I would find that agreeable. Please don't feel the need to return a message, if you show up here fine if not I will see you at the warehouse tomorrow morning at 8:30 A.M. Thank you Haley." He tapped the ITC to send the message. Then he went to the refrigeration unit and took out a bottle of Champaign and the strawberries he had been thinking about. He put the bottle in a pail on ice and set the strawberries in a tray on the side board. Then he stepped into his room for a change and a sonic shower. Water was used on earth, but on a facility in space water was a precious commodity.

Hawk wore his bathrobe, and nothing else. He had decided to give Haley all that she desired and so make her life complete. He was sitting in an armchair not ten minutes later reading the thirtieth reprinting of Stephen Hawking's <u>The Universe in a Nutshell,</u> when the door tone sounded. He said out loud to the computer, "Identify." The computer scanned the visitors ITC and reported, "Haley Orson." Hawk rose and said, "Enter."

The door opened and Hawk was gratified to see Haley walk in with nearly the same poise as he had with the Velcro slippers. She was smiling broadly, her eyes open wide to take in all of her heart's desire. He admired her for a moment. She had long auburn hair tied back and up in a jaunty fashion. She was wearing a long dress, the lower hemming was flowing up and about her legs freely for lack of gravity. She stood there before him, expectantly, almost awkwardly.

Hawk said, "Haley, I'm so happy you were able to come this evening."

She said, "Thank you Pro…uh, Hawk. I was surprised that you called upon me, let alone invited me this evening. I didn't think you even knew my name."

"Oh, my goodness, yes Haley, I took notice of you long ago." Hawk said with his natural charm, "You are my prized pupil. I would like to get right to the point, Haley, I wish to offer you the internship position recently vacated by Stephen Bryant. In this position, you would be directly under me, servicing my needs." He said this with a bit of a lurid smile, allowing his eyelids to lower as well to be sure she understood his intent. She was sure to see and succumb to his wiles.

Haley's eyes grew wider, if that was possible, she said, "Oh Prof.. Hawk, thank you. I would love to accept the position. I would love to work… under you."

Hawk smiled and said, "I'm so glad. I have some Champaign and strawberries… shall we celebrate your new… position?"

She smiled with nearly as much lasciviousness as he and said, "I think that would be wonderful."

They retired to his bed chamber where they allowed their passions to take them.

CHAPTER THIRTY SEVEN

Cy sat alone on the patio thinking about Lexi. It occurred to him that if he should fail, he could go to 1706 and watch over her until she came of age and they could marry again. Yeah, right. Dave and Annie were gone to dinner together. Cy decided to give them time to talk, alone. What an incredible hardship to overcome. They now had a one hundred eighty year age difference. Most people had two or three, perhaps up to ten but one-eighty seemed significant.

Cy was trying to decide if Detective Plante believed anything he had heard the day before. He had listened intently to the story he and Dave told. He seemed to believe them but Cy had to face it, this story was out there. After Plante had left, Annie wanted some time alone, so Dave and Cy went to the library to consult the archives about the Craig family. They both felt they needed to learn as much about him as possible in the next few months. If there could be a chance of stopping him it would be in the small details. They decided to begin with his family history in Sheldon. There were no more news papers, for the last hundred fifty years that medium had been replaced with hand held technology. If you wanted a Sheldon News you simply entered authorization for payment into your hand top computer and the news was immediately transmitted into it. You could read at your convenience. The library had a mainframe, or what would be considered a mainframe in this time, that sat on a table in the center of the reading area. You could be issued a hand top specifically designed for access to the archive memory banks and investigate from the comfort of an armchair. This differed from when Lexi and he were looking up Dave's obituary on microfiche down in the basement.

Cy had entered Craig's info as search criteria and received an impressive amount of data in return. As follows:

"Craig, William Jonas. DOB; 9-Sep-2142.
Parents; Father, Alexander William Craig, 2073 – 2169
          Mother, Marian Eileen Craig, 2077 – 2169
Siblings; Sister, Helen Marie Craig, 2139 – 2151
William Jonas Craig attended Sheldon Elementary School until third grade when he was transferred to the Massachusetts State Institute for the Academically Gifted. He earned his H.S. Diploma at age twelve, Baccalaureate Degree at fifteen, PhD at eighteen. Dr. Craig is a Professor at University of Massachusetts Space Campus leading research into Quantum Physics as related to the spacetime continuum. His current project is the Quantum Particle Accelerator Project currently in assembly. The project is expected to be tested in April 2186." There were more details regarding Craig's childhood that Cy scanned over. Nothing seemed to jump out at him. What did seem odd is the deaths of Craig's family members.

Later when they were together Dave and Cy discussed the information. Dave said, "Plante is on the right path, I think, suspecting this guy in these deaths."

Cy said, "Yeah, it seems like too much of a coincidence that these people buy it and he benefits."

The estate had been purchased in 2065 by Craig's grandfather. There were photographs of the manse that stood on the property. It had been built on a field that Cy recognized. He and Zeke worked that field not more than two weeks ago. There wouldn't even be a field there if it hadn't been for Dave. Everything would be under water. Ironic.

Cy asked, "Dave, what do you think, should we go check this place out?"

Dave grinned and said, "Sure, let's do it tonight."

Cy said, "I wonder what kind of security is in place."

Dave said, "Ask the computer."

Cy said, "You don't honestly think there will be any information about security systems in here?"

Dave said, "Just punch it in, bonehead!"

Cy grinned and typed 'security' into the blank space provided for questions about the current topic. What came up surprised both of them. "Hill Security Systems Inc.'

Cy sat back in his seat. Dave said, "Well, I didn't see that coming."

Cy said, "Dude, this IS too much of a coincidence to be real. We must check this company out."

"Yeah, let's go now."

They took note of the address and returned the hand top to the librarian. The business was located about a mile from the library. They decided to walk. The streets were primarily for parking transports and pedestrian traffic. The sounds along the way were different now from both their own time and from 1906. No horses nickering or neighing, no cars engines roaring or horns blaring as they drove down the road. The traffic coursing overhead was silent. People were out walking to their local destinations. Children were playing in the streets without worry of being hit by a car. Society had changed, and from what they had seen so far, for the better. The stroll to the security company took only twenty minutes.

When the building came into view Cy stopped in his tracks. He turned to Dave, a look of puzzlement on his face and said, "Dude, wait." He looked at the building and then back at Dave, "Something's odd here. I was the only son in my family. There weren't any other Hill families around, 'cause my father moved here from up state New York. Sarah was my only sibling, so why is the Hill family name associated with this outfit?"

Dave said, "You know Cy there could be a million different reasons for that. This may be a different family, maybe it doesn't have anything to do with a family name at all. Then again maybe your Dad started the business after you disappeared and the name just stuck. Let's go find out shall we?"

Cy thought about it briefly and said, "Yeah you're right. After all, there is only one way to find out isn't there?" So with great trepidation on Cy's part, they walked in.

The door was a wood frame with a transparent poly-resin window pane that ran the full length of it. A bell hung on a spring bracket above the door jamb and rubbed against the top of the door as it opened and closed to alert the proprietor of customer's coming and going. The air inside the shop had a hint of mustiness and disinfectant cleaner. Clean but lived in, a comfortable space to enter. A man behind the counter seemed vaguely familiar. At first Cy looked to find a family resemblance, but couldn't see one. The man stood about Cy's height but thinner; sandy blonde hair with a touch of gray at the temples. He walked around the counter and approached Cy and Dave. There was a noticeable limp in his gait. The shopkeeper asked, "So, when're you fellers from?" And he grinned broadly.

Dave laughed out loud. He had the moment of recognition. He said, "Well, we're from whenever! Howdeedo Steve?"

At Steve's name Cy couldn't believe he had not recognized him. He laughed and said, "I see you changed your name."

Steve said, "Yeah, we thought that would get your attention." Then he tapped his ITC and said, "Dee, their here," and tapped it off. He said, "Well, how about we play catch up. When did you guys arrive?"

Dave said, "We've been here for five days now, how about you?"

Steve said, "Oh, I never really left. I've been waiting here for you for a long time now. I watched you two grow up. I was here when you disappeared Dave and when you and Lexi took after him Cy. I've been watching it all from my own distance trying not to interfere. I figure I'm pushing close to four hundred and twenty years old. These nanites keep a body pretty well."

Just then the front door opened causing the bell to chime. Cy and Dave turned to see Olive walk in. She said, "Hi guys!" and ran to Cy first then Dave and gave them hugs. She stepped over to Steve and kissed him and said, "Hi hon."

Steve said, "It took about fifty years for us to see that we were two peas in a pod. Zeke had passed away and in order to not raise suspicion Olive here faded away from the family. After a generation she was invisible to them. She's been able to watch generations of her children grow up. She changed her name back to Deirdra and I changed my last name to Hill, we figured it would get your attention. We opened this home security business about eighty years ago." Steve grinned, "We managed to get the Craig estate as a client about fifty two years ago."

Deirdra said, "We have unlimited access to the estate. It took you long enough to find us!"

Dave said, "Three days? That seems pretty quick to me!"

Cy said, "So you're telling me that we can get inside the estate any time we want to?"

Steve said, "That's right, there's a few things I think you boys should do first. Get ITC's, we'll have to get some uniforms for you too so you don't look suspicious."

Dave asked, "How or where do we get ITC's?"

Steve said, "I'll set you up at the clinic, tomorrow morning. Let's get the uniforms in the back room and get you guys set up."

Cy was looking at Deirdra, waiting for the right moment. She beat him to the punch though, she said, "Ezekiel got her home alright Cy."

Cy looked away. His eyes were filling as he choked up. He said, "So that's it then. You know, when I kissed her good-bye three days ago I knew I was sending her to her death."

Deirdra said, "No Cy, she got there fine."

Cy said, "Don't you see, Deirdra, by the time Zeke got back to you, Ezra had lived her life out to whatever end she had. I left her three days ago. She died over four hundred years ago. And now, after this, I'll never know her."

Deirdra just said, "I understand Cy, I'm sorry."

Cy got up from the seat on the patio. It was mid-afternoon and there seemed to be some clouds rolling in. He reached up behind his right ear and rubbed gently. The ITC installed that morning had caused some slight swelling and some minor itching. They had activated and tested it immediately after the install. Having this thing in his head would take some getting used to. He could see the sense in it, even if there were only a few people he could call.

Tonight they would go into the Hawk's lair. They knew Detective Plante would be out on a date and wouldn't be poking around.

Now all they needed to know was what they were looking for. It seemed unlikely that this guy had incriminating evidence kicking around that would jump out and bop them over the head. On the other hand, nobody expects that. The general idea was to gain insight into his head, to understand what he is capable of. They needed to know that.

CHAPTER THIRTY EIGHT

That night, Plante sat across from Trish Cody. They were in a secluded booth in the back of an Italian restaurant. There was a candle burning on the table which made it difficult for Plante to see her face. He reached forward and moved the candlestick to the left a bit. The glow of the candle resting on her face made her appear softer than he remembered at her office. He struggled, trying desperately not to appear clumsy or oafish. He smiled a subdued smile, and he could feel himself blushing right down to his toes, unsure how much redness she could make out in the dim light.

He said, "Well, how about we get the business out of the way then."

Trish smiled and said, "That will leave all the more time for the pleasure."

"Sure," he said not wanting to linger on it, "What do you know about this quantum particle acceleration technology?"

Trish smirked and shrugged her shoulders and said, "Nothing. I don't get any of that gibberish. Why?"

Plant said, "Well what I am able to understand about it is that it's supposed to make time travel possible. I'm completely lost on the math part of it, but the layman's terms explanation that I was able to get boiled it down to that."

Trish said, "Time travel. That loony tune has been able to convince a University to sponsor him to build equipment that is for time travel? I'm in the wrong line of work."

Plante said, "Well, I met two guys yesterday that claim that it worked. They even claim to be from another time, in the past, and they got here by using the rips in the fabric of time created by Hawk's machine fired in the future."

Trish asked, "Did you have a few before you came to pick me up tonight big fella? It's alright, but you should let me catch up before you start throwing this stuff out at me."

Plante hung his head, grinning, but somewhat embarrassed about what he was telling her. He said, "Have you ever heard of Annie Boudreau?"

"Sure, everyone knows who she is, why?"

"Trish, she's the one who is vouching for these two guys. She positively identified one of them as her husband."

Trish's brow wrinkled as she thought, "I thought he went missing about a hundred years ago."

"One hundred seventy is more like it, 2005 was the year. The second man is their childhood friend Cy Hill. Mr. Hill and his wife went missing about two years after Dave Boudreau. Mrs. Hill is still missing. They claim she went home to her parents."

"Well, it sounds like she's the only one with any sense."

"Her parents live in 1706."

"Aw geeze." Trish laughed out loud. "Frank Plante, tell me this has all been a joke that you made up just to ask me out. You're a bit shy, that's cute. So you manufacture this elaborate tale to lure me out of my safe haven of a home into the public domain where you can get me drunk and take advantage of me. Go ahead, you can tell me."

Plante was still grinning. He looked down and then at Trish and said, "I really wish I could tell you that. The fact is the story keeps getting better. They claim to have spent an extended amount of time in 1903 through 1906 with two other Sheldon missing persons. They claim that one of them said he was the right hand man to none other than Professor William Craig of UMass Space Campus. Trish, they want to stop this project. There is one other thing. My transport is being monitored by someone. It recently rebooted itself. I had the motor pool tech run a quick diagnostic and he confirmed that an outside entity had downloaded something into it."

Trish thought for a few minutes and finally said, "The thing is Frank, none of this is evidence. So far all you've told me would get both of us locked up in the cuckoo's nest if we used it as reasoning to investigate him. Do you have anything tangible?"

Plante said, "No. Just a good enough story to ask you out on a date, lure you out of your safe haven home, get you drunk and take advantage of you." He managed to deadpan through it but when he finished, he smiled.

Trish said, "Fair enough. I'll dig some more on my end. We'll see if we can ground the time lord." Then she reached across the table and took Plante's hand and said, "Now, no more talk of Hawks that fly in space. He's off limits for the rest of the night."

Plante said, "Deal. So tell me about yourself."

The night before, Hawk had allowed himself to indulge in a dalliance with his new assistant. She was attending to project concerns presently, but would be back in the next hour or so. Hawk took the opportunity to reacquaint himself with Detective Plante's transport and determine where he had been. He logged into his personal terminal and touched the icon to acquire the connection to the transport. After a moment the transport logs appeared on his screen. For the most part nothing seemed out of the ordinary. Then Hawk saw something that raised his curiosity. Thursday, April 15, 2184 at 9:00 A.M. what was the good detective doing at Annie Boudreau's home. So far as Hawk was concerned there was nothing Annie Boudreau knew or could possibly contribute against him. Perhaps she could be of use; the world renowned Annie Boudreau, known far and wide as the oldest woman in the world. Who would suspect anything but natural causes if she were to die. Hawk smiled. He could demonstrate his genius through the reprogramming of the nanites in her body. After all, if he could trace the transport and not be detected, how could Plante find a way to connect him to her death. With his natural cunning and technical expertise, this fool Plante would never even pick up a trail.

He called up the files in the mainframe for nanite programming. After only a few moments he had found the inroad within the program that would allow him to accomplish what he wanted. Exuberant, Hawk loaded his program into a laser guided microwave transmitter and set the coordinates to transmit the program in a tightly collimated beam directly at Annie Boudreau's house. He configured the transmission for a three hour duration beginning at 7:00 P.M. This way he would be sure the program changes would reach the nanites.

He confirmed the send command and decided this would be a good time for a cup of tea. That would do it, a nice hot cup of tea before Haley returned.

The commercial transport was surprisingly comfortable. Cy and Dave sat on a couple boxes in the back, while Steve and Deirdra sat on the seats in the front. Steve had contacted Dr. Craig and told him that there were upgrades to the security system that he wanted to install and asked if tonight would be acceptable. The good doctor agreed and confirmed that he would be remaining aloft at the space campus for the next few nights and to take all the time needed.

Annie had remained at home. She hadn't met Steve and hadn't seen Deirdra since she had disappeared. Now she would be nearly four hundred years old. That made Annie want to take a serious look at how she approached her future. As she told Dave, it was one thing to think that she was two hundred years old, and another to think that she was two hundred years young.

Dave said to Cy in a low voice, "I think Annie may be softening to the possibility of she and I getting back together."

Cy smiled and said, "That's wonderful Dave. You need to get some of those nanites so you can keep up with her."

"That's for sure. She's in better shape now than when we got married."

Cy asked, "What do you think of these ITC things we've got stuck in our skulls?"

Dave laughed and said, "If it wasn't for the fact that we're in the future, I'd say it seemed futuristic."

Cy laughed.

Steve said, "Alright guys, we're coming into the estate now. Put your caps on and remember where I told you the cameras are. Hawk could be watching from space, it's his house and his right to look in on us. I don't believe he ever has, but you never know. Do you all know what to do?"

Dave said, "We carry the tool box and replacement multiplex panels into the security control room, when we get in we wait for you."

Steve said, "Right, Dee and I walk the perimeter once together and smile for the cameras, then Dee will come in and join you two in the control room. I'll set the transport in a surveillance hover pattern around the structure and await Dee's call."

Deirdra said, "Once I'm in, I initiate the camera shutdown, I call you when they are all off."

Steve said, "Then I go in, Dee and I can handle the installs and you two can poke around the house while you sweep for surveillance equipment. Remember, do a thorough job, if he has his own bugs in here I want to report that to him. If I don't report a bug of his, then he'll know I didn't do a very good job of sweeping. I'd tell you where to look but he moves this stuff around so check everywhere."

"We should take about three hours to complete the hardware changes. The two of you on a bad day should be able to sweep a house twice this size in half that time. So that leaves you with at least an hour to an hour and a half to search." Deirdra said, and added, "Remember, only search a room after you've cleared it and even then, make sure the door is closed."

Steve added, "Use your ITC's, keep them open between you until we finish."

Cy said, "We've got it."

With no further discussion, and in silence, the four exited the transport. Deirdra and Steve each went in their own direction they would meet up on the far side and each continue their circle while maintaining ITC contact. Cy and Dave lifted the equipment from the rear of the transport and went for the front door. Cy took the remote door opener from his coverall uniform and depressed the open switch. The main entrance clicked, then opened. They continued up the stairs and into the front entrance. The door remained open after they passed. Steve would close it once he came in.

6:05 P.M.

Annie opened the door of her transport and stepped from it. She had been out visiting a friend. With so much going on around her she needed to just get out for a while and not think. She left the transport and pressed the park button. The transport rose and glided easily to the docking port. She felt weary tonight and looked forward to getting to bed early. She entered the house at the back door.

6:55 P.M.

Hawk had just finished his tea when he heard the tone at the front door announcing Haley's presence. Her punctuality pleased him. Perhaps he had made the wrong decision initially by naming Stephen Bryant as his intern assistant. Haley Orson was proving herself to be an exemplary assistant. She was punctual, intelligent, paid attention to detail and best of all, much more comfortable to curl up next to in bed than Bryant would have been. She crossed the central chamber with a sultry gleam in her eye. When Haley had come within arms reach she stopped and waited for her master to give her permission to come nearer. Hawk looked at her approvingly and said, "Report!"

Haley submissively regarded Hawk and said, "The first day of freight went as planned. I was able to procure an additional cargo transport for tomorrow. That will allow us to complete the move from the warehouse a full day ahead of schedule."

Hawk grinned. He said to his love slave, "You may wait for me in my bed."

This was the approval she desired to hear from him. Haley didn't utter a sound but turned and with a carefully controlled gait, strode from his computer room across the central chamber to the bedroom.

Hawk turned his attention to earth. He tapped in the commands to perform a confidential inquiry as to Annie Boudreau's whereabouts. The computer came back almost immediately with its results, reporting a 99.99% likelihood that she had returned home.

Hawk smiled. He stood and walked away from the computer console to his bedroom. He needed a diversion.

7:00 P.M.

Annie felt very tired. She decided she must be fighting a virus of some sort; something the nanites hadn't encountered before. Whenever that happened she found that by just going to bed and sleeping she freed them up to isolate the new bug and fight it. She made a cup of tea and brought it with her to bed. When she got there she felt over come with fatigue. She was only able to take one sip of tea, then she lay herself down on the bed, fully clothed. As Annie drifted off to sleep she thought of Dave, and with his image on her mind she lost consciousness.

7:10 P.M.

Cy and Dave were making their way through the rooms with the sweeping equipment. As they entered each room, one would go left and the other right. They would step around each other at the far end and continue until they were both back at the door. Then they would compare the results of their individual sweeps. If the data agreed they would proceed accordingly. Some rooms had listening devices only. Those rooms they could search as long as they didn't talk. The rooms that had cameras were off limits for searching. Clean rooms presented no threat and they searched them freely.

When two and a half hours passed, Steve called on ITC. He simply said, "Thirty minutes gentlemen."

Cy and Dave were in the last room to be swept. They had catalogued the entire house, finding 12 cameras and four microphones that had been planted for them to find. They had also had ample opportunity to search as well. So far they had turned up nothing. The room they were in now seemed to contain a very large computer system. It seemed to be on but the screen was inactive. They both knew that this would be a very likely place for a bug. Oddly nothing showed on the sweep. When they reached the main entrance to the room and compared results, Dave gave Cy a suspicious and inquisitive look. Cy leaned his head toward the door and they stepped from the room and returned to a room they knew was clean.

Dave asked, "What do you think?"

Cy said, "Well, the equipment tells me one thing but my gut says different."

Dave said, "You know, these sweepers are designed to detect transmissions from microphones and mini-cameras with high frequency transmitters. What if the mic or the camera were hard wired?"

Cy thought for a moment and said, "You know, for someone who is stupid enough to lose a hundred years in the woods, you're a pretty smart guy."

"Well, I managed to land right in front of you, didn't I?"

Cy said, "Yeah, in a pile of cowshit."

Dave shrugged and said, "Okay, since you're the smart one, what do you propose we do about the computer room?"

Cy said, "I know that room has something in it. I also know that it's supposed to look easy. It's too easy, don't you think?"

Dave said, "Yeah, I agree." He tapped his ITC and said, "Steve Bryant."

Steve responded, "What's up, Dave?"

"Steve, we just swept the computer room, it's clean but we don't trust the results. We want to check the computer. What do you think?"

"Whoa fella, the computer is tied in with his system in his quarters on space campus. Accessing either panel displays identical echoes on the other panel. So he'll be able to watch every thing you do. Even if he isn't at his console, he will see it later. And he'll know who was playing on it, that system has an onboard camera, hardwired, which is why you got a clean sweep result in there."

Dave said, "So we're clear and done."

"Well, I didn't exactly say that. Go back in and sweep the room again. Start the same way as before. This time the first one of you to pass the console should "accidentally" touch the screen, only once. This will bring it out of sleep mode, but not record a stroke. He won't have any report of it at his console in space. It's a 50/50 chance that the camera is on, and worth getting a look at the screen. Second man can get a pic of the screen and we can look it over back at the shop. Sound like a plan?"

Dave said, "Okay, we'll do that and meet you outside." He tapped his ITC and related all Steve had told him to Cy.

Cy said, "I have the camera on my sweeper, so you get to the screen and touch it, I'll take the shot."

Dave nodded and they left the room. In under a minute they were sweeping the computer room again. He arrived at the computer and as he touched the screen he cleared his throat as he moved away. Cy stepped up to the screen with his head down looking at his sweeper panel. He aimed and pressed the 'Save Image' button. Then Cy, in his turn cleared his throat and they made their exit from the room.

Hawk rose from bed. He went to his computer room to check on the progress of his nanite virus download. As he approached the console he noticed a flashing icon on the screen, an alert signal from his estate system. He switched the screen to display from the monitor camera on earth. The room stood empty. He pressed "Playback" and was not surprised to see two amateurish sweepers making a circle around the room. What did puzzle him came after, when they returned and each swept half of the room and left. He made a mental note to call that idiot at Hill

Security tomorrow. He made a cursory check of the home log and felt gratified to see that there had been no tampering with the computer. Hawk then checked the nanite virus. The download was complete. Annie Boudreau, if not already dead would soon be.

CHAPTER THIRTY NINE

Trish Cote's transport was parked on the aft deck of the world cruiser. The artificial atmosphere smelled as fresh as an afternoon by the lake. They were cruising at sixty-four thousand feet, there is very little breathable air at that altitude. Plante and Trish were sitting on the plush deck chairs provided on the cruiser. They had left the restaurant and caught the cruiser as it made a Boston stop. A stop for this vehicle meant descending to twenty thousand feet where personal transports could reach it and to two hundred fifty miles per hour so they could catch it and park on its deck.

Plante said, "I really like riding these cruisers."

"Well, anytime you want to go for a spin on one, I'm game." Said Trish.

The cruiser had ascended again and they were out over the Atlantic. They would descend again in London, after about a twenty minute trip 'across the pond.'

Plante held Trish's hand and thought about stealing a kiss when he heard a tone from his ITC. He tipped and shook his head and said, "I've got a call, excuse me." He didn't leave, he just tapped his ITC and said, "This is Plante." A look of disbelief came over his face, and he said, "Are you sure?" then, "I'll be there as soon as I can."

Trish recognized the look. She said, "Let's get to the transport, we can catch the next cruiser back to Boston."

Plante just nodded. They got to their feet and made their way to the transport bay. The cruiser slowed and descended to twenty thousand and the transport bay depressurized as transports exited and entered. They exited the bay and Trish commanded the transport back to Boston. At lower altitudes with a denser atmosphere, the trip would take a much longer time this way, but it would take longer to wait for the next cruiser bound for Boston.

He finally spoke saying, "You may want to come along on this one. SPD received an ITC alert. Annie Boudreau."

ITC's were programmed to alert the local police departments when the owners body temperature dropped, signifying either hypothermia or death.

Trish said, "Are they sure?"

"Patrolmen are en route. They expect confirmation soon."

"Listen Plante, first; you owe me a romantic cruise around the earth, second, I'll come with, and third, you were just at her place interviewing her yesterday, this can't be a coincidence."

Plante sighed, "I know. This Hawk guy is all over this thing, I can feel it."

Trish took his hand and said, "We'll get him."

The Hill Security crew had returned to the shop. The equipment from the nights work had been stowed and secured. Dave and Cy were milling about the shop, disappointed with the nights discoveries, which seemed minimal at best.

Steve said, "Don't be too disappointed, at least you know where there isn't anything to find."

Deirdra added, "Yeah, and this place was the toughest nut to crack when it comes to getting in."

Cy said, "I bet if were going to find anything it'll be in the computer. We need to get the image out of the sweeper logs so we can see what was on the screen."

"Right, there may be a clue there for us. I'll get the decoder, you set the sweeper up on the work bench." Steve said and he went to the storage room to get the decoder. When he returned he set the unit on the bench next to the sweeper. He switched on the interface transceiver and jacked the decoder into the back of the sweeper. They went to the computer console and Steve touched the screen. The monitor illuminated before them. Steve selected an icon on the screen and the image that the sweeper cam had snapped of Hawk's home computer came on the monitor.

"It's out of focus," said Dave.

"I can clean it up." Steve said, and he started to enhance the image. In less than a minute the image became clear. "Dee, do you know anything about this programming language?"

Deirdra looked at it for a moment and said, "It looks like an old form of a very old program, ForTran they called it; it stood for Formula Translation. That was used back in the twentieth and twenty first centuries. These are the most simplistic of command strings though, and fragmented all over the place; almost as if each command line were independent of the other. This doesn't make any sense."

"What's wrong with it?" asked Dave.

"Well, a program should run all inclusive. Each of these strings is a short command unto itself. There's a codec in each one that seems to tie them all together, but in no logical structured sequence, it's like a collective hive program."

Cy asked, "What would run a program like this?"

Deirdra sighed deeply and said, "Well, a CHP is used in technology like in our nanites. But it doesn't make sense that Hawk would have such a program on his console. Does his project use a CHP environment Steve?"

Steve said, "Not unless he changed things a lot since I went for my spin, which was just last week."

Dave said, "Why is Annie's address on the top left corner of his screen?"

A mystified realization came over Steve's face as he said, "You know something, this is a transmission screen. Whatever this program is, it's being beamed into Annie's house."

Deirdra stayed behind and examined the program closer as Steve, Dave and Cy ran to the transport.

They were half way to Annie's when Steve heard a tone on his ITC. He tapped and said, "Steve here." After only a few seconds he tapped off. He said, "That was Dee, the program is a nanite virus.

The transport rounded into view of Annie's house. There were police transports hovering curbside with their blue strobes flashing. They landed a half block away. Dave and Cy ran from the transport even as the doors were still opening.

When they reached the police line Dave said, "I'm Dave Boudreau, this is my Wife's home. What's happening?"

The officer said "Wait here." He went to the center of the crowd of cops and came back out after only a brief moment and waved Dave in.

Cy decided to not be left behind and stayed on Dave's tail.

When the two got into the crowd of police they were surprised to see Detective Plante there with an attractive woman at his side.

Plante said, "Mr. Boudreau, do you have nanite technology in your system?"

Dave said, "No, neither of us do." Gesturing to Cy.

Plante said, "Look, this isn't going to be easy, we received an ITC alert which only happens when someone dies. We think your wife is dead. We cannot go inside for another hour when the Nanite Control team arrives." There were three other alerts in this neighborhood tonight and that's too much to be an accident.

Cy said, "You're right it's no accident, it's Hawk. We'll go in."

"This place is technically a crime scene." Said Plante.

Steve waited at the police line waving to Cy and Dave.

Cy said, "The crime happened here but the crime scene is somewhere else. That man can explain in great detail," pointing to Steve, "Let us go in, please."

Plante looked at Trish as she saw Cy and Dave for the first time, studying them. He said, "Were you expecting something really far out there?" Then to Cy he said, "I can't let you go in there. Even if you two don't have nanites inside of you, the nanites in there could get inside of you and tear you apart. Two officers who initially responded are dead now as a result of walking in there. That's a lot of nanites looking for human flesh."

Plante gestured to the cop at the line to let Steve pass. When he came up, Plante asked, "Who are you, sir?"

"My name is Stephen Bryant."

Plante threw his arms wide and looked up to the sky. He said, "Of course you are." He looked at Trish and said, "This makes the third old case file that gets solved this week." He returned his attention to Steve and said, "You don't have Deirdra Evans in your back pocket do you?"

Steve said, "No, she's back at the shop."

Plante said, "Back at the shop."

"Yes, that's right, call her, she'll tell you."

Plante tapped his ITC and said, "Deirdra Evans."

After only a few seconds, Deirdra answered. She said, "This is Deirdra."

Plante was incredulous. He stood shaking his head and said, "Ms. Evans, I'm detective Plante, What can you tell me about Annie Boudreau's death?"

Deirdra immediately began explaining, "There was a program launched from the quarters of Dr. William Craig on board the UMass Space Campus, transmitted by microwave carrier signal and directed at Annie Boudreau's home. The program signal duration was two hours, from 7:00–9:00 P.M. The program carried a codec that had been altered from the original. Instead of the nanites working in sync to preserve the human they occupy, it causes them to destroy it, and then themselves."

Plante said, "So, the transmission is terminated and any remaining nanites inside should be neutralized?"

"That's right"

Plante asked, "What evidence do you have of this?"

Trish said, "We have a still frame of his echo screen taken tonight in his estate."

Plante said, "I look forward to meeting you Ms. Evans." He tapped off. He said, "You two can follow me in. But you stay with me, do you understand?"

Dave and Cy nodded. The three of them went into the house, Plante leading the way. They searched the downstairs first, then went upstairs. The upstairs hall had the bodies of the two policemen lay twisted and contorted. They appeared to have been in a fight with an unseen foe. There were black and blue splotches on their skin from the damage that the nanites had caused inside as they were dying. Annie's bedroom was at the end of the hall in the back of the house.

As they entered the room it took both, Plante and Cy to hold Dave back from the body of his wife. She lay bruised and broken on her bed. She was fully clothed and hadn't pulled the covers over her. Her youthful appearance had been rescinded in death. She looked all of her two hundred years.

Dave's cries could be heard outside the house.

CHAPTER FOURTY

Plante allowed Dave to remain with Annie's body. He gathered Steve and Cy together and said, "I want you to take me and Detective Cody here, to meet this Deirdra."

Steve asked, "Do you want to follow us in your own transport?"

Plante said, "That's fine, let's go."

Cy was still reeling from seeing Annie dead. His heart ached for his own grief and for Dave's grief as well. Steve took Cy by the arm and led him to the transport. The trip back to the shop had been brief, and soon they were stepping out into the street in front of Hill Security. They walked to the front of the shop and waited for the two detectives.

Plante stopped in front of the shop and looked at the sign over the door. He asked, "Why 'Hill' Security?"

Steve said, "I wanted to get Cy's attention when he arrived in this time."

Plante smirked and said, "Let's go inside."

The door bells jangled overhead as the four passed in. Deirdra came running to Cy and seeing his tear stained face, hugged him and said, "Cy, I'm so sorry." Then seeing the two detectives she stepped back from Cy and asked, "Where's Dave?"

Cy said, "He's with Annie for the time being."

Plante said, "I'm Detective Plante, this is Detective Cody. You and I spoke earlier. Would you show me the screen frame, please.

Deirdra said, "This way please." She led them into the back room to the console. The screen frame was still up on the monitor. Plante and Cody stepped up and were examining the screen. "You can take the sweeper and download the image at the station. We'd like the sweeper back, please."

Plante looked at her and said, "So you're Deirdra Evans. You're supposed to be missing too. How long have you been here under our noses?"

"For about three hundred years." Deirdra said, "I actually even saw myself when I came to visit Aunt Annie. I've been living in Sheldon since 1886."

Plante looked at Trish and said, "Some detective I am, huh?"

Trish said, "I'm having a hard time buying all of this. You people talk about bouncing all over time like you have a time machine or something. Come on, someone explain this to me so it makes sense."

Steve said, "I'm probably the most qualified to do that Detective Cody"

"Who did you say you are again?"

"I'm Steve Bryant. Until I took a spin in the ether, which was two years ago for you people, I was Dr. William Craig's intern and assistant. I worked on the Quantum Accelerator Project along side him and whoever else he has up there."

Trish asked, "How is it that if you are missing, you are here? Wouldn't that mean you aren't missing anymore?"

Steve said, "That sure is true Detective Cody. The fact is I haven't been missing so much as a bit out of time with the rest of you. That accelerator Hawk is building fires in two years from now. The purpose of the experiment is to gather feedback on the effects of a concentrated stream of quanta on the fabric of spacetime. The truth is, according to his and the late Dr. Fish's calculations, this stream of quanta should have opened a wormhole to allow controlled time travel. Something had to have gone terribly wrong. These eddies popping up every couple of years must be a result of some kind of accident. I wasn't there for the first firing, but I'll be there for it this time, I'll stop it if I can."

"You mean he's fired this accelerator before?" Trish asked.

"No, but that doesn't matter with spacetime. When this accelerator fires it's in our future, it affects both that future and the past. Myself and Deirdra were caught in ethereal eddies and taken back in time. I went back to the 1850's, Dee to the 1880's. Well, we waited out the centuries. Nanites kept us going when the contemporary western medicine wasn't enough. Dave and Cy both came back as well. There were no nanites in there own time, so they couldn't wait around. The eddies come every two years, so they moved forward to this time through the ether. You see, we have to stop the accelerator from being fired two years from now. We have to stop Hawk. Who knows how many other people have gone missing farther back in the past. Who knows how many people go missing in the future into a different time."

Trish looked at Plante and said, "This is either the most bizarre case in history or the most highly orchestrated inane ramblings of madmen ever heard."

Plante said, "Trish, there are three dead bodies that we just left that are demanding a full and thorough investigation."

Cy was beginning to come back around and had heard Trish and Plante's comments and said, "There are three bodies that are demanding that we set things to rights. You can investigate this if you want Detective, but I'm going to change it." He then got up and left the room.

Trish asked, "How does he think he's going to change anything?"

Steve said, "By stopping Hawk's accelerator from being fired. You might be able to help there Detective Cody. You're a Boston cop, the accelerator is being constructed in a Boston warehouse."

She looked at Plante and said, "I'll look into it."

Steve added, "A warehouse in the back bay."

She turned to Steve and said, "Thank you, like I said, I'll look into it."

Plante said, "I'll be up all night here, how about I take you home. It's been a busy first date."

Trish smiled and said, "Okay, that'd be nice."

Plante said to Steve, "I'll be back in about twenty minutes, we'll talk more then."

Dave stayed with Annie for as long as they would let him. At the morgue, when the medical examiner was ready to begin his autopsy Dave had been asked to leave her. He went looking for Cy. He was on foot and walking in a hurry toward the shop when he heard a tone in his head. At first he ignored it, forgetting the new ITC. Then as it persisted he remembered and tapped it, saying, "Yeah?"

Cy said, "Where are you?"

"I'm looking for you. This is messed up Cy, this is really messed up!"

"I know Dave," Cy said, "We have to change it. You have to go back, man, you have to go back to Annie like you should have in the first place."

Dave, silent at first, then said, "No. No Cy, that's wrong. I don't care if I die here, I have to stop this bastard. That way I'll be sure to never leave Annie in the first place. Look, I think we need to do this on our own. I don't think these two detectives can really do too much for us, not unless laws have changed a lot since our time."

"Where are you man, I'll pick you up."

"I'm outside of the Sheldon Police station. Out in back where the morgue is."

"Sit tight."

Within a minute the midrange humming of a transport overhead could be heard. It lowered itself to the roadway alongside Dave. The door slid open and Dave stepped in, taking the remaining seat by Cy. When the door closed and the transport had ascended into traffic, Cy reached across and pulled Dave to him. They hugged as Dave let go the anguish he had been holding in since they had found Annie dead in her room. When some time had passed he let go of Cy and sat back. Cy too sat back, and Dave could see that he had been crying as well.

Cy said, "I want to show you something." and placed his finger on his lips to stop Dave from responding. Then he said, "Did you know that these transports operate in manual mode as well as fully automatic?" With that he flicked a switch on the side of the computer console and a joystick came up from a compartment just in front of the screen. Cy gripped it and immediately the onboard computer voice said, "Manual mode not recommended at freeway speeds." But in spite of the warning, the transport lurched as it went from computerized navigation to manual. Cy pulled back on the joystick and then to the left, the vehicle responded by rising up and out of the traffic lane and swooping around in a long arc only to rejoin a traffic lane in the opposite direction. They were returning to Sheldon. As soon as they had settled into traffic Cy touched an icon on the screen and said, "Computer, shut down." The onboard flashed a few lights in its shutdown sequence and finally went dark. Cy said, "I don't really trust computers sometimes, especially when there's so much connectivity between them. The lights of Sheldon came up fast and Cy dropped out of highway speed, slowing to navigate around the city. He directed the transport toward Sheldon's south village district.

There Dave recognized the neighborhood that Cy had bought a house in. He said, "Cy, is that your old house ahead?"

Cy said, "Yep, it sure is. Stood up well didn't it?"

"Do you know who is living there now?"

Cy smiled and said, "Yeah, my little sister Sarah lives there now. She isn't expecting us, so be ready for just about anything."

The transport came to rest on the old paved driveway along side another transport. They got out and walked around to the rear of the house. As they approached the back door it suddenly burst open and Sarah came running out. She seemed much the same as Cy remembered her. She still wore her brunette hair down on her shoulders, though now there were a few silver strands. She was fit and looked well, and Cy felt overcome with happiness to see her. This night had become turbulent with emotion. She ran straight to Cy and threw her arms around his neck. After a quick hug she backed away and slapped him in the face. She said, "That's for letting your family believe you were dead." Then she went to Dave and gave him a hug, when she stepped back from him he blocked his face. But Sarah didn't try to slap Dave.

Cy asked, "You knew we were here didn't you?"

Sarah said, "Annie told me. She and I have become great friends over the last century. I've been waiting for you to come find me."

Cy said, "Yeah, Sis, there's something you need to know. It's about Annie. It's bad Sarah, she's been killed."

Sarah looked at Cy in disbelief. She had a hard time understanding what he was saying. She said, "What are you talking about? How?"

Dave said, "That bastard Hawk, that's how. He gave her nanites a virus. They turned on her body, they killed her."

"Who is this Hawk? Do they know for sure he's responsible? Why would he do this?" The questions were coming from Sarah faster than she could give them voice. She wept while at the same time talking, and could not accept Annie's death. After a few moments she said, "Come inside." and she led the way.

The inside of Cy's old digs had changed considerably. Sarah's taste in decor and color schemes differed completely from his. Cy thought that had Lexi been given a chance to live here it might have ended up much like it was now; with strong feminine touches.

A man sat at the table in the kitchen. He got up quickly when he saw Sarah's tears and went to her directly. He took her in his arms, in a way that gave Cy to realize that he must be this man's brother-in-law.

Sarah cried into his shoulder for a few minutes and then turned and said, "Cy, I want you to meet your brother-in-law, Marc, Marc this is my brother Cy and our family friend Dave Boudreau, Annie's husband." Then she lay her head back on Marc's shoulder and let the tears stream down her face. "It's Annie, Marc, she's dead."

Marc shook Cy and Dave's hands and said, "I've heard all about both of you from Annie and Sarah. It's good to meet you."

Cy explained to Marc as he had Sarah the circumstances of Annie's death. When he was finished he added, "We're going to stop this. We're going to stop this experiment from happening so spacetime remains undisturbed."

By this time Sarah felt sufficiently in control to ask, "So, Captain Bonehead, where are you staying?"

Cy's face turned a subdued grin, he said, "We're staying in the Colonial Hotel, but not for much longer. I heard we can get rooms out at the Wright Farm. That's been ground zero for so long now that it seems the most logical place to stay."

Dave said, "I wonder if we can get our old rooms back."

"I bet they don't look like they did when we were there." Cy looked at Sarah and said, "Sarah, I'm going to leave now. I've hit your emotions pretty hard tonight and you look like you could use some rest. I just didn't want you to find out about Annie in a grocery line. Dave and I have a lot to talk about so we'll head back to our room. If you want me I'm just a tap away, we had ITC's installed."

Sarah stepped from Marc's protective arms and gave Cy another hug. She said, "Okay, just don't you wait another hundred eighty years to come again."

Cy and Dave left the house and returned to the transport. Cy said, "I overheard Detective Plante talking to another cop about his suspicion that his transport was being monitored by someone and he was liking Hawk for it. I don't know if Steve's is being tracked or not, but if we use it in manual mode it shouldn't be accessible."

Dave said, "Ahh, that's why you didn't want me to speak."

"Right, but I'm not sure if the devices require the on-board computer or not. So anything we say inside this thing may be listened in on."

"We'll just keep our comments to the weather and lovely landscape."

They boarded the transport in silence and Cy switched the transport to on, but directly into manual mode. Without a word they rose up over the rooftops and cruised directly to the Wright Farm. It was getting late and the farm was closed but Cy wanted to get a look at the place. From the air at night there was very little that seemed discernibly different. Cy pointed the transport toward the Colonial Hotel and they headed in for the night.

Plante stayed true to his word, he returned to Steve and Deirdra's shop twenty minutes later. He entered and went straight out back to the workshop where Steve and Deirdra were waiting. A patrolman had been left in the room with them to make sure there would be no tampering with the screen frame. Plante considered it a mere formality. He knew that the frame could have been a complete fabrication, but he didn't believe that. He firmly believed that Hawk had orchestrated Annie's death.

Plante went back over to the console and looked at the frame again. He asked, "How is it that you were inside Craig's house?"

Steve said, "We set up the security system in the mansion when it was first constructed, over eighty years ago. We go in every so often, with the owner's permission of course, to perform periodic maintenance and install upgrades. We routinely sweep the premises for audio and video eavesdropping devices that may have been planted in the owner's absence."

Plante said, "It doesn't speak well of your security system if bugs can be planted on the premises that your system is supposed to be protecting."

"Well Detective, the fact is, there are other utility companies that gain access to the mansion regularly with permission from the owner or his agent. There is also the caretaker to consider, who has unfettered access to the grounds. The fact is, Hawk him self plants listening devices throughout the mansion and moves them after our sweeps. His way of testing whether or not we actually do what we are paid to do."

"I see. This image of his console monitor, what was the purpose of capturing the image?"

Steve said, "We occasionally shoot a random image as we go about our sweep patrol. It's in our contract to do so. If we see anything that we aren't sure of we shoot the picture and if later on we aren't able to understand it, we contact the client and ask them if they are aware of it. If they aren't then we've identified a breech; if they are, then all's well. In this case it may well have been someone accessing his computer that did not have permission to do so."

"So this image is likely to be admissible in court. I'll have to check on that, do you have a copy of that contract?"

Steve looked at Dee and she immediately produced the handheld screen with Hawk's own signature on it. She said, "Our contracts renew every five years with our long term customers. This one was renewed three years ago. Would you like a hard copy?"

Plante had a broad grin on his face, he nodded and said, "Yes please, along with your sweeper. I can't guarantee we'll be getting it back to you anytime soon. It's evidence now. We have to keep the sweeper unit intact with the camera to preserve the continuity of evidence. Will you two be willing to testify?"

Steve smiled and said, "As for my self sir, I would be happy to."

Deirdra added, "Yes, absolutely."

Plante said, "Well then, we're well on our way to taking this guy down!"

CHAPTER FOURTY ONE

Trish contacted her captain the next morning and requested permission to reopen the Fish Case. While she awaited the decision she made some inquiries and found the location for the warehouse that Hawk had leased in the back bay. She decided to take a spin by and see what she could see. As she descended between the traffic altitude and the rooftops and she could see that there were several men engaged in moving the contents of the warehouse out.

The transport landed and Trish got out. She approached the entrance of the warehouse and walked up to the man who was directing all of the others. She held up her detective's shield and said, "I'm detective Cody, can you tell me whose warehouse this is that you're emptying?"

The man said, "Sure, this place is leased to a professor up on UMass Space Campus, ah let's see," he scrolled through the pages on his hand held, "yeah, Dr. Craig is his name. He contracted us through his agent to transfer all of the contents up to the space campus. We're almost finished up, this ought to be the last load. Is something wrong?"

Trish looked at the equipment and said, "No, go ahead and do your job, I'm just checking. There've been some warehouse break-ins lately and I just wanted to be sure that your presence is legit. Thanks."

She left the warehouse and returned to her transport. Punching in a few commands she activated the nose camera that came standard issue on cop transports and began a recording of the remaining instruments that were being removed. She stayed until the job was done, only twenty minutes, and left after the work crew left. She entered Sheldon P.D. into her onboard console. The transport rose and arced smoothly into the stream of westbound traffic. Five minutes later it decelerated from two-hundred fifty miles per hour and dropped out of the traffic lane, cutting another smooth arc and descending into the Sheldon P.D. lot. She found Plante in the investigative tactical room sitting behind a cluttered desk, exactly as she had pictured him when she first met him. His hair was mussed up from not sleeping, and he still wore the same clothes from the night before.

Plante looked up from his desk with fatigued and bloodshot eyes. He saw Trish standing there and at first it didn't register that she had come to visit him. She seemed to fit into the surroundings, almost too well. When he realized that he had been staring stupidly he snapped out of it and smiled saying, "Hey, what are you doing here?"

"What, you want I should leave?" Trish quipped.

"No, no, sorry, I didn't mean to make it sound like that. Here have a seat." He pulled his coat off of the chair next to his desk and made a place for her to sit down. When she had settled herself by him he asked, "So, what brings you out here at this time of day?"

She looked at his disheveled appearance, smiled and said, "The same thing that kept you out all night; Hawk. I have some surveillance video I shot this morning that you will be interested in seeing." Trish reached into her handbag and removed her transport remote. She touched a playback key and then asked, "What's your console key code so I can stream to here?"

Plante looked for a card in his desk that had the information for his console, he found it and said, "a32fd7e"

Trish inputted the hexadecimal number into the remote and immediately the video she shot at the Boston warehouse streamed onto his computer.

As he watched he asked, "Is this where I think it is?"

She said, "Yes, Hawk's warehouse. It's empty now, this is all that I could get. The worker told me it was going to the UMass Space Campus to Dr. Craig's lab."

"He cleared out. He's onto me, like I said, he tapped my transport and he's been watching my every move. Annie Boudreau's death was a shot across my bow. He wanted me looking this way so he could be moving out of town and dammit, it worked."

"Do you know what any of this stuff is?" Trish asked.

"No, but I know who will." He tapped his ITC and said, "Deirdra Evans" "Deirdra here." "Deirdra, it's Detective Plante. Do you think you and Steve could come over to the station for a few minutes please?" "Sure thing Detective, we'll be right there." Plante tapped out. He said to Trish, "I'm glad you came without calling me first, I don't know if my ITC is secure or not. That's why I called Deirdra instead of Steve. Hawk would recognize Steve's name as his recently gone missing assistant."

Trish said, "If you think your ITC is compromised you should have it replaced."

"Well if he's tapped into this one, how long do you think it would take to tap into a new one?"

"Good point."

Plante stood up and said, "Come on, while we're waiting I'll buy you a cup of bad coffee."

Trish got up and followed him to a vending machine in the foyer just outside of the tactical room. He stepped up to it and placed his eye near a biometric scanner, then pressed a button marked coffee. He asked, "Cream, no sugar, right?"

"That's right, you remember, how sweet." Trish said with an exaggerated honey tone.

Plante blushed right down to his toes and placed her coffee order then his own. As the coffees were dispensing Steve and Deirdra came into the foyer. Plante said, "Just in time, you two want coffee?"

Dee said, "No thanks, I just had some."

Steve said, "I'm all set too, Detective, thanks just the same."

They went inside to Plante's desk to let Steve get a look at the equipment being loaded and moved from the warehouse. Steve sat in Plante's chair so he could have the best view.

Steve said, "This is bad. He's pulling out of here because he's ahead of schedule. That was the quantum generator, and accelerator gun. He's ready for final assembly in space." Steve looked at Plante. "For Hawk to have gotten this far ahead of schedule, he couldn't have done much testing on the equipment. This mechanism makes a Swiss watch look like something out a Rube Goldberg catalog. It's no wonder something went wrong."

Plante looked at the screen. Steve had frozen the frame on the generator. He drew a deep sigh and said, "Thanks Steve. I need to go talk to my captain about all of this."

Steve and Deirdra said goodbye and left the tactical room. Trish said, "I spoke to my Captain this morning and asked to reopen the Fish case. As much as I hate to admit it, you were right."

"About Hawk?"

"No, about this coffee, it's really bad." Trish smiled and turned to walk out. Over her shoulder she said, "See ya later sunshine!"

Plante chuckled at his good fortune with Trish as she left the station, then became very serious at the realization that he was caught in a deadly game with a homicidal sociopath. There were three dead in this round alone, and a good chance that many of the remaining players could be Hawk's next victim. He turned him self toward the captain's office and went in to push his case to get a warrant.

Steve and Deirdra left the Sheldon Police Department with an elevated sense of anxiety. Hawk being ahead of schedule had Steve shook up. He knew that the firing of the quantum accelerator had been moved up but by just how much he couldn't be sure. For all he knew Hawk would fire the accelerator whenever he felt ready. That scared him because he remembered that the only check and balance for Hawk, was Dr. Fish. Somehow, Steve felt sure that the only way to stop this guy involved direct intervention. He knew the layout, he also knew he had to bring more people into the plan.

Steve said to Dee, "We need to link my ITC to our computer console. I want everything recorded and I want to be able to send and retrieve information at will. How long?"

Dee said, "It'll take me a few hours to set up the programming and then it's just a matter of initiating it. What are you planning?"

"I have to get myself, Dave and Cy to the space campus, and somehow onto that platform." Steve felt frantic. His mind was racing, he knew he needed to slow it down if he were to make any sense of the puzzle ahead of him. He tapped his ITC and said, "Message to Cy Hill, Cy I need you and Dave to come to the shop immediately, we're going to space."

Hawk stood in the test platform control room where Haley would monitor the experiment. He would be out on the platform making certain there were no equipment failures. He wasn't happy about the need to advance the project so, but he felt sure that if he waited until the scheduled time he would never see the experiment through. He heard a tone in his ITC, he tapped it and said, "Yes, this is Hawk."

"Professor Craig, this is Steve Hill from Hill Security calling. Do you have a moment sir?"

Hawk responded, "Yes but hurry, what is it?"

Steve said, "Sir everything went well last night at your home, we detected seven devices during our sweep, I hope that matches your count. Your upgrades have been installed and everything looks tight."

"Very good Mr. Hill, submit your bill as usual and thank you for your service."

"Your welcome sir, if you have any further security needs, I hope you keep us in mind." Steve tapped out.

Hawk's mind was busy solving equations during the conversation, he could solve complicated calculations in his head while carrying on conversations with very little effort. After the conversation ended his mind spun in a new direction. It occurred to him that perhaps he would put his security outfit to work here on the station. He paused from his spacetime fabric folding calculation and tapped his ITC saying, "Steve Hill."

After a moment Steve answered, "Hill Security Systems."

"Mr. Hill, Professor Craig here, I have a job for you here at the Space Campus if you have the availability."

"What is the scope of the job, Sir?"

"I need a project that I'm working on to be kept under wraps. I don't want anyone snooping around. The facility is 35,000 cubic feet, I'll require 24/7 surveillance. Can you accommodate me?"

"Yes sir, I can get my team in place within twelve hours, we'll rig for closed circuit within two hours of arrival. If that's satisfactory I'll contact you on our approach."

"That will be fine, until then." This time Hawk tapped off before this commoner could beat him to it.

This was just what Hawk needed; somebody to watchdog the intruders and minimize interruption. It's bad enough that he had to stop as often as he did for sleep. He told Haley she would have to control herself until after they fired the accelerator, he simply had to devote all of his energy to the project. That proved to be all the motivation she needed to go all out with effort. She performed her tasks with her previous energy now. Hawk's only worry now was that busybody, Plante. Presently he had very little information as to the detective's whereabouts. Either Plante had figured out that his transport had been compromised, or he had become just plain stupid lucky. Of course Hawk knew that Plante was stupid lucky. But for the time being that meant that he didn't know the detective's whereabouts or his activities. Perhaps the time had come for the more drastic measure of tapping into Plante's ITC. Ah, just the thing to put an intern on.

He singled out his programmer, Scotty Holland, and contacted him via ITC. He instructed him saying, "I have been consulting for a large corporate security group, I can't name them you understand, and a concern was raised regarding ITC security. They want to determine whether an ITC can be compromised without the owner's awareness, and just what it would take. I want you to examine the problem from all angles and give me a report first thing in the morning."

"Yes sir, Professor Hawk." Said Scotty, and the intern went immediately to work on the project. Hawk knew that he could do it if he set his mind to it, but there was a lot of work to do.

"Now... back to that generator."

CHAPTER FOURTY TWO

"When we are in transit, we put these slip on space walkers on our feet. They have Velcro on the soles. Just be aware of where you are walking, not all of the surfaces have the mating material." Steve stowed the space walkers in the van and asked, "Any questions?"

Cy asked, "Do you know the layout up there?"

"No, I've never been to the facility that we're going to. I'm not too worried about that, I'm more concerned about Hawk recognizing me. Look, just ignore all of the things that are going on in the room, we're wearing enough recording devises to catch everything that's happening around us. We can review all of that data when we get back. Concentrate on putting the cameras in place; one in each of the four upper corners. There are markers everywhere designating floor, wall and ceiling surfaces and you only need to stay on the walker paths to get there. It might be a bit disorienting, but just stay relaxed, and focus on your tasks."

Dave said, "We only put cameras in the upper corners?"

"Right, the lenses can pick up 180 by 360 degrees. Theoretically one in the center should be adequate. This guy likes redundancy, we can use that to our advantage. Anything else?"

Dave and Cy shook their heads. When the last of the equipment had been loaded they boarded the transport. Steve said, "Let's do this." He punched in the space campus as the destination and settled in for the ride.

The transport rose and made an imperceptible arc toward the space campus facility aloft in geosynchronous orbit over Massachusetts. At eight thousand feet the oxygen tanks could be heard as the valves opened. The transport automatically sealed itself against the lessening pressure as it ascended. As if on cue Steve removed his shoes and stowed them, Dave and Cy followed suit, and they all donned their space walkers. After only a few more moments they began to notice the lightness in their seats as gravity began to fade.

Steve said, "Better strap in."

The harnesses used for space transport were five point buckle systems and were much more effective at holding a body in place than a lap belt with a single shoulder strap. The curvature of the earth was apparent along the horizon and the atmosphere no longer reflected blue from above. Stars were visible in the sky as the transport continued to climb. A bright object, too distant to discern grew perceptively as they approached. The station grew and as it did its full scope gradually became apparent to Dave and Cy as they took it all in for the first time.

As the transport approached the station the Traffic Control Program picked it up and requested destination and control override. Steve punched in the destination as platform j-6, and granted the TCP its override access.

The transport veered to the left and rotated clockwise to reorient its attitude to match the station plane. Once oriented and in alignment with the bay final approach began. The transport moved toward the behemoth and as it did, a steel door opened in their path. At first it looked like a tiny door, but as they finally passed through it they could see that the door was at least thirty feet across and fifteen feet high. The transport continued on as the door closed behind them. They floated past what could only be described as a parking lot of transports standing on end and packed in like sardines. There were hundreds of them on both sides. Then they traversed what seemed to be city streets, only there were no cars or pedestrians. There were only occasional transports just arriving like them, or just departing. People could be seen inside of the compartments on both sides of the street. They turned a corner to the right and proceeded down this street for a short interval before turning what seemed to them to be straight upward. This street brought them to their final destination in the campus facility. Another steel door opened for them, this one shaped like an iris, and allowed them to pass. The transport entered and docked itself precisely in the bay. The iris door closed behind them and the bay pressurized. The transport had been adjusting the internal pressure slowly to match the atmosphere in the bay, so by the time the room was pressurized the doors were safe to open and the passengers could comfortably disembark.

Steve said, "It's been a long time since I've made that trip. How did you guys enjoy your first soiree into space?"

Cy responded first by saying, "This is really going to make it difficult to go back to riding a bicycle."

Dave said, "You couldn't ride a bicycle before."

"Yeah, so now it's going to be all the more difficult!"

Steve said, "Alright guys, it's time to get serious. Hawk is going to be here real soon. Remember, I'll do the talking, you two stay on task we get in, and get out. He'll be able to tell that you've never been in a weightless environment so don't try faking it. Just do your best to get around. Get the equipment from the back of the transport and follow me."

Dave stepped out onto a smooth surface with his right foot and learned his first real lesson about watching where you step when in space. He placed his body as though he were trying to put his weight into it thrusting himself from behind with his left leg and launched himself from the interior of the transport. He yelled, "Whooa!" as his body went hurling out. Fortunately he caught the door frame, so instead of floating away, he found himself hanging horizontally, facing the floor; the Velcro that he was supposed to have placed his foot on three feet from him, and it may as well have been a mile.

Hawk gripped Dave's right ankle and said, "You need a hand?" Bending down with Dave's ankle he guided the foot directly to the deck's Velcro surface. Then standing erect, he said, "There is a training module for first time space travelers. I would highly recommend that you attend such a program before you ever consider returning to space."

Steve came around the transport, he wore a cap with the visor down low over his eyes. He saw Dave slowly standing to face Hawk. Dave was looking into the eyes of his wife's killer who had just come to his rescue and who was now speaking to him in a very condescending manner. He said to Dave, "Get the gear!" then looked at Hawk and said, "Professor Craig, I'm Steve Hill, Hill Security Systems. I'm sorry about that sir, he's a good man, just never been to space before. Would you show me to the compartment that you want me to secure for you, please."

Hawk looked at Steve and said, "I don't believe we've ever actually met before Mr. Hill." He reached out his hand which Steve shook. "However, you do look familiar." Then turning abruptly he said, "This way please." And he strode quickly away.

Over his shoulder Steve said, "Dave, Cy, wait here, I'll be right back." And he walked away behind the professor.

Cy and Dave were standing at the rear of the transport. Cy had managed to get out of the transport behind Steve and followed his example. Now they were just the two of them, and Cy asked, "Are you alright Dave?"

Dave drew a deep breath. He said, "Cy, I almost took care of the problem right there. I saw those eyes looking at me, that smug tone in his voice and I swear to God I wanted to strangle the son of a bitch."

Cy said, "That's what separates you from an animal like him. Uh, remember what Steve said about bugs?"

"Yeah, shutting up now." Dave held the cargo doors at the back of the transport with a white knuckled grip. He wriggled his feet to test the grip to the floor, and with great reluctance forced himself to let go of the door. "Maybe a little practice walking is in order" He said. Slowly he stepped, being sure to place his feet on the woolen surface only. The walkers made a ripping sound with every step. He tried to mimic the stride that Steve used as he left the docking area. The oddest thing was no sensation of weight on the bottom of his feet. The stride was more of a shuffle and thrust that kept his body moving in a forward direction while allowing his slippers to maintain their tenuous grip on the floor.

Cy was right behind him trying to make the same adjustment to the new method of ambulation. After three minutes of shuffle and thrust they returned to the transport doors. Cy said, "This is bizarre. We had best get the gear out of the back."

They reached inside and undid the container from the sidewall harness that had held it in place. The expectation of the container falling out on them had them braced to catch it. However it floated from it's resting position and simply drifted into the middle of the transport.

Dave looked at Cy and said, "Another thing to get used to." He gripped one of the handles on the container and gently drew it to him. Then he turned and began to do the space shuffle with the container in tow. It simply stayed with him, but when he stopped it kept coming, bumping the back of his legs.

Cy said, "Dave, there's a Velcro patch on the bottom of the container, stick it to the floor."

Dave guided the container to the floor and pushed it onto the woolen surface. It stuck.

They rolled their eyes at each other, grinning. Steve returned through the door that he had gone through and motioned them to follow. Cy had the transport remote and he pressed the secure button. The transport closed itself up and locked against access. Dave pulled the container free and they trailed off behind Steve.

The door led to a long corridor that had airtight compartments on either side. Each door had an airlock. When a compartment was empty the computer would seal the airlock and pump the atmosphere out of the compartment. This ensured against items being sucked out of the compartment in the event of a hull breech. It also allowed for conservation of breathable air. There were red and green lights above each airlock portal indicating the atmospheric condition within; green if breathable and red if a vacuum.

After passing several compartments they arrived at the portal they would be securing. The door had a green light on over it. Steve entered a security code into the keypad and the door opened outward. One by one they entered in.

Once inside the lab, Steve looked at Cy and Dave and said, "Like this." He took the case from Dave and affixed it to the woolen surface on the wall alongside of the door. Once it was secured he lifted one foot from the floor and placed it on the wall next to the case. He slowly leaned way back and placed a hand on the floor as he pulled his remaining foot from the floor. Then he put his second foot down by his first on the wall and stood erect on the wall with his body parallel to the floor. He bent and pulled the case free and began to do the shuffle thrust up the wall toward the ceiling.

Up, down, left and right were all subjective and a matter of the individual perspective in this environment. Cy and Dave were struggling to contain their exuberance.

Dave followed Steve first, however he had no case to carry along. He planted his right foot on the wall and leaned toward the floor. Mimicking Steve he braced himself with one hand and freed his left foot only to place it on the wall aside his right. He found himself facing the ceiling and looking upward at Cy, who now seemed to be standing on the wall. He smiled and said, "Oh, man this is mighty strange!"

Cy followed suit and soon he too found himself doing the 'shuffle thrust' up the wall to the site of the first camera install.

Hawk felt disturbed. It had occurred to him that in all of the eighty years that Hill Security Systems had been handling the security at his estate, he had never met either of the principals of the company. There seemed to be something about this man Steve Hill that was familiar. He looked remarkably like Stephen Bryant but considerably older. Perhaps he was a relative of his missing young protégé. Perhaps the time had come to perform a full background check on this security company. Yet, they were impeccable in the performance of their security arrangements.

Then there was that man who didn't know how to get about in the docking bay; one might excuse a newcomer to space his obvious lack of coordination in a weightless environment. Yet, something malevolent shown in that dullard's eyes when there should have been gratitude.

Hawk found his finely tuned mind to be hard at to puzzle through these inconsistencies. It would be only a matter of time and he would understand. He always did. Currently he had only a few moments to check on the whereabouts of that imbecile Plante back on earth and then he needed to attend a boorish meeting with the Dean of Astronomical Studies. At his console he tapped the icon and brought the tracking program up on the monitor. The report showed Plante right where he ought to be, at the Sheldon police department, at least his transport was. Plante could have been anywhere. Hawk made a mental note to check with the intern working on the ITC eavesdropping program to get status on his progress. Unfortunately he would have to meet with an untimely end as well once he completed the task. Martyrs all who have died for the cause of the quantum particle accelerator being realized, and the young intern would be added to the list. He added a mental note to find out his name, again.

While he was not satisfied that things were completely under control, he needed to leave them as they were for the time being and go listen to the Dean drone on about some inconsequential point of red or blue shifted galaxies and their gravitational effect on our solar system and some liberal 'Save the moons' sentimentality. This is the price that he himself must pay for his own great cause.

Chapter Forty Three

On earth, the only indication of anything ominous going on in space was the activity in the back room of Hill Security Systems. Deirdra monitored all three of the men as they installed the surveillance equipment. The separate feed on the number three camera had been finely tuned to a frequency band reserved for police. This particular frequency had been reserved for Detective Plante and information had already begun streaming from space. Every fifth image from the camera was duplicated encrypted and transmitted through a separate channel to a transceiver that had been planted in the docking bay. That transceiver then linked up with the space station's communications array and sent the encrypted images to the small shop in Sheldon. These signals were all piggybacked together in an environment that piggybacked signals were the standard means of carrier. The professor would have a difficult time finding the signal let alone breaking the encryption. Besides which, it would only be on to transmit stored surveillance or to look in on the bay, after which it would be shut down until the next time they chose to look in.. All according to the specifications of the warrant that Detectives Cody and Plante were able to secure.

Deirdra felt nervous about the whole business. She didn't feel that Dave and Cy were up to the space environment task. She knew that Steve could handle it, but didn't like seeing him in harm's way. She didn't like having law enforcement types hanging over her shoulder. Cops didn't bother her, except when they were observing her and how capable she was with a computer. She refused to let them see her full capability, they would likely confine her. She could hear everything Steve said through his ITC and could see through the visual provided by the camera. The real test of the visual capabilities would come when they left the docking bay and there would be no way to repair any malfunctions without returning to the station. She wasn't worried about equipment failure. The equipment and the software that operated it was all of her own handiwork. Deirdra's concerns were with Hawk's murderous capabilities and Steve's proximity to him. They were near completion on the install. Soon she would relax.

Plante sat behind Deirdra and observed all that took place. He and detective Cody had secured a warrant that morning to place the tap on the feed from the cameras. They were able to use the screen frame that Cy had taken from the Craig estate the night before. Because neither of their jurisdictions typically extended to the space campus they needed to go to a Federal judge.

Cy and Dave had just finished stowing the empty container in the back of the transport when Steve came into the docking bay. Cy closed the cargo doors of the transport and they all got into the vehicle. Steve tapped the control console and the docking clamps released. The transport autopilot took control backing the transport out of the cargo bay, and began its trip back to earth. In only a matter of minutes they were outside of the space campus and had begun their decent. Steve tapped his ITC and said Deirdra's name.

She responded and said, "It's all right Steve, the transport is clean."

Steve said, "Well, thank god that's over."

Deirdra said, "Detective Plant is here, and he's quite pleased with the result."

"That's good. I'm going to talk with Cy and Dave now; We'll be there in ten minutes." Steve tapped his ITC to disconnect.

The transport had begun its controlled decent through the upper atmosphere. Steve said, "Well guys, that actually went well. Hawk is curious about me, but I don't think he realizes I was his assistant. You guys got around real well after a while, you should be proud."

Cy said, "Once we got the hang of walking on the walls and ceiling it wasn't so bad."

Dave said, "When we first arrived and he caught me and spoke to me, well, I never knew I was capable of such hatred. I wanted to kill him. I have to say, I could have. I could have."

Cy put his hand on Dave's shoulder and said, "It may come to that yet Dave. We may have to test your resolve."

Dave just nodded, haunted by Professor Craig's cold eyes and condescending manner. He felt more than hatred, he also felt anger, wounded pride, vengefulness. The emotional cacophony playing inside deafened his normally calm and gentle heart. He decided he would nurture the anger, feed his hatred with the pain of his loss. He kept Annie's face in the forefront of his mind whenever he thought of 'The Hawk.'

The transport had slowed its rate of descent now. The earth rose up to meet them and they were clearing the travel traffic lanes on final approach to the shop. They saw Sheldon growing beneath them. At last the transport settled into it's parking space located in the ally behind Steve's shop. They disembarked.

Cy said, "I'll get the empty container."

He took the container from the back of the transport and secured the doors. Steve stood by his side with his finger at his mouth. He said only, "Sweep it, inside and out, before you bring it in."

Cy nodded.

Steve pressed the 'dock' button on the transport remote and the vehicle lifted off and smoothly navigated to the docking clamp on the side of the building to shut down and recharge.

Cy brought the container to the front end of the shop where the sweeper was kept. He placed it in the designated 'safe' location as he got the sweeper. Carefully, he ran the signal sensitive nose around the entire outside of the case. On the bottom near a hinge there was an audio hit. Looking very carefully at the surface of the case he saw a patch, about the size of a dime in diameter but paper thin stuck to the case. It could have been a piece of tape. He logged it on a piece of paper to show Steve, and continued his sweep. He opened the case and pointed the nose around the entire inside of the case. He had another hit inside; this one an audio and video hit. He did a careful visual inspection of the hit location and located the camera and microphone tucked into a corner. The patches were the same kind of equipment Steve used in his shop so it may have been his. Cy noted it as well and closed the case after he completed the sweep. He placed the case in a transmission dampening field that had been deemed secure and brought the report to Steve.

Steve, Deirdra and both Detectives Plante and Cody were in the back of the shop looking at the video feed from space. Dave hadn't come in yet, he had gone out back to try to sort through the feelings of anguish and anger. Steve identified people and equipment in the lab for the detectives. Deirdra operated the computer console. She was possessive of her equipment and didn't even like Steve to touch it. Cy realized he would only be in the way here so he left his report on the table and without a word he went out back to find Dave.

Cy sat next to Dave on a bench in the back alley. Dave had leaned way back against the wall of the building absorbing the early spring heat from the sunny afternoon. His eyes were closed and he seemed at peace when Cy found him.

Cy said, "Hey, everything alright?"

"Yeah," Dave said without opening his eyes, "I'm just thinking. We've got to stop this guy Cy; we can't leave it to chance. I'm willing to wait and let the police do what they can to get him, but if it starts to look like the project is a go and they're still dragging their feet, I'm telling you man, we may have to do the job ourselves."

Cy said, "I couldn't agree with you more. I'm ready to do what it takes."

"We don't drag Steve and Deirdra in, they're out of this, right?"

"Right, it's just you and I."

"Cy, this may be suicide. You know that right?"

"Yeah, I pretty much expect it to be a one way trip. Look, I loosened a screw on a wire on the number four camera. With the vibrations on that station it ought to work its way completely loose in a few days. Hawke will contact Steve to come and repair it. I'll convince Steve to let you and I go take care of it alone. If the cops haven't made a move by then we'll make ours."

Dave opened his eyes and looked at Cy. He nodded his head and said, "Did you ever think that we would have a conversation like this?"

Cy shook his head and said, "No. I sure wish Brian were here to help out though."

Dave said, "Hey, let's go get an ice cream."

Cy nodded, "Yes, I think that's a fine idea!"

Plante sat across from Trish in the café. They had spent the afternoon pouring over the images being sent from the space campus. There was much to learn about quantum mechanics and the equipment in that field, but they weren't interested in learning about that. Steve could tell them anything they needed to know about that, they knew what they needed to know to recognize a killer. They were in agreement that the professor was a killer. They only needed some physical evidence that would get this guy behind bars and shut this project down. The scope of their warrant only allowed them to tap into the feed from the space lab. It didn't allow them to access anything more, for the time being.

After two weeks the warrant would be subject to review by the judge and if nothing significant became apparent, then it would be rescinded. Two weeks could be a long time to wait, but it may not be long enough to give them what they needed.

Trish said, "So, what do you think?"

"I think we're screwed. This guy is all business in that lab, there isn't even a social nicety to his interns and other students. It's like he knows we're watching."

"He may be behaving like that because of the possibility of being watched. Hell, he may have hired Steve because he suspected that we would be tapping in; maybe he wants us to watch!"

Plante scratched at his days growth of beard with his fingernails. He said, "Yeah, I though about that too. At least he doesn't seem to realize who Steve is. That'll be our ace in the hole. At the very least we'll be able to monitor and forecast a time frame for his project firing. Steve already seems concerned that it will be soon. He's studying the feed and trying to recollect all of the components and their assemblies."

Trish was pensive. She asked, "Do you really believe this whole time travel business?"

Plante took his fingers away from his whiskers. He said, "Trish, I've looked back through the archives and done some investigating. Do you know how many disappearances there have been in Sheldon? I'll tell you, since the territory was first settled in the late 1690's there have been seventy-two reported and recorded disappearances. All unsolved, all random demographic, and all of them in the proximity of the Wright farm. That has been laying under our noses for centuries. Hind sight is twenty-twenty. I can't help but wonder if there isn't some guy four hundred years into the future that is sitting there ticking off all of the reported and recorded unsolved disappearances that seem obvious to him."

Trish said, "Well then maybe we should be looking at the Wright farm."

"It's been done; turned upside down on more than one occasion looking for missing folks. There's never anything suggesting foul play."

"Well maybe we should go there anyway. I like ice cream."

Plante smiled and said, "Alright, just let me go get a few things back at the precinct and we'll go for ice cream."

Chapter Fourty Four

The transport had brought them safely into the docking bay and nestled cozily onto its teat suckling the stuff of life support for the return trip. Dave sat inside making his last preparations for the mission. Cy had already disembarked and began removing a tool kit from the back of the transport, a much smaller box than the first trip. It too had the strips of hooked talons for the Velcro brand of gravity. With the box in hand he did the thrust shuffle to the side of the transport where Dave would be coming out soon. He rapped on the side of the chassis and said, "Are you about ready, Nancy?"

Dave replied, "I'm just finishing my hair, give a girl a break will ya?"

Cy grinned, he said, "I'm going to head inside. Come when you're ready."

He had no sooner begun to shuffle away and the side door of the transport opened. Dave extended his leg, this time placing his foot securely on the woolen surface, and stood beside Cy. They were both wearing Hill Security jumpsuits, the same suits they had worn to Hawks house, and on their first trip to the campus.

In the three days since their last trip into space no progress had been made by the police to arrest the professor. There was nothing nefarious about carrying out an experiment in space, especially when it had the sanction of multiple institutions of higher learning and several earth governments. Soon even the monitoring warrant would expire and the authorities would loose all interest in allowing the two detectives to continue investigating him. They would be ordered to return to other cases and abandon this one.

The loose wire on camera four had done the trick and here they were, as Cy had hoped, going to fix it and fix the time line as well. The corridor to the staging bay bustled with students, professors, techs, and myriad others thrusting and shuffling with varying degrees of ease and unease. They tried to move along with the crowd and not be conspicuous, and must have met with some success because for the most part no one took notice of them.

They arrived at the portal to the bay and found a red light glowing above the door. A small round window allowed for a view inside, here Dave and Cy stood looking in on the staging bay in complete awe. The two people inside were dressed just as they were, no special suits or helmets, no tethers, nothing other than the walkers that kept their feet Velcroed to the floor, a tenuous lifeline at best. A slight green aura surrounded each of them, with a ray of the same color running back to a wall. Hawk was one of them; intent in his concentration, focused on the task at hand. He stood a mere few feet away but seemed totally oblivious to their presence. The entire ceiling had split along the middle and opened upward on hydraulic arms and hinges exposing the entire bay to the vast ever tenebrous universe beyond.

Dave saw what appeared to be a control booth to the left of the room. On the other side of the glass sat a pretty blonde girl with keen eyes and an almost stern look on her face. She surveyed the bay and all in it, not missing a move before her. He looked at Cy and nodded toward her. Cy turned his attention to her and watched intently. Then he looked down the corridor and saw that the next door opened into the control room and the light above it was green. He looked back at Dave and saw that he had followed his gaze and come to the same conclusion. Without a word, they made their way to the door and stopped just outside, looking in as at the first door. From here the view of the bay was obstructed partially by equipment in the room. The girl was not alone inside. A young man worked the control console beside her.

Dave said, "Can you see what they're doing?"

"I can't make out the screens from here," said Cy, "one of them must be for life support though, and probably the other one is operations."

"The way she's concentrating I'll bet she is life support."

"Yeah and if I took that bet I'd lose money. I think we have our opportunity being handed to us right here, right now." Cy looked around them, "We're alone in this corridor and we have a green light. We can take out the professor and stop the project in one move."

Dave held his hand out to Cy and said, "I love you brother."

Cy nodded and shook his hand saying, "To a better life next time around, for all of us!"

Dave put his hand on the door latch and pressed it down. The airlock hissed and the door opened.

They entered the room quickly and quietly, but not unnoticed by its inhabitants. Without turning around to see who entered the young intern, Scott Holland, who was at the operation controls at the console barked, "Whoever you are, you aren't supposed to be in here, this room is restricted to project operatives! Now get out before I call security."

Cy and Dave looked at each other and nodded. Everything happened quite quickly from there. Cy secured the door from the inside by setting the electronic lock. Once he had done this they converged on the two operators. Dave subdued the girl by tossing her across the room. She bumped her head when she hit the other side. Weightlessness made it very easy to toss a person. Cy went for Scott, first he threw the case at him, and then he advanced. The intern was better prepared to put up a fight than the young girl, but he had two adult men to contend with. He lunged at Cy with his arms out in front of him and floated across the room. Floated, not flew, as he headed for Cy, he drifted almost in slow motion past Dave. When his feet were passing, Dave reached out and took hold of his ankles. With the intern suspended, Cy knocked him out with one punch to the jaw. With both operators compromised, the fate of those in the cargo bay rested in Cy and Dave's hands. Realizing they needed to take control of the situation, they went to the consoles. Dave took the life support console and Cy the operations. The console layouts seemed fairly simple. On life support; each person had their own avatar which identified them and allowed life support as well as monitored their vital signs. By selecting an avatar, the operator could isolate a person within the room and customize gaseous mixture to increase or decrease oxygen or nitrogen as needed. Dave selected the hawk avatar and looked out in the bay. The crew had just noticed that something had gone awry in the control room. Professor Craig strode toward the window, an angry and inquisitive expression on his face. He shouted accusingly at them though they could hear nothing of it. Cy, studying his console, had just isolated the icons for the bay doors when he looked up to see the professor shouting at them.

Dave said, "I didn't notice headsets on those two, did you?"

"No," Cy said, "they must have been conferencing with their ITC's.

At that moment the overhead doors began moving back inward to close up. Cy looked back at the console and saw the status of the doors as 'closing'. He touched the screen and fingered the 'open' icon. The doors stopped and reversed their course. He scrolled down through the menu items and selected control lock, and heard, with satisfaction, the bolts securing the doors open. He looked at Dave and said, "Okay, he's all yours brother."

Dave looked at the console and fingered through the fields of selections until he found the item he was looking for. He looked out, straight at Professor William Craig's eyes and smiled. Then he touched the 'Off' button. Craig's protective green aura immediately disappeared. The result was instantaneous. All of the air in Hawk's lungs belched out of him, ripped into the vacuous environment in a vane effort to fill some of it. His eyes bulged and his tongue extended, he took on a slightly inflated appearance for a brief moment as all of the remaining gasses in his body were similarly drawn from him. He stood there before them, lifeless in a weightless room held to the floor by Velcro on his feet; a dead reed wavering in the ethereal wind. Cy took in a deep breath and said, that's half of the job. He stood and leaned toward the thick plexi-glass that stayed him from suffocation, and gestured to the two remaining men in the cargo bay. They were just a couple kids working an internship. He and Dave had no more desire to harm them than they had to hurt the two in the control room, he waved his arms to get their attention. One of them noticed and said something to the other. Their eyes had never witnessed the specter of death before. It was difficult to get them to understand what he expected of them. But after pointing at the generator repetitively and then at space above them they finally understood. Slowly and with trepidation they uncoupled the generator from the framework that held it. They looked again at the control room. Cy gestured upward. They released it upward, as Cy released the lock on the bay door and pressed close. As the doors moved toward each other the generator slipped upward and out into the void of space. Cy felt satisfied for the moment. He searched the icons for the corridor door, found it and pressed 'secure' to keep the two from getting out.

Dave set the life support to automatically restore pressure and breathable atmosphere in the bay as soon as the doors locked shut.

Cy said, "Are we ready?"

"Let's get while the gettin's good." Dave said.

They checked the two students in the control room again and found that they were unconscious but breathing, they would be alright. Dave went to the door, unlocked it and pressed down on the lever. The door opened and they stepped out into the corridor. There were a few students and professors meandering up and down the corridor but no one seemed to suspect that there might be anything wrong in the great Professor 'Hawk' Craig's bay. Dave and Cy began their shuffle and thrust and joined the line of traffic going in the direction of the transport bay.

They had regained their transport and launched themselves from the space station. Cy piloted the craft and they had managed to find the outside of the bay where Professor Craig stood lifelessly among his students. With a bit of imagination they determined about what direction the generator had coursed as it left the bay. It had only been ten minutes so it couldn't have gone very far out into space. Cy pointed the nose of the transport at right angles to the bay doors and pressed 'forward' on the console. They moved and slowly accelerated. After another ten minutes a slight glitter in the distance caught their attention, just a bit to the right of their course. Dave saw it first.

Dave said, "There, just to the right, do you see?"

Cy looked and said, "Yes, I see it." He turned the transport toward the glinting piece of debris and gradually it became larger and larger until at last it was there, directly in front of them. Dave pressed the outer cargo hatch release icon on his screen. Using a little finesse that Cy didn't realize he possessed he maneuvered the transport so the generator was just about inside of the outer cargo hold. Dave pressed 'close', and the door shut, trapping the generator inside.

Dave sighed and said, "Home, James!"

"With pleasure." Said Cy.

THE ETHER

He touched 'Home' on the control console and the transport made a slow and gradual arc toward earth. They sat back and relaxed for a long and slow return.

The transport had reentered the atmosphere and was making a slow descent toward the planet's surface. Cy prompted a course change and they immediately turned to the east and at their present altitude they were over the Atlantic in minutes. When they were at 20,000 ft. and about a hundred miles out to sea, Dave opened the outer cargo hold and the generator spilled out into the air. It tumbled from their sight end over end and was lost to their vision as it made for the deep. Again, Cy pressed 'Home' on the console and the transport turned for Sheldon.

CHAPTER FOURTY FIVE

The news feed gave the following account of the story:

Professor Killed, Terrorists Believed Dead
By Alphonse Forillo, Earth News International

Two men gained access to a top secret project being conducted at the University of Massachusetts Space Campus. Two students were injured and the professor in charge of the project was killed. The incident leaves parents with unanswered questions regarding the level of security at the orbiting facility and just what type of work are their children involved with.

Injured in the attack was Haley Evans, 21 of Spokane Washington and Scott Holland, 20 of Greenville Virginia. Professor William Craig, 56 of Sheldon Massachusetts was killed. According to Holland and Evans, two heavily armed men forced their way into the control room that they were working in. They were compromised and rendered unconscious. The men then cut life support to Professor Craig in the open cargo bay that had been converted into a laboratory. Craig's death was instantaneous. The two students remaining in the bay are not identified because of their age. Their account from this point on is puzzling. They claim to have been gestured to by the men in the control booth, under the threat of life support termination, to release into outer space a component of the project that they were working on. The cargo bay doors were then closed, however the compartment was not re-pressurized and the students were unable to raise the alarm over the incident until they were freed twenty minutes later when the control booth team regained consciousness.

The transport left the space campus and was routinely tracked at departure. The video shows the transport tracking and recovering the device before returning to earth. EarthNav Satellites tracked the vehicle reentering the atmosphere and setting a course over the Atlantic Ocean. When the Transport turned west again to return to the North American east coast it disappeared.

The transport is believed to have crashed into the ocean approximately two hundred nautical miles from the shoreline.

The terrorists are as yet unidentified and believed dead.

No claims of responsibility have been made as of the time of this publication.

Plante sat in the backroom of Hill Security talking about the case with Trish, Steve and Dee. They were discussing Cy and Dave and the entire affair.

Steve said, "And that's it, everything I know about it."

Plante nodded. He said, "I'm supposed to tell my boss that this psycho that I've been investigating gets whacked by a couple of guys that have been helping me gather evidence? That they acted alone without anyone knowing their agenda? That they were even trusted enough by the victim to receive security clearance onto the station? And oh yeah chief, they were the same two guys who were active missing persons files just a week ago! But on the upside, they aren't missing anymore!"

"Sounds good to me." Trish said, and got up to leave.

"Yeah me too." Said Plante, "I'll see you guys around."

"Have a good one." Said Steve.

"Bye." Said Deirdra.

The detectives left the shop. Steve said to Deirdra, "Do you think we'll ever see them again?"

Dee said, "Well we could just do a search for them. If they were able to get nanites during their lives they would be around somewhere."

"Mmm, but they wouldn't know us." He chuckled, "that might be fun!"

Dee smiled, she said, "Do you ever think about retiring?"

Steve said, "Now that this is over, maybe. But I think it might be a bit boring, don't you?"

She smiled and said, "I could use a little boring."

CHAPTER FOURTY SIX

Cy stood with his back to the kitchen sink; the window behind him open. It had been a long day at work and he felt ready to call it a night. The cool night air rolled across Cy's shoulders making him feel as though there could be something alive in the ether. The breeze caused the hair on the nape of his neck to stand up on end. Cy was not prone to believing in spooks in the night or alien invasions; those things were for horror movies and sci-fi nuts. He considered himself much too practical for that, yet he knew certainly that he felt something more than a breeze. Cyrus Theodule Hill often wondered how his parents could have been so cruel at his birth. Jeez Louise, 'Cyrus?' Who names a kid Cyrus? Nashville's Johnny Cash had his 'Boy named Sue' and Sheldon's Owen and Eve Hill had their boy named Cy. At least his kid sister Sarah had a normal name. When he was younger he always found himself the smallest guy in the crowd. Adulthood brought an extra few inches in height and a broadened chest and shoulders. These days, Cy looked the bruiser at about 225 pounds, he shaved

THE ETHER

his head and face. His inner self was nothing like the image he projected. He wanted the same things most guys wanted; hearth and home, the love of a good woman, the perquisite 2.5 children running around in the backyard chasing the family dog, and so on and so on. The faint breeze brought Cy back to the moment, the night air felt balmy and warm but it sent a chill up his spine. He stepped out onto the back deck turning to face the air current, breathing it in and daring the bogeyman to come out of hiding. Nothing, just the sound of Crickets, a nearby tree frog, freight trains in the old Depot Square changing tracks and a few late night trucks rolling down route 2 in the distance. Cy thought it curious how the night can play games with your head. This was a night just like any other autumn night. Dave and Annie were married and had their reception on a night much like this one three years ago now and they were pregnant with baby number one. Brian and Charlie already had two kids and plans for one more. Perhaps it would be a good time after all.

Soft rain began to fall adding to the nocturnal symphony. Perhaps, tonight, a breeze is just a breeze after all. Cy decided to move it back inside, his pillow is calling and he felt ready to answer it.

He went inside and made his way upstairs to bed. Quietly he stripped and climbed into bed. He cuddled up behind his wife. She had been his childhood sweetheart and one of his best friend's cousins. Her name was Ezra, after one of her great, great grandmothers. He looked into her eyes when they were kids and he was lost for anyone else. He looked into them now and saw his unborn children. As he reached his arm over her from behind she stirred.

"Is everything alright?" Ezra asked.

"Yes," Cy said, "I think everything is going to be just fine. In fact, I think maybe it's time to start that family."

She turned to him and said, "You know, some times it feels like I've known you for centuries!"